MW00944889

THE TIME BENDER

by

Debra Chapoton

This is a work of fiction. Names, characters, places, and incidents either are the product of the author's imagination or are used fictitiously.

Printed in the USA
Cover art by Boone Patchard

ISBN-13: 978-1546559986

ISBN-10: 1546559981

Other works by Debra Chapoton

EDGE OF ESCAPE

THE GUARDIAN'S DIARY

SHELTERED

EXODIA

OUT OF EXODIA

A SOUL'S KISS

THE GIRL IN THE TIME MACHINE

THE TIME BENDER series

Children's chapter books:

THE SECRET IN THE HIDDEN CAVE

MYSTERY'S GRAVE

BULLIES AND BEARS

A TICK IN TIME

BIGFOOT DAY, NINJA NIGHT

TUNNELS series

Non-fiction works:

CROSSING THE SCRIPTURES

BUILDING A LOG HOME IN UNDER A YEAR

THE TIME BENDER

Book 1 in The Time Bender series

CHAPTER 1
#SnowAndStars

I ANSWERED TO loser, elf-skin, slobberer and Lady Blabla, to name a few of the less contemptible slurs. Everyone labeled me. Now my high school guidance counselor, Mrs. Smith, added a new one, classifying me as having an avoidant personality disorder. What the freak? Her analysis came after only three appointments during which I barely spoke.

This appointment was now over and she dismissed me from her tiny office with a smile. I, however, remained majorly stunned. So stunned that I stomped out. And by stomped I mean I slipped quietly around the door jamb, my lips tightly pressed together. I made a feeble attempt at a smile and mouthed my thanks—I'm nothing if not polite—though my eyes lingered on a piece of gum stuck to the floor. Whether or not she heard me was another thing.

I kept my eyes averted from her secretary and fixed them on the bowl of leftover Halloween candies on her desk. I was dying for some chocolate.

"Here's your pass back to class, Selina," the secretary said. She held out the pass, and also a piece of candy and a tissue, which motivate me to shuffle close enough to receive the objects.

I honestly tried to produce an acceptable word of thanks before she turned around and kicked the copy machine. Two seconds later the bell rang. The last bell of the day. I stood there crumpling the pass and judging the safest path through the corridors. The halls filled and so did my tear ducts. I focused on my feet and coaxed my ugly shoes into alternating steps all the way to my locker. My best friend Alex was waiting there. He had my locker open and was holding my winter coat out. I knew this not because I'd lifted my gaze, because I hadn't, I knew it because coming from the counseling office instead of my last class took longer. Naturally Alex would be there to make sure I wouldn't miss the bus.

I stuffed my arms into my jacket without a word, grabbed my backpack and shoved most of my textbooks in it. We walked out together with me a step behind and to his side. If I got too close to him someone would mock me and he'd spring into action. It was easier if there was no hint of our special relationship.

But it was one of those days. As we inched down the school bus aisle two junior girls whispered some choice gossip about why my skin looked icy blue. Alex looked back at me, wiggled his cocoa brown eyebrows and kept his temper in check. The wiggle was an effective distraction. It kept him from going ballistic and me from crying. I made a noise indicating grateful appreciation of his feeble attempt at humor.

The girls repeated their taunt. Louder. Honestly, it wasn't the worst thing they've ever said, but they continued with another dig about me being a virgin. Followed by tittering. Every kid already seated lifted their heads in unison. I could feel it; I couldn't bear the unblinking mass of judgmental eyes, so I focused on the back of Alex's head, willing him to look back again while I blocked out the snickering.

He did and gave me another eyebrow wiggle. Okay, that one was a bit over the top. I knew Alex was struggling to keep his cool. His dancing eyebrows didn't match his tight lips and clenched jaw. He flashed me a smile, a phony one for sure, but with good intentions. I matched it with a forced upturning of the corners of my own mouth. Some moron farted loudly and all the attention on me switched to him. I let my breath out. We took our seats and cradled our backpacks on our laps. Alex visibly relaxed. Me, not so much. I stared past him out the grimy window, forbidding my facial muscles to pucker my lips or quiver my chin while he searched for a particular song to listen to. A few snowflakes started falling as the bus pulled away from school.

I got a grip and concentrated on what was positive in my pathetic life: Alex. Sweet, sweet Alex. He was devotedly protective of me, had been since we were seven, but we were just friends. No racing heart or sweaty palms, at least not on my part. And not that I'd want there to be. Not with Alex. Only in books and teen movies did the girl end up with the dork-turned-dream-guy who had been right there under her nose all along.

He cleared his throat. "So ... how about we pray for a snow day tomorrow, Selina? Or would you prefer an alien abduction?" His voice was deep, smooth and low, rich as homemade hot chocolate—a singer's voice. His tone and the silly questions meant he was calm again even if I wasn't.

I considered the options carefully. I rarely spoke in the close quarters of the bus—huh, maybe I did have an avoidant personality disorder—but, anyway, I thought of a clever answer and knew Alex would appreciate it. "Stand by, snow storm. Cue clouds."

The girls across the aisle giggled through their sneers. Crap, they heard my stage directions. Stupid habit. Kill me now.

The bus rumbled over a speed bump and the seat ahead punished me with a smack to my knees ... well, I definitely deserved that.

"You okay?"

I nodded and Alex handed me an earbud. "Good. I'll cancel the aliens, then, and we'll pray for snow. I found a song about winter."

I closed my eyes and listened. Thank God for Alex. He was one of the very few who accepted how I looked and acted. His humming along with the tune soothed me. I squirmed in the vinyl seat, squeezed my eyes tighter, and fought the urge to do something radical. Like glare at my tormentors. Too bad making eye contact with cool kids was not in my social skill set.

"Selina." Alex nudged me.

"Huh?" I opened my eyes. Usually such uncomfortable moments lasted forever, but somehow we were at my bus stop already. This wasn't the first instance my perception of time seemed skewed. I handed Alex the earbud and almost winked at him. Oops. Emoji: troll face.

I pretended I had something in my eye. Sure, I can talk to Alex like I talk to my own soul, but I'd sooner flirt with a Martian—if I could flirt at all. "Call me later," I whispered, code for *you don't have to get off at my stop today*. I rose and carried my backpack like a shield.

Now if I could get down the foot-littered aisle and then the steps without tripping that would be good. Even better if no one tossed any barbed comments at my back. That thought was enough to knot my intestines.

My toes caught on the ribbed rubber of the last step and I fell into gray slush, dropping my pack and wetting both knees and one hand. Sweet. The driver took his time closing the mango-colored door behind me. Muffled guffaws rippled along behind the windows and the bus snailed ahead a mere inch or two. Diesel fumes puffed a noxious cloud around me. I kept my head down. I focused on the slurry oozing up between my fingers and tried my hardest to rise. It took forever.

In that eternity the strangest scene played out in my head like a fantasy movie. I saw two scarecrow figures running inside a large enclosure. They stopped next to a nebulous structure the size of a bus. In my mind's eye they morphed into fuller, well-muscled bodies, but I couldn't distinguish their faces—I knew intuitively they were good-looking though—and one entered the bus-thing while the other jogged toward a larger bus ... no, it wasn't a bus, it was a spaceship. They were going to pilot stolen ships to come to Earth. To come and get me. My heart lurched and my whole body, even the icy fingers still in the slush, tingled not with fear, but with excitement. The startling images withered faster than they formed and as soon as I rose they completely vanished, but that didn't stop my body from dumping a dose of adrenaline into my bloodstream. My heart contracted like a squeezed balloon.

"Changed my mind." I knuckled a wet strand of hair out of my eyes as the bus turned the corner. "Forget the snow day," I said to no one. "I'd prefer an alien abduction."

❄ ❄ ❄

COREG JABBED AN elbow in Marcum's side, jogged ahead, and claimed the newest starship available to the young recruits: the celestial blue *Intimidator*. Its name matched Coreg's temperament.

The vessel's underside drained away an oily sub-stance that ran along the hangar's grooved floor. In the low gravity it left a dull mechanical odor.

Marcum reached the ship a moment later. Coreg laughed at him. "No time-pacer blood in your veins, is there?" Coreg pulled his thumb ring off and showed Marcum the inner readout. "Here's the extended leave code." He elbowed him again. "And, hey, I won't speed, sunny."

"I don't believe you." Marcum ignored the throb in his ribs and the loathsome nickname. He adjusted his thumb ring to accept the code. "Your time-pacing will be a good diversion if we start near the space alley before the guard ship gives chase."

"Technically we'll be exceeding the distance limits there, but it's absolutely worth the risk of banishment."

Marcum gave a reluctant nod and a grunt from the back of his throat. "*Ehk*. I've jeopardized my future twice by listening to you. What's once more?"

He and Coreg, rivals since they entered the Interstellar Combat Academy, held nothing back in trying to best the other in both simulated and real battle.

Coreg snorted. "There were no consequences either time, thanks to me. The odds favor us again and the guard will never suspect we're going to pierce the space alley. Especially if you take the *Galaxer*."

They both glanced at the old spaceship Marcum had trained on, its sides and underbelly a faded cerulean frost, the nose and topside a dull copper. Both also kept their emotional excitement hidden from one another by not letting their ears flap in obvious anticipation. Coreg continued, "You translated the uncorrupted radio waves from Earth with me. You know how high the probability is of finding a human time-bender there."

Marcum's grunt was enough to concede. He moved toward the *Galaxer*.

"Don't back out on me, sunny," Coreg called out. He pressed his ring into the side of the *Intimidator* not waiting for Marcum's response. He was already fixated on how he would use the time-bender. And as a time-pacer himself, he might be awarded total control of him.

Or her.

The thought of the time-bender possibly being female caused Coreg to hesitate. Before he could initiate take-off Marcum's old ship lifted off ahead of him. He pressed his feet into the piloting divots and stretched his hands up to the ceiling levers. He gave a warrior's shout and blasted off without checking the immediate airspace.

❄ ❄ ❄

FOUR LONG HOURS later I finished my homework and the laundry. My tears had retraced their tracks a couple of times. It sucks to be me.

The snowfall had changed from light flakes to frozen crystals as soon as the bus finally lumbered out of sight. Wisps of swirling snow rose like genies escaping an enchanted lamp. After my little brother got home the weather steadily worsened, transforming into a whiteout with huge flakes. The heavy wet kind. They made the spruce tree branches bend low to the ground and the pine boughs push threateningly across the power lines. I guess they did more than threaten because five minutes after the dryer buzzed the electricity went out. Could this day get any worse?

Unfortunately, stomping one's feet in protest of the weather has relatively little effect, especially when executed in bare feet on carpet. I stepped on something sharp—a piece to one of Buddy's toys—yelped and limped a few steps before reaching the smooth floor of the kitchen. I found the candles in the junk drawer and the matches on the highest shelf. Buddy was at my elbow, whimpering, but at least he wasn't throwing a fit. I lit the candles and lined them up on the table. Their orange glow reflected in my brother's glasses in a most unnerving way.

Michigan winter. Something else to cry about.

"Cue the scary music," I mumbled. Sheesh, it wasn't even mid-November yet.

"Thelina?" Buddy's voice trembled as he lisped my name and asked for the tenth time, "When ... Mom ... h-home?"

"I don't know, Bud. Soon, I hope."

Nine years ago Alex got a puppy for his eighth birthday; I got a special needs brother. I wouldn't trade him for a thousand puppies.

Of course I might trade him for an honest-to-goodness boyfriend. Not to sound desperate or anything, but you could leave out the "goodness;" I just wanted a boyfriend. Good, bad, tall, short, blonde, brunette, as long as a check appeared in the box marked Human. And it would be nice if he had his driver's license. Okay, so I *was* desperate, especially since I'd come to terms long ago with the medical fact—*all right, suspicion*—that I probably wouldn't make it to eighteen. Mrs. Smith thought I had APD, but I had something much worse, something I couldn't explain to her. Yeah, a lot of tears over that.

Not likely to find a boyfriend though. Not if it meant I'd have to talk to a guy, let alone flirt with one.

A loud booming noise made Buddy and me jump. "It's the outside deck, Bud," I assured him—and myself. "The wood cracks that way when the temperature drops so fast." That sounded like a reasonable explanation to me. Yes—*pep talk to self*—I was going to believe that was the deck cracking and not some crazed murderer with a gun or a psycho-maniac breaking the basement window. I looked through a gap in the clouds where stars pin-holed the night and forced my imagination to fly to safer orbits. There couldn't be any murderers or maniacs up there ... and it had to be a zillion times colder that far out in the universe. I imagined a spaceship racing toward Earth. No, two spaceships ... like I envisioned before. *Cue the science fiction adventure.*

Echoes of the shock of hurtling through space wavered through my flesh, and I tried desperately to stop the vision. Then I drew a long, painful breath, and found myself shaking, the shock turning to a very real feeling of danger.

❄ ❄ ❄

"TWENTY LIGHT YEARS is stretching it, isn't it?" Coreg's voice crackled through the minuscule speaker in Marcum's helmet.

Dying stars—lances of red and green against the cold black universe—dove past Marcum's viewing screen as his heart beat double time in anticipation of an illegal contest with Coreg. "What's the big deal?" Marcum goaded, a cockeyed smile playing at his lips. "Too hard for you to speed up time for one hundred twenty trillion miles?" He kept an eye on the readouts as Coreg maneuvered his spaceship within inches of the sparkling bio-metals that framed the exterior of his own craft.

"You Gleezhian fart, you know I can." Coreg's ship latched onto the port side of Marcum's older, wider vessel, clinging like a persistent leech so both ships could fly as one. "The real question is: will you be able to communicate with the females? You'll need some skills there, Marcum."

"I learned English, Russian, and Chinese, same as you. Shouldn't be a problem. Your job is to time-pace us there fast." Marcum sniffed and crinkled his nose at the stink the interior bio-metals were releasing: oily vapors from living machines. He sat forward and relaxed his hands which on their last partnered training excursion had been busy firing anti-flames at Coreg.

"Oh, I'll get us there fast. You can count on it." Coreg's lips were halfway to a cocky grin as the gray light of the upper screen cast shadows along his jaw.

Memories intruded: forbidden shouting matches with his father, filled with words too harsh to take back; running away; being forced to join the space school. He shook off the memories and squeezed his eyes tighter as he pushed himself to pace the ships onward. He'd show them. He'd show them all, especially the Commander who gave him the secret Intel.

❄ ❄ ❄

I BENT DOWN, not too far since I'm short to begin with, and gave Buddy a squishy hug—so glad the scented candles masked the odor of his dirty hair—and said, "Mom's probably caught behind a county snow plow. Don't worry, I can make us some peanut butter and jelly sandwiches for dinner."

I nuzzled him some more as a guilty wave of regret came over me. I'd had an awful shouting, or rather pouting, match with my dad the day before he left. About something stupid: sandwiches for dinner.

I gave Buddy a final squeeze and looked him in the eye. "You love peanut butter and jelly sandwiches, right?"

I watched his round face as he gazed at me; words visibly trembled past his lips but were muddled. "Peanahbutta en chelly," he said. The tip of his tongue stole out again, wetting his upper lip. His therapist worked so patiently with him. Two steps forward, but then one step back.

"I cold." He pressed his fat fingers onto my face and I grabbed them, held them in my own, and blew hot breath on them. I sure hoped the power came on soon or it would be more than frozen fingers I'd have to deal with. There was an upside though: we might get a day off school. I helped Buddy into his winter coat and mittens then pulled my orange and black Panthers sweatshirt over my head and smoothed the front over my virtually non-existent boobs. No upside there.

My imagination took off again. I saw Black Holes and interplanetary passageways where astronauts had to shield their brains from debilitating radio waves or radiation or maybe cable reruns. But again it didn't feel like my imagination. It felt real. And I felt a little less afraid. For a day that had been filled with a boatload of tears I almost, almost felt happy.

CHAPTER 2
#Shorcuts

WITH THEIR OWN planet millions of miles behind them Marcum and Coreg entered a space alley that not even their enemies the Gleezhians used anymore. Their shielding helmets blocked the majority of radio waves; it was still painful for the young warriors to pass through the anomaly, but they'd decided to take the shortest way to Earth so sacrifices had to be made.

Earth. Marcum reviewed what he'd learned. He squeezed his eyes tightly shut against the piercing pain and recalled the messages he'd been given to translate. He was sure, absolutely positive, that there lived at least one time-bender on that particular planet. And it could be a female.

He'd been practicing his languages ever since. He'd blend in even if he had to shave his head to hide his blue-black hair. He didn't know what to do about his skin color though. Coreg sported the perfect blend of palest green and light yellow, but Marcum's own face and arms always looked pasty white. What if the female showed off skin of brown or red or dark blue? He'd made fun of the tales of a human-inhabited planet where size and color and weight made a deadly difference. His instructors had provided insufficient data to come to a reliable conclusion regarding Earth.

"Are we there yet?" The pain eased up and Marcum opened his eyes to the sight of a wan and ghastly moon filling his viewing screen. The next moment the image changed. The planet seemed to be rushing toward him instead of the other way around. The broadcasted sounds of Earth—voices, music, clicks, bangs—filtered through his helmet, confusing, but not painful. The transmissions echoed like the current, translatable radio data that he'd studied, and not the corrupted, amplified frequencies of the space alley.

He stared in shock at the readout indicating human life: there was one race on the planet comprised of more than seven billion beings. He couldn't comprehend it. His own civilization barely reached a million before the first invasion drastically reduced their population. How would they ever find a single time-bender among so many? The subsequent readout answered that question and he had a clue.

Alerts gently sounded across the dashboard in low-pitched chimes. His ship rocked as Coreg disengaged the locks that held the two ships together. Coreg shouted into his speaker, "First one to find the time-bender wins."

He shot away with such force that Marcum nearly lost his balance as the automatic anti-spin rockets engaged. Dust motes danced around him, then glommed onto the static screen. He drew in a stabilizing breath, tasting the stale air, but ignoring its bitter moldiness.

"That will be me," he whispered to himself, following the faster ship toward Earth. Speed wouldn't win this. Knowledge would. He waited until Coreg fixed his trajectory toward the continent's brightly lit coastline before aiming his own lumbering vessel toward a peninsula shaped like a hand.

Marcum glided in for as dark a landing as possible. No bounce, no burn. His parents would be proud. He took the first few moments on Earth to record into his thumb ring a concise summary of his actions.

❄ ❄ ❄

I GAZED OUT the door wall to the deck, thought I saw a shooting star and switched my mental point of view to Disney theme music. I imagined Alex humming ... *when you wish upon a star...* Yeah, I knew exactly what to wish for. Another light streaked across the sky. Something flared then faded into a black shadow and fell into the woods beyond the neighbors' darkened houses. Goosebumps and chills fought for space on my arms and neck. I grabbed Buddy's hand and moved away from the window.

❄ ❄ ❄

MARCUM REMOVED HIS helmet and employed the data retrievers. According to the feedback the area was populated with concentrations of hundreds of humans in the larger domiciles, quite like the western cities on his planet. But the scanners also showed two to five humans in each of the individual units, not unlike the residential composition he was used to.

Some places included four-legged beings. That concerned him. He grunted his usual *ehk* and doused himself with repellent, smeared it head to toe over his tight-knit black uniform, and hoped it would make him undetectable to the sensory receptors of any hostile creatures these humans undoubtedly kept as guards. He'd earned high commendations in evasion tactics, but this was a new frontier and he would take no chances.

He checked the oxygen and poison levels before stepping outside the ship. Too high a level of nitric oxide would be fatal, but all tested within the non-lethal limit. He trembled, too excited about searching out his objective to pay attention to the feeling that he'd forgotten something. The low visibility surprised him. He recognized snow from his studies of the Gleezhians' planet and the dark side of his own, but he had no idea such an enormous concentration of it commonly fell all at once. This must be what it was like at the banishment colonies on Klaqin.

He stepped away from the vessel, plunging each foot up to his ankles in snow, and ignored the involuntary shivers that fluttered from his shoulders to his knees. It wasn't the cold that affected him; the magnitude of this adventure could no longer be denied. He had betrayed his parents' trust and the force's regulations. He might talk himself out of disciplinary measures with one, but not the other.

"It's so quiet," he whispered in his native language. He reached a hand up and tried to catch a few flakes. "And wet. And cold."

He noticed his breath in the glow of the ship's concealment lights. He blew out several times, observing how the swirls of air and snowflakes spiraled away. The lights blinked out; the ship finished its automatic shut down and began cooling into the snow. It creaked a final time as the bio-metals finished re-coloring and lacing themselves into a tree-like silhouette, effectively blending into the woods.

Marcum brushed the snow from his uniform. Its bio-materials should have been reacting to the temperature, but something was wrong. The suit didn't puff up and provide the automatic insulation he expected. He shivered, but didn't let the suit's failure concern him.

He didn't wheeze or cough as he had on foreign planet simulations. He expected to be dizzy in the higher oxygen level, but this was not much different from his own planet. He drew in and out a few more deep breaths and felt invigorated. He cleared his throat and tried his Russian, his Chinese, and then his English: "Hellew, I am Marcum." Naively confident he would blend in with people as well as his ship had conformed to its surroundings, he set off to explore.

He swatted away snow-covered branches as he made a path toward a settlement. Small rolling vehicles with fuzzy lights crept along the second street he came to. That made sense to Marcum—these humans had most types of advanced land, sea, and air transportation. However, the lack of adequate lighting in the houses bewildered him. Even his own home was equipped with lights despite the constant sun. His house sat in the middle of the farming region of Klaqin, where the sun's angle left the smallest shadows and a geographical aberration protected the region from Gleezhian attacks. The house's windowless interior rooms were designed for sleeping, but appointed with artificial lighting. He wondered why these Earth people's vehicles had lights, but their homes did not.

He peeked in windows and analyzed the humans. Some were wrapped in bulky coverings sitting quietly beside tapered fingers of single flames. Others had built larger fires inside and were moving around. He wished he hadn't arrived at night. He'd have to shiver for quite some time before dawn came and warmed things up.

❄ ❄ ❄

I SHOULD HAVE used that wish for the electricity to come on—*slap forehead*—or at the very least wished for mom to call. I mumbled the more important need aloud: "Come on, mom, call us." I'd left two messages on her voicemail. She probably had her phone turned off. It was unlike her not to check on us. She was usually quite annoying, calling hourly on days she had to work a long shift. The world's most dedicated nurse was also a dedicated mom.

For some reason time was dragging. Nothing new there. It always went slowest when I wanted it to go fast. And now my inconvenient illness was manifesting a new symptom. I'd have to tell Alex about these interstellar hallucinations.

I hiccupped then I coughed. Buddy didn't notice, thank goodness, or he would have grabbed his toy medical kit. I cringed as I remembered the time my dad caught me and Alex taking turns playing doctor. About a thousand years ago. Before things got awkward.

The house directly behind us sat in total darkness, but the colonial next to it, Alex's house, flickered with wandering flashlights. I went to the table and grabbed a candle.

"Me too," Buddy begged.

"I'll hold it for you." I carried two to the window. If there was a gun-wielding psycho out in this storm maybe he'd think twice before breaking in where kids were playing with fire.

A flashlight's beam swept across the yards, aimed down from Alex's bedroom window. "Look, there's our friend Alex."

"Alekth," Buddy said, the candle forgotten. He pounded on the glass and waved, hollering at the top of his lungs.

"Shh, he can't hear you." But then, as if he had heard Buddy, Alex shined his flashlight at his own smiling face, then up under his chin making it ghoulish even at a distance, and waved back. I lifted my candles in a careful wave and wished we were ten years old again. It was a lot easier being best friends with a boy before the hormones kicked in. Now I wasn't sure what I felt for him, but I was pretty sure he wanted to be more than friends. Maybe I should give in and let him be the answer to my wish. But I didn't get butterflies around him. You're supposed to get butterflies, get giggly, be at a loss for words—

My phone vibrated in my pocket. It better be my mom. I set the candles on the coffee table.

Not my mom; it was Alex.

"Hey, Selina. You guys getting cold yet? I don't see any smoke from the chimney."

"Yeah, you know I can't build a fire. And my mom's not home yet. Do you think if I turn on the gas stove it'll keep us warm?" I raised my voice in sarcasm as I asked because a couple years ago Alex got in major trouble for doing that when he stayed home from school sick. After that his folks took the knobs off the stove if they left him alone.

"Funny. No, really, if your mom's not home you and Buddy can come over here. My dad's going to start the generator and run it off and on to keep the furnace going."

I balanced the phone between my shoulder and ear in order to tuck my fingers up my sleeves for an extra bit of warmth. "Thanks. If she's not here in an hour I'll pack a bag for Buddy and bring him over." I tried not to dwell on the fact that Alex and I had numerous sleepovers when we were little kids, and backyard camp-outs, and a single scary night in his tree fort. Long before he grew a foot taller than me. No way was I going to accept an invitation from his mom to stay in their guest room now. Awkward. Even without butterflies.

Alex kept quiet on his end of the line. No doubt he knew what I was thinking. He always did.

"Okay, then," he said at last. "Call me back. And, hey, ignore what those girls said on the bus. You're awesome."

I smiled. "Thanks." Alex always had my back. But I was so tired of the hurtful comments by people I've known forever. I may not be cool enough for their cliques and parties and inside jokes—me being the laughingstock of their jokes—but at least I'm not unkind.

Like nobody else daydreams in class? Guess I simply have to live with the rep of a drooler. And ignore their mean comments about my brother. And so what if I don't have a driver's license? Neither does Alex. Maybe if I told them the doctors thought my daydreams were seizures and I'd figured out there was something fatal in my blood ... no, I'd rather be laughed at than pitied.

I withdrew my hands from my sleeves, said goodbye to Alex, and clicked off. I texted my mom again. I wasn't afraid to be home alone with no electricity. I wasn't that big of a scaredy-cat—I didn't actually think there were psychos roaming around. My phobias ran more toward spiders, snakes and needles. And heights. But I'll admit I freaked out when I glanced up from my phone and saw a shadowy figure dash between the houses. No hat, no coat. Murderers and psychos aren't that goofy. Had to be Alex. What the heck—*confused hand motions*—was he doing out in the cold after a blizzard without even a scarf? Was he coming to my rescue to build a fire? A face hovered pale in the dark, not close enough to recognize.

CHAPTER 3
#FriendMe

A FLASH OF candlelight drew Marcum's attention as he sprinted along a path between two of the houses. He stopped under a sheltering pine to watch a small female employ what struck him as tremendous strength to push aside an entire glass wall. At first he didn't comprehend that she had seen him, but then she shouted into the darkness at him, "Are you crazy? It must be ten degrees out there!"

Marcum stood transfixed. His eyes darted from her face to her chest; he noted the bulky body covering she wore with the outline of an animal printed diagonally across it. A cat, he thought, like the feral kind on his planet. He remained statue-still. The female squinted against the snow gusting into her face. "Is that you, Alex?"

"Hellew. I am ... *ehk* ... Marcum." Spit scattered as he enunciated every syllable.

"*Hellew*? You're not from around here, are you?" The female retreated, pulling the glass wall almost entirely closed, leaving her head and neck outside. A normal-sized female head. A pure white neck.

Small frozen drops fell from the boughs above, startling him. Marcum thought she spoke too fast, but he understood most of what she said. He had an answer memorized for this. "Hellew, I am lost." Both ears twitched.

"Oh, hello. Well ... um ... I ... uh." A gust of icy cold wind blew snow into her face. "Oh, for— Get in here." She pushed the transparent wall wider again, waved him forward and stepped out of the way. Marcum covered the distance quickly and entered without stomping the snow off his feet. Cold air and plenty of white flakes swirled in behind him.

A small human, a child with a round face and curious eyes, threw its arms around the female's waist and latched on. She dragged-stepped him along with her as she pushed the glass wall closed.

"Um, you said your name is Marc? Uh, hi. I'm Selina and this is my brother, Buddy."

Her voice sounded friendly, but her body language expressed something between fear and reluctance. Based on her actions he concluded that she found the gray floor covering of more interest than his face. Maybe, as Coreg had teased, he didn't have the skills to attract an Earth female.

Marcum bobbed his head, his English lessons failing him. By the candlelight he saw that both of them were nearly as pale as he was. Good. He blended in already.

"So ... how'd you get lost? And with no coat ... or anything ..." She lifted her eyes to scan up and down his form-fitting, regulation, all-in-one uniform. She quickly looked away.

He took a deep breath and tried to construct an answer, but the small one, Buddy, spoke first, scrunching up his nose. "He thtinkth."

"Buddy, that's not nice. Please, don't pay any attention to my brother. Here, sit here."

The female patted the sofa. She kept her head down, snorting her breaths in and out in ragged fashion, her body trembling. She stepped back, tore the child's hands from her waist and made him sit on a chair. Marcum lowered his tall frame onto the cushion she had touched. She picked up a fuzzy blanket-like covering and held it out to him. He took it expecting their eyes to meet, but she kept hers cast to the side while she spoke.

"So, um, you're lost? Are you an exchange student?" She moved to an adjacent chair and sat down. "I noticed your accent."

Marcum nodded. He drew the covering tighter around his shoulders and marveled at his luck in finding the time-bender without even trying. He didn't need to analyze it; he knew she hammered the air around him with time-manipulating force in exact opposition to the time-pacing he endured when Coreg employed his unique gift.

He checked his thumb ring's readout; he'd been in this dwelling for a few time units, but it felt like a double-moon. Her reluctance to meet his gaze and her engagement of the time-bending gave him a chance to study her.

His heart raced.

Her name was Selina. How amazing; *selina* meant heaven in his language. Her hair waved over her shoulders with all the grace of natural curls, brown he thought. He couldn't make out her eye color, but those eyes captivated him all the same as she started to steal glances his way. She was diminutive, not tall enough to pilot a ship by herself, but that didn't matter. *English, think in English*, he told himself. He needed to come up with an answer.

"Yes. 'Change student."

The time-bender had nervous and halting questions: "Can I ... call someone ... for you?"

"New. New, thank you." His confidence grew. He intended to keep his answers short, with little embellishment.

"No? Uh, have you been outside ... very long?" Her eyes flitted from the floor to the window to his knees.

He stuck with the negative response, this time rounding out the O as he answered, "No."

The child complained of being cold. She moved to his chair and pulled him onto her lap. Either mitts or bandages hid the child's hands, Marcum wasn't entirely sure which.

Perhaps they made him wear protective sheaths if his fingers ended in claws like some Gleezhians' hands.

No one said anything as the Earth minutes and the Klaqin time units lengthened. The awkward silence deepened until the child made funny faces at him. Marcum memorized each one, drew his own lips into a similar pucker, and mimicked the head tilting and eyebrow narrowing. Suddenly the child laughed. With the silence broken, Selina laughed too, and then Marcum allowed himself to replicate her giggle, though he hoped it didn't sound like a Gleezhian gurgle.

Time slowed again. Stopped.

Suddenly several lights popped on and Marcum observed the time-bender and the child as they exhibited excited yet reverent reactions to the bursts of light. The time-bender marked the event by repeating a single word he didn't know: hic. The child hopped off her lap and blew out the candles with wheezing puffs.

Then the house seemed to shudder. Warmed air spewed through holes in the floor.

Brown. Yes, her eyes were brown. But her skin ... she was not the color he thought at first. She had a different hue. Bluish pink? Or pinkish blue? The artificial lights bothered his eyes. If she was blue that would be fine. He'd had his eye on a blue beauty named Renzen who had watched him fight in bridge battles. He could get comfortable with blue.

The young male pulled off his hand coverings and Marcum noted the short, stubby fingers and even shorter nails. He became vividly aware of certain other details too: his own long, lean reflection in the wall of glass, the stiff stillness of the walls, and the furnishings—so typically human they could have come from his own planet. Then there were the smells. The female gave off an unfamiliar yet pleasant fragrance, but the child reeked of something more animal.

A question formed in his head and he struggled to translate it into English, but the time-bender spoke first. “You can borrow a coat and gloves, if you like.”

“I like.”

The time-bender moved more quickly than he expected. She slurred two words together as she rose, but he was certain she meant for him to follow her.

He shadowed her as she moved room to room, Mesmerized by how she stepped, though she walked no differently than females on Klaqin. Her shoulders, hips and feet moved in a flawless rhythm as one motion faded into the next. She opened the door to a tiny storeroom, pulled out an upper body covering and pushed it against his chest. He clutched it before it dropped. She turned back to search out more items. Her hair swung forward and hid her face as she whipped her small hands in and out of a clear container on the floor. She rose, handed him a couple more things, then smiled at his effort to wiggle into the tight coat.

“Sorry,” she said, holding his gaze for the smallest Klaqin time unit, “it’s the best I can offer. At least my mom wears a large. Uh ... do you think you can find your way now?”

Marcum knew, on a technical level, what fear was, though he had never experienced it. For an interminable moment he believed he might be suffering something similar. Anxiety maybe or panic. He looked her straight in her eyes and his tightly coiled heart unraveled.

“I am thankful,” he said, distinctly and with well-practiced though imperfect pronunciation, “for your hospitality.” She nodded and gave him a tight smile before glancing away. He reached out and gently touched her elbow, then drew his hand back as if he’d been burned. She reacted by quickly opening the nearest door. A blast of cold air surprised him. She turned her face away and wished him luck finding his way home.

Once outside, he hurried up the street without looking back. He avoided running between houses, most of which now beamed brightly with lights inside and out.

❄ ❄ ❄

EVERY INCH OF my body bristled with guilt and relief. And something else: elation. I'd done it! I'd survived an unexpected social encounter. With a stranger!

I couldn't believe I let a stranger into the house. What was I thinking … and why did I feel such a strange pull toward him? Like my blood wanted to leap out of every vein and, and … oh, I'd never be able to explain why I let him in, but I was so glad I did.

I watched him jog away, the porch light gleaming on his back, making flakes of snow glitter like diamonds on his head. I set the alarm on the door and turned around, not expecting Buddy to be sitting on the floor in the middle of my path. He held his arms up, yawned, and moaned a single word, "Bed?"

I hushed my silent rejoicing and answered, "Sure, Bud. I'll put you to bed. But I'm not carrying you. Come on. Stand up."

It was a struggle to take him through his nightly routine without mom, but I didn't mind since my head was virtually on another planet. Marc was so hot. *Cue the firemen.* When I had pushed mom's jacket against his chest he felt as if he were made of something spongy yet altogether harder than mere flesh. The second he touched my arm lasted about a thousand years. And I saw things.

I tried to make sense of it all while I made Buddy brush his teeth.

I'd seen a couple of visions. The last one was of Marc on a bridge … fighting … it was too weird. Those thoughts turned to vapor as I helped my brother into his pajamas. I forced myself to ignore the imaginary stuff and turned my thoughts to real memories. I replayed every second from the instant I let that stranger into the house. Funny, my heart beat more wildly remembering it all than when it happened. I wished I had kept my head up more, made actual eye contact, and asked more questions. With my luck I'd never see him again.

"Thtory?" Buddy asked. He was way too old to act like he did, but my dad said he'd make his mental advances in spurts. Like I did. Apparently I didn't talk at all until I was three.

I tucked him in and began to tell him about Jack and the Beanstalk, but in my new creative—make that inspired—version Jack kept climbing all the way to the stars and beyond until he entered a land of pale delicate trees and round-faced men where a princess named Selina was betrothed to a prince named Marc, with black hair, a prominent nose and chiseled jaw, who had the magic to extend her life.

I giggled at the silliness of my story then saw that Buddy's eyes were closed. I waited to see if he was faking. His breathing grew regular and raspy; a quiet snore followed.

❄ ❄ ❄

MARCUM FOUND HIS way to his spacecraft, well-disguised except for his previous footprints leading away from it. The prints stopped near what appeared to be a mound of fresh snow over wispy tree branches, but was actually the camouflaged entrance. He opened the hatch and climbed in, intending to remain holed up inside until he could thoroughly assess what had happened to him while under the influence of the time-bender's power.

His usually slow beating heart was still out of control.

He pressed his thumb ring into a groove under the viewing screen. The readouts dimpled the screen with data he wasn't expecting. The sensors in the thumb ring had detected evidence of at least four humanoid beings of Klaqin origin within the vicinity he'd explored. That didn't make sense unless Coreg was nearby after all and the time-bender's protracted influence doubled the results.

He flashed on her brown eyes.

His heart still pounded.

❄ ❄ ❄

I HEARD THE garage door go up and I crept to Buddy's window to look down at the front yard. My mom's car lights swept wide across the snowy expanse of our yard and then up the driveway. My heart skittered past a couple of beats when I thought of how I'd have to explain Marc's visit to mom—*never open the door to strangers!*—and that I'd given away her ski jacket. But I couldn't see his footprints out there anywhere. The blowing drifts had concealed all evidence of my untrustworthiness.

I tiptoed out and slipped into my room without turning on the light, got into bed fully clothed and fake-snored when I sensed her presence in the hallway. She didn't fall for it. We had a short conversation that I fake-yawned my way through. As soon as she went to her room I changed clothes and snuggled under the covers. I wasn't the least bit sleepy. I lay first on my back, then on my side with my knees pulled up, then on my stomach.

I should have been figuring out a way to buy Buddy's silence, but instead I fantasized about Marc and finally dropped off into a delicious sleep full of dreams.

CHAPTER 4
#TMI

MARCUM MADE A pillow of the borrowed ski jacket, not for sleeping, but to keep his head comfortable in the cabin of the ship. The gravity here affected him, enough that he found himself fighting neck cramps. He spent the entire night hacking into various servers, streaming satellite feeds, and familiarizing himself with his surroundings.

And obsessing about the time-bender. He spoke her name aloud several times, just to hear it, then pressed his hands over his ears to calm himself. He chastised himself for not wrestling her away from the strange child and carrying her to the ship during the snow storm. But he had foolishly left his weapon on board—that was what he'd forgotten—and he suspected that she was abnormally strong for her slight size, having moved that transparent wall with one hand. That would have been a mechanical feat on his planet since their glass-like element was heavier than copper.

Then there was the hypnotic power she exerted over him from the moment she commanded him to enter. She had him confused.

But it was fortuitous, he discovered, that he hadn't kidnapped her. His starship would not re-solarize in the vapid moonlight. The sensors needed recharging, too, and electric currents in the atmosphere were interfering with his communication device. He couldn't raise Coreg on the headset or locate his whereabouts.

By morning the bio-metals readjusted in the early light and the chameleon spacecraft glittered white. Marcum sneaked back to Selina's house, this time with his weapon, and caught a glimpse of her leaving. Again he experienced the temporal deceleration that being near her brought on. He couldn't move out from his hiding spot, but mutely watched as she boarded a yellow transport.

He returned to the ship to do some more scientific and specialized investigation. As the sun crossed the sky he finally felt the first tiny pang of hunger and squirted a ration of precisely formulated liquid down his throat. Highly concentrated and blended for his extremely slow metabolism, it gave him little enjoyment in the consumption; his mind lingered elsewhere.

First one to find her wins. Wins what? He wished he had bet Coreg something, such as first pick on the newer space crafts. But winning would have to be enough since winning meant he would own her. And owning a time-bender would be priceless. Those who sped up time, like Coreg, were not as commonplace as they once were, and hence were more highly esteemed. Coreg could speed away from battle fights or, as he had when they locked their ships together, he could loosen the bonds of time around their vast travel.

Marcum imagined the praise he would receive from the First and Second Commanders when he could put Selina to work to slow down his side of the battles long enough to aim superweapons with unhurried precision. Quite possibly he'd operate in tandem with Coreg's ability and together they'd help bring the Gleezhian Wars to an end. It might be fantasy, but it was better to dream of winning accolades than to worry about the punishment he and Coreg were risking. They'd exceeded the roaming distance by twelve light years.

He made a decision: as soon as his ship rebooted he'd go get the female, confine her comfortably in the cargo bay, and search out his comrade.

❄ ❄ ❄

COREG TRACKED MARCUM'S spacecraft to the woods and hid his own ship nearby. At the same time Marcum sat in Selina's house, Coreg charted the city, then went in search of apparel and anything else useful for assimilating into this society. He didn't need a costume like the ones he and Marcum had worn to infiltrate a Gleezhian colony. Those gave them humped backs and twelve fingers. For this illicit mission to Earth he needed some stolen clothes to cover his body-hugging uniform which was not warming him as it should have. He found what he needed at a warehouse-like facility and donned two sets of clothes right in the aisle of the store, between racks of winter clothes for men. The store was practically deserted because of the storm with no clerks around to wait on him and no one to stop him from stealing.

A few minutes outside the next morning in the early angled sunlight, cold as it was, and the exposed skin on his hands and face lost its sickly tinge. He could pass for a native. No one he passed on the snowy street glanced twice at him, if they noticed him at all.

Being a time-pacer allowed him to flash through time alone, unnoticed. On his own planet the leaders had licensed him to use his gift exclusively in outer space or on recovery expeditions to the dark side of Klaqin. He'd been recruited because he paced unlawfully near a weapons post, broke in and stole an array of arc-guns and spikers. Caught and faced with the choice between a thousand doublemoons in prison, a sentence a time-pacer might endure quickly, or enrollment in a government service department followed by mandatory enlistment in the military, Coreg chose service in the Interstellar Combat Academy.

He assimilated into new cultures most skillfully—faster than his peers—and his proficient digital scouting always put him ahead of Marcum. He knew the fundamentals: that time, at very long distances, telescoped; that it moved according to a specific perspective; and that when he moved, he saved time. He moved quite a lot that first night and following morning.

❄ ❄ ❄

I WOKE TO the blackest morning ever and the stupid beep of my super insistent alarm clock. The numbers read 6 a.m., but they continued to flash after I hit the snooze button. I stared, mesmerized, and tried to figure out why they kept flashing.

The power! Duh.

When Marc was here and the lights came on the clock must have restarted at 12:00. I did a foggy calculation and decided it was closer to one in the morning. No wonder it was so dark. I fumbled for my phone and checked. Yup. 1:13 a.m.

1:13 a.m. and I was thinking about Marc. Still.

I sat up, turned on the light and reset my clock.

Then I clicked the light off and tried to get back to sleep. *Cue sandman.*

I've had dizzy spells before, but not while lying down. Such a strange feeling. And it came with visions. Okay, I could do visions. They were like daydreams, something I was famous for and I could work Marc into a romantic scenario like I'd been fantasizing a few hours ago. But this vision came with a faster heartbeat and a new feeling, kind of a cross between panic and joy. I put my hand out to find my phone, sort of an automatic response to reach out to Alex, but the vision grew stronger and I pulled my arm back under the covers.

I squeezed my eyes shut as tight as I could trying to imagine only Marc, but instead I saw a lot of round-faced people, dressed like people from the dark ages. They stood along the sides of the streets of a sun-drenched city, watching me walk by. Me and Alex. I felt electrified. A distant splash echoed in the sudden silence before I sank back under the surface of sleep.

❄ ❄ ❄

WITH A MASS three times larger than Earth's, Coreg and Marcum's planet, Klaqin, had the muscle to hold atmosphere. Their world was tidally locked to its sun, a parent star nearly as old as time, and therefore Klaqin experienced perpetual light on half its surface and permanent darkness on the other side. As a result, temperatures were extremely stable though diverse.

Far from the edge of darkness, in a ruined city centered on a continent freckled with fresh water lakes, stood the military capital building which housed the offices of the highest level commanders. Rooms were five sided, hive-like, and previously capable of launching separately, but not since the last Gleezhian attack.

One particular room, shrouded in copper, lent itself to deadly plans, secret missions and both covert and overt operations. The quiet conversation between Second Commander Dace and an angry alley guard, one of the short supply of adult flyers, took place in front of the fifth wall that blended their golden brown reflections into one.

"Straight through the alley and headed for Earth," the guard growled. "My ship is not licensed to chase beyond one light year. That pretentious little time-pacer, Fifth Commander Coreg, appropriated a new ship. He coupled onto the old moon-chaser Fifth Commander Marcum was piloting and the two of them vanished through the corridor." He huffed for effect and added, "They were out for A and E maneuvers, registered and certified for extended leave. They might make it to Earth."

"Calm down, guard. It's happened before."

"Not on my watch it hasn't!"

"Noted. There won't be any consequences for you since you reported this immediately. I order you not to repeat this information to anyone."

"So ordered; so complied." He clucked his tongue twice and bowed his head.

"Dismissed." Commander Dace's plump face creased slightly as he gave the order.

As soon as the guard left, Dace faced the copper wall and drew both hands outward in a circling motion. Holographic images leaped out of the wall and Dace moved through them searching with his fingers until he found what he wanted. He watched and listened.

"Perfect," he mumbled to himself, "they took the bait." His superiors, the First Commanders, had denied his requests repeatedly; they couldn't afford to lose a time-pacer, especially a prodigy like Coreg. Dace disagreed. He had given the Fifth Commanders specific phone waves to work with, ones easiest to translate, arranged to have their training closer to the space alley, and allowed Coreg to choose the most advanced spacecraft. If the young troopers found a true time-bender and brought her back, the Klaqin scientists who were now sheltered underground could create a race of blended fighters. They'd be able to fend off the Gleezhian invasions; those star cannibals wouldn't stand a chance once the right people had a handle on time manipulation. In the end the First Commanders would be pleased.

He stepped away from the copper, smoothed over the few hairs left on his head that had become electrically charged, and spun the ring on his thumb until it gave off a low summoning call.

CHAPTER 5
#ConfessionSession

"HEY, WHAT ARE you so bummed about, Selina?"

I stood at my locker and wondered how to answer Alex's question. No doubt he noticed how quiet I was on the bus—*cue the crickets.*

"You expected a snow day, right?"

I shook my head no. "Not after the lights came back on and the snow quit falling. By the time my mom got home, she said the major roads were clear. Then they had all night to plow."

"Okay then. Something else has you in a weird mood. What?"

"I don't know. I guess I didn't sleep well."

"That's it?"

"Yeah." Emoji: cold sweat.

"No, I don't think so. I know you. What else is wrong?"

I've never kept secrets from Alex. He does know me. Probably too well. I sighed. "Um, did you see somebody running around the backyards last night, when the snow started again?" I decided not to mention that this particular somebody's tight clothing hugged his body more like a wet suit than t-shirt and jeans. Even before the lights came on I could tell Marc worked out. Maybe it was time to keep some secrets. Alex pierced his eyebrows together and grunted in the negative so I went on, "Well, at first I thought it was you, but it was some poor guy without a coat or anything. I let him in. You know, to warm up." That was going to freak Alex out. He knew better than anyone how much I avoided meeting new people.

"Wait. What? Are you crazy? You let some stranger in your house when you were alone because he was too brainless to be wearing a coat in a blizzard?" Alex's voice got all wobbly and low. "Are you okay? He didn't hurt you, did he?" He half reached a hand toward my shoulder then pressed it against the locker next to mine instead.

"No, no, nothing like that. He said he was an exchange student. You should hear his accent. His o's are like u's and he leaves out a lot of little words."

"He sounds stupid." Alex took his hand off the locker, leaving a steamy little print, and rubbed his nose with the back of his hand, a silly habit he has.

I grabbed my English book, a dog-eared copy of Shakespeare's eighth play, and closed the locker. I ignored Alex's jealous reaction. Then a couple of rowdy kids backed into me and almost apologized until they saw it was me. Instead of *excuse me* they uttered a rude question about my skin color. Jerks. Alex had some stronger words to fling at their backsides.

"Anyway," I said, "my brother didn't like him. Said he stank." Alex smiled at that and we started down the hall side by side. I was too aware of the way my feet tried to hurry us along. "He had sort of an oily garage smell to him. Like a mechanic."

"So what's this guy's name?"

"Marc." I kept my eyes on the ugly tile floor and listened to my shoes tap out a pitter-patter. I thought about those jerks' comment. Some people—

"Last name?"

"Um, I don't know." What did everyone else see when they looked at me? Apparently not what my mirror reflected. Or Alex's eyes. My anxious heart beat ten times faster than the steps I took.

"But he's an exchange student? What country is he from?"

"Uh, I don't know that either." *Focus.*

We walked toward his locker and Alex asked more questions I didn't have answers for. Why the third degree? He knows I'm socially inept.

I zoned out remembering how I could feel Marc staring at me for an interminably long stretch. Until I got the hiccups. He'd smiled then and we'd both laughed when Buddy made faces as soon as the electricity came on. Or was it before? The whole encounter had become as hazy and dream-like as all my recent hallucinations.

"Look," I said as we reached his locker and it was safe for me to lift my eyes, "don't get your panties in a bunch. He was only inside maybe ten minutes."

It seemed like hours and hours, though, but I left that out. I'd never admit to Alex that the guy was extremely attractive and I'd let my guard down. Being sociable was so not my style. But for some reason I'd been instantly drawn to Marc.

Alex said nothing so I babbled on, "You know me ... it was awkward. And we had a language barrier. Then the power came on. I lent him my mom's ski jacket, some mittens and a hat and he left. End of story." *Whew, breathe!*

Alex frowned. "So he'll be back then. To return the stuff."

I hoped so, but I said, "Or maybe I'll see him here. If he's an exchange student at our school and not Central." I didn't know why, but my heart was pounding like I'd been caught doing something terrible. Like stabbing someone in the back.

Or heart.

❄ ❄ ❄

IT WAS PECULIAR how disappointed I was—*pouty lip, tear on cheek*—not to run into Marcum at school. He didn't turn up in my lunch hour and I didn't see him in the halls. Sure, our school had thirteen hundred students, but a tall guy with movie star good looks would be hard to miss.

I didn't see Alex between our last two classes. He had those two periods back to back in the south wing so I always walked to Spanish with Mingzhu, my one and only girl-friend, who today appeared ready to burst with some phenomenal gossip.

She came toward me and did a U-turn to fall into step with me as I passed her locker. "Selina, don't look behind you." Her voice was low and rough as broken fingernails on a used emery board.

"Why not?"

"Oh. My. Gosh." She leaned close enough for me to feel her trembling. "He's like ten feet back."

"Who?"

"The new exchange student from Australia. He. Is. So. Hot." Her straight cut bangs flicked right, left, right, left.

I chanced keeping my eyes up and noticed that all the girls coming our way who usually had a sneer to toss at me, had their eyes riveted on the space behind us. I couldn't help myself; I had to check. I scanned the crowd for some-one tall, dark and handsome, but Marc wasn't there. In-stead an equally good-looking newcomer strode forward with all the confidence of a rock star and all the adoration of the girls in the hall. Mingzhu grabbed my arm to keep me from stumbling and I brought my head back around.

"Who's *he*?"

Mingzhu did her best stage whisper, the rough tone graduating to sandpaper. "His name is Craig, I think. He's from down under but he hardly has any accent at all. He was in my first hour. And guess what? He'll be in our Spanish class! I heard him go over his schedule with Ellory."

We turned the corner, passed the language lab, the French class, and the German room, and ducked into Señora Vargas's *sala de clase*. Most of the desks were already occupied. We quickly took our seats at the rear of the room and watched the door. Unless someone was absent there wouldn't be a single seat left for a new kid, but I had a suspicion the girl in front of me wouldn't show since I hadn't seen her on the bus.

When the new kid almost had to duck to get through the door, Mingzhu let out her breath. Gasps of air skipped over my vocal cords, too. Sorta couldn't help it. He was hot. Physically this guy matched Marc's height and weight. Muscular, slow moving, deliberate. But instead of black hair, his was platinum blond. He spoke to the teacher while his eyes roamed the room, as if he intended to catalogue each of us. I swore he spent a few seconds longer on me. *Cue the blush.* I couldn't look away, but I did manage to puff my chest out a bit. His gaze moved on to Mingzhu and at the same time he answered Señora's questions, took the book she handed him, and started moving in our direction.

I heard the squeak of Señora's marker on the whiteboard, felt the draft from Angie Olsen swinging her backpack up in the next aisle and smelled the stink of Gary Pace's smoke-drenched clothing two seats up. I was strikingly aware of these things, but had no eyes for anything but this ultimate specimen of masculinity.

"Oh, no," Mingzhu stuttered.

He barely lifted his feet to glide down the aisle. He stopped in front of us and spoke in low honey notes. "She told me ... sit here today. I hope not ... to be a block ... in front of you."

I shook my head, more to clear the sound of his voice than to answer, and tore my gaze away from his light blue eyes. I should have been having the same jitters as last night, being so close to another super-stud hunk, but instead my body was telling me something else. Like my gut was saying *watch out, keep away, run.*

Mingzhu stifled a giggle and her voice changed into melodic syrup, *"No problema. ¿Cómo te llamas?"*

Leave it to Mingzhu to get into Spanish mode before the bell rang.

"Coreg," he answered.

"*Mucho gusto*, Coreg." I rolled my eyes at her flawless response. Coreg turned to face forward and Mingzhu gave me the wide-eyed *I-think-I'm-in-love* expression and my eyes arced around again. So it was going to be love for Mingzhu and, hmm, a little nausea for me—*hold back gagging sounds.* I thought he seemed a bit phony, like he knew the effect he had on girls and meant to use it to his advantage. That charming smile was not going to work on me. I was sorry I'd tried to look bigger boobed by puffing out my chest at him.

The class period flew by as I stared at the back of Coreg's neck. His skin gave the impression of being much paler there, almost yellow, which reminded me of when Buddy was born and he was jaundiced. When Señora gave out the homework at the end of the hour, Coreg turned to hand me the last sheet and I saw the skin on his wrist as his shirt drew back an inch. Not yellow, more like faintly green. This kid seriously needed some time in the sun. I had a bizarre feeling about him. Not nausea anymore, something else.

Something relatively novel. Something I couldn't dodge. Something that was going to require a change in my personality. I think I was finally coming out of what my counselor called an avoidance disorder. Here I was inches from gorgeous and possibly dangerous maleness that my instincts told me to avoid and yet ... there was something ... something attracting me.

❄ ❄ ❄

AT THE END of his first and last intended day in this earthly school, every turbulent impulse in Coreg's nature was poised for action. This mission challenged him less than any he'd done in training. He managed to control his emotions—and two distinct physical responses—as the females flirted with him and the males evaluated him. When the time-bender ignored him and kept her special ability hidden, he sped up time to terminate the class period. He followed her to her locker, but kept walking when a hefty male met her there and held her books and bag as she put on a puffy body covering. Since Coreg had stolen clothes from the store but not a coat, he made a tactical decision to acquire one before approaching the time-bender again.

He went into a corner relief station and found a pudgy boy, his back to Coreg, entering a stall. Coreg shoved him to the floor, yanked his coat off one arm and then the other, and put it on himself. He snatched the stunned student's knit cap and adjusted it over his own trembling ears in front of the mirror. Then he turned and left. It all took place in less than what seemed like a second to his victim—the advantage of being a time-pacer.

Coreg had kept an eye out for Marcum all day, but surprisingly enough, Marcum failed to appear and wouldn't witness Coreg's triumph. It was a favorite habit of his to snatch victories away from Marcum in a sudden time-paced moment and he liked to do it right before his eyes. Something on this planet had invaded Coreg's communication device, corrupting the settings, and preventing him from communicating with Marcum. Nevertheless, he made a strategic assessment and decided to nab the time-bender as she left the school—without benefit of Marcum's audience—and take her outside of Earth's atmosphere. There, with her gift employed, he'd have plenty of time to fix and re-engage communication.

"*Hola*," Coreg called to Selina's back. The boy with her turned and gave him a quick inspection. Coreg fumbled to hide his weapon.

❄ ❄ ❄

"SOME BLOND DUDE'S trying to get your attention," Alex said to me. I looked back and smiled at Coreg. Okay, that was so not one of my habits, but I gave him no more than a hint of a smile and there was no chest inflating on my part.

"He's new," I told Alex. "An exchange student. From Australia, I think."

"That's the guy?"

"Not the one that was at my house. Just a coincidence. Funny, huh?" A heat started in my belly and branched out.

"'Scuse me," Coreg said, his voice sweet and slow as molasses.

I stopped before the doors and turned to answer him; he'd caught up to us. I suppressed the fear that he was on the verge of ridiculing me.

"Yeah?" I found myself both uncomfortable—*hold back nervous laughter*—and flattered by the way Coreg stared at me. Alex didn't say anything, but his perpetually tan face hinted at an angry blush and he gave off vibes that Coreg perturbed him. He moved around to block me from going through the doors, which was weird, and Coreg moved, too, as if he meant to hand me something. My eyes went down his arms and I noticed the Spanish book in one of his hands, the sleeve of his coat—too short and obviously borrowed—and a line between normal skin and greenish skin, which resembled the rind of a watermelon. Time stretched. Alex and Coreg stared at each other. It was the ears-back look male dogs give each other before deciding whether to fight or sniff crotches.

The tense moment strained, expanded and tightened before Coreg finally answered. "I wondered..."

"What? You have a question about the homework?"

Alex butted in. "Hey, we have to catch the bus. Sorry." He leaned against the door and pushed it open with his whole body. Good, no fighting, no crotch sniffing. But I did note a bit of chest inflating. "Come on, Selina, or we'll miss it. It's too cold to walk." And just like that the moment snapped back with rubber band speed.

"*Mañana*," I said. Not too clever, but I didn't want to talk to this guy because I knew Alex didn't want me to. I guess I picked up on a subliminal message—*surprise, new social skill.*

I stepped through the door and Alex followed. I wanted to look back, smile and be nice, because, when you come right down to it, I'm a nice person and I know what it's like to be shunned ... but I also didn't want to miss the bus or tick off Alex. The entire innocent dialogue had taken forever, though Coreg only spoke a few words.

"You were a bit rude," I said to Alex after we took our usual seats, mid-way on the left side of the bus. No one said anything nasty to me, probably because they were staring out the window at that white-blond super-model exchange student.

Sitting next to my best friend made me feel normal again and settled my stomach. Nice ... but a sense of something sour persisted. I had the window seat this time and I saw Coreg moving off across the parking lot. Long strides. Hat in hand. Hat striking thigh. The cloud cover parted for a moment and the low afternoon light touched the edges of his physique, making him look gilded, like an angel. Crap. My conscience kicked in. I felt guilty. I was the rude one.

"You didn't see what I saw," Alex mumbled.

"What?"

"Never mind." He pulled a yellow sucker out of his pocket, held the good end and licked the white stick. Of course I laughed.

CHAPTER 6
#SecretAdmirer

MARCUM HUDDLED IN his ship and pulled up all the information he had on his shipboard data concerning both Earth and Gleezhe. Cruel humanoids known to his people as Gleezhians, or in Klaqin lore *star cannibals*, populated a planet that orbited a red dwarf star smaller and cooler than Earth's sun. These adversaries had first been nomadic, peaceful tribes, progressing technologically at various rates until an advanced race of aliens ignored other viable planets and landed on Gleezhe intending to colonize it. The invasion succeeded with minimal bloodshed; the Gleezhians succumbed, were enslaved, and eventually assimilated over five hundred years into a new, highly combative society. The present day Gleezhians, a hybrid species, evolved through interbreeding. Or so Klaqin scientists believed. Gleezhians most notably lacked the benevolence the earlier inhabitants manifested, though that hadn't been Marcum's experience during the six double-moons he and Coreg had spent with Gleezhian renegades in an underground colony.

From time to time a child was born with ten fingers, a throwback to the aboriginals, but it was believed that the modern Gleezhians promptly disposed of him or her; sanctity of life was a forgotten concept. Marcum's scant data on Earth reflected a similar trajectory.

The modern Gleezhians built great cities, continued their space exploration, and eventually tried to colonize the sun-drenched side of Marcum's own planet, Klaqin. But the

Klaqins, who were at first welcoming, quickly hardened into defensive guardians of their precious civilization. The space wars began and for three generations both sides took heavy casualties, held prisoners, and refused to negotiate.

The Klaqins searched the galaxies for allies, for resources, and for life forms that manipulated space or time while the Gleezhians conducted galactic searches of their own—for weapons and, presumably, edible flesh. Marcum was afraid that if he and Coreg didn't return with a time-bender soon, Gleezhian forces would not only overwhelm Klaqin defenses, but they would reach Earth where they would certainly find an available food source and snatch the time-bender for themselves.

❄ ❄ ❄

ALEX USUALLY GOT off the bus with Selina, saw her safely inside and then trudged through the backyards to get home, but with so much new snow on the path he decided against it. Besides, the threat—that new kid—was nowhere around. He sat back down after he let her out from the window seat.

"Wimp," Selina called over her shoulder as she reached the steps and realized Alex hadn't followed. Mocking voices taunted her, which she ignored, but Alex didn't. He growled a wordless threat at the tormentors, two girls who made it a habit to heckle Selina.

The doors closed and the bus rumbled. He looked across the aisle and out the right side. Selina was almost to her door, the bus slowly passing her house, when he spotted a guy in a pink flower print ski jacket watching her from behind the Wilsons' van. He lurched out of his seat, but the bus's simultaneous gear-shifting momentum knocked him back down.

The short ride around the block seemed to take twice as long. Alex leaped up before the doors opened, but several sophomores and juniors who sat nearer the front blocked his way, taking their time to leave.

He jumped down the last step and pushed through a small crowd of lingerers. "Move it." He pressed through the group of boys, two of whom were pulling out packs of cigarettes. He ran, reached his house, flung his backpack onto the porch and continued on through the yard, making new, deeper tracks along the snowy path to Selina's place.

He slowed when he reached Selina's deck. He saw her standing at the kitchen island, the light from an open refrigerator behind her outlining her slight frame. She was safely inside. She still had her coat on which didn't surprise him. She'd be back outside in less than ten minutes to meet Buddy's bus, a routine he'd done with her hundreds of times.

He stood stock still, noted the fringe of November's icy cold on his warm cheeks, and heard the slightest whistle from a gust of air. Feathers of snow spun over his head as the wind carried the voices of the smokers: laughing, swearing, coughing. But another sound came from the opposite direction. He imagined a footstep on Selina's porch and feared the next thing he'd hear would be her doorbell, her voice, and then a stranger's accented speech.

He raced around the garage and slid to a cautious stop at the corner. But no one was there. No pink coat. Another breeze whipped a branch from the leafless maple against the porch beam. He stomped the snow from his pant-legs and hurried down the sidewalk toward the Wilsons' house. The footprints were obvious. The snow had been trampled in two spots as if the pervert had hidden by the front bumper of the van and then moved to the side to have a better view of Selina as she headed home.

Alex's labored breaths filled his ears. He let the curse words steam out between his lips. First one foreign student was coming after Selina, trying to flirt with her, and now another. He had a bad feeling about both of them.

He hurried to the end of the street, the direction it appeared the stalker had taken, and eyed the condominiums down the next road. He glanced briefly toward the woods that bordered his subdivision, eight acres of oaks and scrub pines poised to be phase two of the development ten years ago, that no one built on. The perv probably wouldn't head that way. Alex walked in the other direction, toward the main road, and stood at the corner, his frozen hands tucked under the armpits of his coat. He scanned up and down the road, but saw only Buddy's short bus slowing for the turn.

The boxy shape of the bus reminded him of the object he'd seen in the hand of Selina's second admirer, that tall white-haired exchange student who'd stopped Selina after school. The object, not at all different from a brown and gray box he'd found years ago in his own garage evoked a memory. When his father had caught him getting ready to open it, he quickly locked it away, cautioning a young Alex of the dangers of touching things he knew nothing about.

❄ ❄ ❄

I STEPPED OUTSIDE as my brother's bus pulled to a stop at the end of our driveway. Alex trotted behind it, a scowl on his face. We reached the door at the same time, before the attendant finished unbuckling Buddy.

"Why were you coming from that direction?"

He glanced all around before answering. "I was following your mom's ski jacket."

"What?"

"I saw your other foreign exchange admirer." He pulled a white-frosted hand out of his pocket and pointed toward the house three doors down. "The perv was watching you get off the bus. I ran back to catch him at your house, but I guess he got spooked and took off. I followed the creep up to the main road."

"Are you kidding me?" I took Buddy's backpack and then his hand. Alex moved to his other side and gave him a warm greeting and took his other hand. We walked up the drive the way we'd done lots of times, pulling and sliding Buddy along the slick surface. I kept glancing at Alex waiting for him to relax and tell me he was joking. I doubled up on meaningful looks. Alex kept silent.

"Again," Buddy begged when we reached the porch, but I wasn't in the mood to play winter games. My mind raced around the idea of Marc spying on me. That could be interpreted two ways, good or bad, and obviously Alex chose the bad.

"Not today, Buddy."

Alex grinned at me. He begged on Buddy's behalf, "Aw, come on, Selina. Just once more."

Buddy repeated the plea. "Come on, Thelina. Juth wonth more." His eyes gleamed extra-large behind his fogged up glasses.

"All right, but only once. Poor Alex doesn't have his gloves. Look how cold his hands are, Bud. They're nearly as blue as mine sometimes get."

I tossed the pack by the front door and we slid Buddy down the driveway and pulled him back up the slight incline. I couldn't have done it alone; Buddy was getting hefty. Alex outclassed angels when it came to dealing with my little brother, who could be quite obstinate at the worst times.

"Coming in with us?" I asked Alex.

"Sure."

He helped me get Buddy's coat off him, a difficult task when my brother doesn't want to cooperate. Then Alex made himself useful in the kitchen by nuking us some hot chocolate—with lots of milk to cool down Buddy's—while I situated Buddy at the table with his homework video started on the laptop. I turned the volume up and made him promise not to spill, then we took our drinks into the family room. Alex plopped down on the couch where Marc had sat. He couldn't compare to Marc's superstar good looks and formal posture; he relaxed into the cushion more like a cowboy or—dare I think it?—a shaggy pet.

"I'm staying till your mom gets home. That creep could come back."

"Alex. Come on, you can't call him a creep, okay? If he was still wearing my mom's jacket then he probably hasn't gotten one of his own yet."

"So why was he sneaking around, spying?"

I stared at my hands, watching them grow pinker from the warmth of the mug. "Maybe he wasn't. Maybe he's staying with the Wilsons. Did you consider that? Or maybe he couldn't remember which house was mine. They're all alike."

Alex slurped his drink instead of answering. It used to be we'd play games, watch TV, hang out, whatever, without a smidgen of awkwardness. The silences we had lately were becoming uncomfortable. Neither of us wanted to say the wrong thing. If my current thoughts came out of my mouth it would hurt Alex. And he was holding back, too. For one dreadfully long minute I wished for an attraction to Alex like I had with Marc. But I couldn't get around the fact that he was just a friend. My best friend. I didn't want to lose that. I couldn't even imagine kissing Alex, but I'd spent most of the last twenty-four hours wondering what Marc's lips would feel like—*sigh*.

"I know what I saw," Alex said after too long of a pause. "You have a stalker. Two, if you count that dude at school. There must be a special on signing up foreign exchange students who have a knack for lurking." He gulped down the rest of his chocolate, probably burning his throat, then said, "I forgot I left my bag outside. I gotta go. See ya tomorrow."

He took his mug to the kitchen and I followed him, trying to formulate the right thing to say short of lying. Alex stood by Buddy for a bit and watched the lesson with him. When Buddy hit the right key to answer correctly, Alex gave him a high five and a bunch of praise.

"See you tomorrow, kid." He gave my brother a sideways hug that made me want to cry. No other guy in the world could be as cool and kind as Alex and it made me feel like a jerk that I didn't return the feelings he had for me.

❄ ❄ ❄

ALEX TOOK THE long way home around the block. With his head down and his hands in his pockets, he followed the last car's snowy tire tracks but didn't see them or anything else as he visualized Selina's pretty face, long brown hair, puppy dog eyes, pert nose.

Once, when they were twelve, he told her that he liked Emily. Selina laughed and told him he had to make Emily jealous. They'd worked out a plot, but by the time he was supposed to act it out he'd lost interest in Emily. All through middle school he had told Selina the names of girls he thought were cute or special and each time her reaction had been supportive. He kept hoping that eventually she'd be jealous, but it hadn't happened yet. Now here he stood with more jealous bones in his body than stars in the sky. It was all he could do not to knock that white-blond exchange student on his butt when they left school. And he wanted to find that guy in the pink jacket and ring his neck too. He'd never been in a real fight in his life, martial arts classes not included, but he felt so protective of Selina, and of Buddy too, that he knew he'd flatten any guy who tried to bother them.

He stopped when he got to his driveway. A strange reverberation caught his attention in the crisp, frigid air. He listened. It sounded again. He perked up his ears as he did before. It wasn't a branch on a porch; it wasn't a car door; it wasn't like anything he'd ever heard before. And for some reason it made his bones ache.

CHAPTER 7
#ShipShape

THE TIME-BENDER HAD managed to affect the time around her again as Marcum spied on her from behind a bulky land vehicle. He shivered when it occurred to him that he was experiencing the fourth principle he'd studied: that time, like space, could dilate. He witnessed the way she hopped off the yellow transport vehicle—a school bus, he'd learned—how she kept her head down against the wind, and how she carefully picked her way up the driveway to the front door. He sensed his heart changing rhythms as she shifted the time around him. He observed her breath stiffen in frost along her collar and he peered down his own nose to see if his did the same. Small clouds of steam puffed around his face. *Ehk!* He looked back to see her tap a code into the door lock. It seemed to take too long for the bus to move on up the street and for her to open the door.

When she closed the door behind her time began its normal pace.

Marcum put a hand on the land vehicle, stared at the iron sky of early winter, and shook the snow from his hair. Here he was, light years from home, and obsessing over an Earth girl. He wondered if his parents would approve of what he planned to do. He wanted to snatch Selina straight away. Fear didn't hold him back from acting, but compassion did.

He flicked his thumb ring and recorded a swift synopsis of his reconnaissance. He included a brief word about his feelings—something he'd never done before.

On his planet genetic manipulation routinely occurred as an ordinary part of conception. Pay more and you could eliminate a particular characteristic or ensure another. He was sure his father paid for fearlessness, having always claimed he wanted nothing but a son who'd be heroic, courageous in battle, and daring—that trait certainly helped him cope with the serious situation he was presently in—but his mother bought him compassion. He had difficulty tempering the two. He'd rather be ruthless, because right now compassion was winning out as he hesitated to steal Selina away from her world.

A sudden far off popping sound, a reverberation alien to this world, sent a curl of disappointment through his body and he knew it would be pointless to take even one slippery step toward her house. Then the monitor on his belt, the one part of the communication device that still functioned, echoed the sound. He had a problem at the spaceship. He took off down the street and followed a narrow animal trail into the woods unaware that he'd been spotted by Selina's protector.

Snow shrouded the craft. Intermittent flashes from the bio-metals glinted gold in places where the flakes had melted. The camouflage had lapsed even though the snow did a fine job on its own, for the most part.

Marcum entered and tried to reset the alarm. He worked on the controls for half an hour. When he thought he had solved the problem, the alarm popped again. Not loud enough to alert most humans, he thought, but it might draw the attention of those four-legged pets.

Then his communication device began to crackle. He grabbed his helmet and worked the controls. He didn't hear English, Spanish, or Gleezhian when he found the right channel. His own native language, Klaqin, burst through in the rough voice of his comrade, Coreg.

Coreg's first words were expletives that would have earned him extra duties on Klaqin, followed by, "I found the time-bender! I win."

"What are you talking about? I encountered her last night. And I saw her now and you were not around." Marcum snorted into the speaker. "Where did you land? Maybe we found different time-benders."

Coreg gave his coordinates and Marcum confirmed that they were within a mile of each other.

"Is your ship well hidden?"

Coreg laughed. "Of course. I've collapsed it and fed the bio-metals enough galactic lard to keep the camo working as long as we need to be here."

Marcum took a turn at swearing then. "I forgot to feed the bio's. That must be my problem. Hold on." He checked his supplies and found that he didn't have enough grease to service the entire ship. "Listen, Coreg, do you have any extra? I seem to be a little low. I wasn't planning on this twenty light year trip when I re-docked after our last scouting run."

"Maybe. First answer this: who won?"

"I saw her first. I won."

"But you don't have her. I can grab her anytime I want. I got the highest mark in infiltration tactics, remember?" Coreg touched the clear band of purlass that encircled his wrist, the prize for his spectacular score, though Marcum knew he didn't deserve the prize. Coreg continued his boasting, "I sit right in front of her in their youth training center."

Coreg's revelation that he'd infiltrated a school astonished Marcum. That was incredible. But Coreg hadn't captured her yet. "I believe the bet was 'first one to find her wins,' was it not?"

Coreg breathed loudly then said, "You need the galactic lard, yes? Let's say we tied and the new bet is whoever grabs her first wins."

Marcum answered in English. "Whoever gets her to come willingly onto his ship wins."

"That might take more time, but I still have the advantage. If you're sure you want to do it that way, it's a deal."

"I'm sure. I know where she lives, you don't. She thinks I'm an exchange student. If you can infiltrate a school, then so can I." Then in Klaqin Marcum added the standard oath that had been missing from their first wager. Coreg broke the connection and Marcum suppressed a growl.

❄ ❄ ❄

MARCUM WAS AT Coreg's mercy regarding the galactic lard he needed, but Coreg carried two buckets of the stuff from his ship into the woods that night and helped distribute the necessary greasy proteins into the system all the while berating Marcum for forgetting something they'd learned on the very first day at the Academy: never leave base without extra galactic lard. The metal-based cells resumed their programmed functions, replicating themselves and evolving.

Coreg laughed when he saw Marcum's pink print coat. "You chose wrong. That's a female's covering. Your reconnaissance failed."

"It belongs to the time-bender's mother. I intend to return it."

Coreg shook his head. "I can't believe you were in her home and didn't steal her." He laughed in short spasms. "As far as warm weather goes, we won't be here that long. This planet doesn't warm up around these big lakes for—" he checked his thumb ring—"one hundred fifty Earth days. It might take *you* that long to coax a female into your cabin, but I plan on being back on Klaqin, with the prize, long before that." He patted Marcum on the top of his head. "Do your homework, Commander." He pulled on the orange and black Varsity jacket he'd stolen. "Or maybe you can cheat off me, as usual. I'll send you my data. You'll be enrolled in the time-bender's school by morning."

"I don't need your help."

"Really?" He picked up the two empty buckets. "So you didn't need these?" Coreg mocked Marcum who kept his mouth closed. "I'll send you the data now that our comms are working. Call it a handicap. After all, you're going to be watching *me*. And we both know my moves are fast."

"You couldn't get a Gleezhian slave to look twice at your green face."

"Ah, but it's not so green now, is it? The sunlight here is transformative. You should try it."

❄ ❄ ❄

MARCUM DISCOVERED A basket of unattended laundry on his after dark canvass of the businesses in the area. He helped himself to a pair of blue jeans and a shirt. When he returned to his ship he found Coreg's data awaiting his review. With a ration of nourishment, some motivated study —the vision of Selina's face helping him—two hours of sleep, and the first rays of light, Marcum rose ready and eager to make his way to the school.

He wouldn't recommend standing stark naked in the snow to soak up the seven fifteen sunrise, but it was worth the temporary physical discomfort which he hardly noticed. His attention was riveted on the long shadows, something that only happened on the frozen edges of his planet. Five minutes did the trick; his skin tone lost its anemic pallor. With no mirror to check his face he had to assume his complexion matched the color on his arms. He dressed quickly in the jeans and shirt he'd stolen; their peculiar odor mystified him, but he didn't find it unpleasant.

The new wager held higher stakes because of the oath. If he couldn't tempt the time-bender into his ship, and Coreg could, he would return home to worse than humiliation. He knew what would make a Klaqin female accompany him anywhere, but he hadn't foreseen the need to have expensive inducements with him in his spaceship. He had no idea if he could charm Selina. Had she found him attractive the night before last? She seemed more concerned with Buddy. She behaved in a protective and attentive manner toward the boy. Maybe he should abduct the child first. He needed to figure this out soon. He and Coreg had signed out on a training excursion and, if they didn't return in a Klaqin month, they would be hunted down by punishers and parents alike.

❄ ❄ ❄

I WAS A ZOMBIE getting ready for school. I woke up a dozen times during the night with the oddest feeling that someone was staring at me. And the dreams I had—*call the police*—were super real, much clearer than those visions I'd been having. The last one freaked me out. I was crawling up a chute, sort of like the long covered slide at the park, and Alex was pushing me from behind, which was odd because he'd never go on that park slide due to his problem with enclosed spaces. I surfaced into a room with a blasted hole in the ceiling. The dream stopped there, but I had reruns of it in the shower, on the bus, and at my locker. Alex noticed my zombie-ness.

"Did your alarm not work again?" he asked, leaning against the locker next to mine. He had his arms folded, his backpack at his feet, and I knew he was acting as sentry.

"Bad dream."

"Well, then I must not have been in it."

"Actually you were," I teased. I grabbed my book for English and closed the locker door as quietly as I could. No need to draw attention.

"Tell me about it."

"Later. I want to get to class." I'd usually stand and talk to him until the last minute when he'd rush off to his first hour, but I had an insistent feeling that I should be in my classroom early. A tiny bead of adrenaline burst in my heart as I imagined that I was going to see Marc seated in Mrs. Buckley's English class. *Romantic day-dreamer, that's me.*

Alex picked up his bag and walked me across the wide hallway. "Okay, Selina, see you in," he checked the clock in the hall, "the time it takes to listen to twenty songs on iTunes."

"Don't get caught," I said.

He turned with a wave of his free hand and his usual eyebrow wiggling. "I never do."

I slipped into the classroom, head down, heart pounding and slinked to my seat as inconspicuously as possible. I hadn't needed to try so hard; the room was empty, except for Mrs. B. who was writing on the white board.

❄ ❄ ❄

MARCUM ARRIVED LATE to school. The paperwork he manipulated to precede him could not be found. Some of Coreg's data was deviously faulty. The secretary sent him to the counseling office anyway.

The counselor exhibited rude superiority. "You're the second Johnny-come-lately in two days. This is unacceptable. It's November, for crying out loud. Parent conferences commence in a few days. Sit down."

Luckily Marcum caught the last two words of her tirade and lowered himself onto the tattered chair across from her. He tried to imagine how Coreg influenced this elderly human into giving him access to a class with Selina. Must have been luck, he couldn't see how time-pacing would have helped. He glanced around the small office. The corners were piled with thick manuals that couldn't find space on the cluttered shelves. An aromatic black liquid steamed from a drinking vessel. The harried woman took a sip from it before she started fingering the lettered board on her desk.

Marcum got an idea. "Pardon. Hellew," he began, clearing his throat, "easy for you ... give me same classes as Selina."

"Selina Langston? Oh, sweet girl." The woman's attitude instantly changed; she tapped a few keys and stared at the monitor. Her phone rang and without taking her eyes off the screen she answered, maintained a monosyllabic conversation with someone, scrawled on a square notepad, and hung up. She tore off the paper and pressed it to the top edge of the screen where it stuck. "Sorry about that. Lots of angry mothers this time of year. Report cards went home yesterday. Okay, then," she said, lowering her voice to an intimate level while she studied the screen, "do you speak Spanish?"

"No, I speak English and—" he almost said Klaqin, Gleezhian, Chinese and Russian but he stopped himself.

"And?"

"And that's all." Best to stick with yes and no answers. He smiled without showing his teeth, his lips curling up more on one side than the other, his ears not quite still.

The counselor clicked a few more keys. "That," she murmured to herself, "changes this. And Humphry's class is full. Okay, that works. And print. Oh, crap, the printer's down again. Hold on a minute." She pulled a sheet of paper from a drawer and made a column of numbers. "There you go. First hour, right now, you're in room 218. Then second hour you go to 109. I got you into four of the same classes as Selina. Nice girl. Too bad that she's ... uh, never mind. I'll send an aid with the complete schedule once the printer's up and running. Don't worry. Tell the teachers that you'll be in their system by the end of the day."

Marcum stared at the list of room numbers. He wasn't particularly adept at handwritten English letters and had even less experience with numbers. His brain spun on overload from listening to this woman's confusing instructions, but he had passed stressful intrusion and subversion exams in Gleezhian and this wasn't much different. He flashed another lop-sided smile. "Thank-ful...thank you."

❄ ❄ ❄

SECOND COMMANDER DACE took a bite of the frozen delicacy impaled on his knife. He nibbled around the edges as he viewed the live feed of the combat raging high above the dark side of his planet. An entire battalion of Fourth Commanders, boys who'd barely passed their exit exams, were being introduced to a bloodless space battle and disappearing rapidly in cosmic vapor. They hardly stood a chance without an experienced time-pacer to work the edges. Their disappearance reminded him of a similar catastrophe when he trained as a youth.

There were no more than a dozen time-pacers left on the planet now that Coreg had gone rogue with Marcum. In spite of the propaganda assuring the populace of military superiority and a surplus of soldiers with gifts such as pacing, Dace knew a devastatingly different truth.

He had to face the First Commanders at the next moon passing and give the small council a full report. He wasn't prepared to resign; no one resigned from such a high position and he was sure they wouldn't allow it given their reduced numbers, but he fully expected to be reprimanded and then sent to retrieve both Coreg and the possible time-bender. However, they might reluctantly deem Marcum expendable. And he couldn't let that happen, not after sharing restricted and confidential information about Marcum with Coreg. Dace was in a precarious position. He spit the remains of his frozen treat into a vacuum port and then waved his hands in front of the copper screen. Maybe he could propose a way to save Marcum too without revealing his incredible suspicions. He scrutinized the genetic reports.

CHAPTER 8
#BFF

HE WORE A white shirt and scruffy jeans, and I squirmed at the sight of him. I couldn't believe my eyes—*restart heart*—when Marcum sauntered into my first hour class with fifteen minutes left. Mrs. Buckley didn't appreciate someone interrupting one of her Shakespeare readings. She spoke to him at the door and seemed hesitant to let him in. We had rules about not bringing a coat to class and Marcum stood there clutching my mom's jacket. Yeah, like he planned on smuggling in booze, drugs, or a cell phone in a girl's coat. After a few moments Buckley relented. He no doubt enchanted her with his accent and those dark eyes—*cue mysterious theme music.*

She gave him a copy of the play, introduced him to the class as Marc Marcum and assigned him to the front seat, two rows over. I usually avoided eye contact, but he caught me staring and smiled as he sat down. I smiled back and got goose bumps. I endured the glare of every girl in the class. No matter. I saw him first and it was time for me to find a boyfriend. I tried hard not to puff out my chest.

I sat far enough over and behind that I could mentally drool over his profile with little chance of him catching me staring again. I watched him roll my mom's jacket in a ball and stuff it between his lap and the desk. The girl next to him reached over and turned his book to the right page. He turned his head enough to peep my way which made my stomach cartwheel. I totally lived out Act II, Scene 2, of Mrs. Buckley's dramatic interpretation of both Juliet and

Romeo. Instead of following along in the text I watched Marc as he held his book flattened against the desk and moved his finger across each line.

When the bell rang it startled me almost as much as it did Marc. The others filed out of the room, but I took my time as Mrs. Buckley assigned him a locker and told him to leave his coat there from now on. I ducked out as soon as I heard the locker number and hurried across the hall to open mine. I swear I could feel his eyes on me as he came out. In that instant the loud hallway chatter, the slamming of locker doors, the breezy rush of hurried bodies passing by all seemed to fade like in a movie scene. My ears went deaf and my sight darkened around the edges; I couldn't clearly see the padlock in my hand as I slowly twisted the dial.

"Hellew."

I turned my head to the right. He stood in front of the locker two down from mine. My eyes made it from the floor to his waist. With a little extra effort I raised them to his face. "Hi. Need help with your combination?" I tried to keep the breathlessness out of my voice. *What was I doing!* The romantic notion that his eyes were speaking to my soul struck me as a noteworthy possibility and I worried I might drool for real.

"Oh, speak again, bright angel." His accent disappeared for the brief quotation and my heart stopped somewhere on its way to my throat.

"Have you studied that play before?"

"No."

I swallowed hard and reached for the slip of paper in his hand. "Sometimes kids switch out locks." I memorized the numbers, 13-4-33, and started twisting the dial around for him. One good yank and it opened. A coat hung on the hook and some books filled the top shelf. "Looks like you're sharing." These were more words than we'd exchanged in my house. Marc stood there staring at me, all tall and handsome, and my thoughts raced between fearing I'd been too forward or too condescending—he could certainly open his own lock—and fearing I had breakfast stuck in my teeth —I made a quick tongue inspection. Prickles of heat swarmed my shoulders, neck, and face. I struggled for something clever to say, another line from Romeo and Juliet, anything. My inadequate conversational skills underwhelmed me. The best I could do was, "Stuff that pink thing in there before some bully sees you and makes a big deal out of it." *Wow, I was speaking to him as easily as I did with Alex.*

Marc doled out a sly smile millimeter by millimeter and fed me another line from the play, *"I have night's cloak to hide me from their eyes."*

I laughed, I actually laughed, pushed my locker closed, and begged my scattered brain to come up with the perfect response and I did: *"Parting is such sweet sorrow."*

I grinned, feeling less inferior than usual, and turned and walked straight into Alex's chest.

❄ ❄ ❄

ALEX ALWAYS MET Selina after first hour and escorted her to choir, the one class they had together. He sat with the tenors directly behind the only alto who mattered—Selina. He whispered jokes to her and mimicked Ms. Hartoonian quietly enough that, aside from the kids on either side of them, no one heard him. It was his favorite class of the day, mostly because she was there, but also because he had a natural ability to harmonize and to recall virtually every song lyric he'd ever heard.

It had stunned him to see Selina flirting at her locker with a tall kid he'd never seen before. The big guy had hair so black it looked blue, like the comic book version of

Superman. He stopped behind her at the moment she quoted the sweet sorrow line and his heart did a nose dive. When she turned and saw him, almost stepping on his toes, he took a mental snapshot of the scene—muscular dude, open locker, pink coat, two grins—and then time went into a funeral pace: Selina dropped her grin, the dude fumbled with latching his locker, and the one minute warning bell buzzed, though for Alex it sounded more like a hiss.

"Oh, Alex, sorry." Selina stepped back, caught her balance. "Um, this is Marc, Marc Marcum, the exchange student I told you about. He was in my first hour. Mrs. B. gave him a locker here. I was helping him. Marc, this is Alex."

Selina's breakneck introductions fizzled out with the last of her breath. He couldn't think of a time he'd heard her speak so much in front of an outsider.

"Hey."

"Hellew."

"Where ya from?" Alex tried his best to hide his irritation.

"Klaqin."

"Where's that?"

"Long way from here." Marc pulled a piece of paper out of his jeans and held it out to show Selina. "Where is one ... zero ... nine?"

Alex groaned and Selina beamed. "Oh, you're in choir with me and Alex. Come on, we have to hurry now."

They walked down the corridor, but not at all in a hurry, and took the stairs, Selina on the railing. They rounded the landing and took a short hall past the drama room and slid into the choir room as the bell rang.

Alex bluffed a smile, easing off his initial irritation, and said, "Ms. Hartoonian, we brought you a new singer."

During music class Alex watched Marc watch Selina. He didn't welcome the competition. And he couldn't bear the way Selina bubbled up around this foreigner—she never interacted with people unless absolutely necessary.

Something about that dude didn't add up. When the bell rang Alex stayed a few steps behind as Selina walked wordlessly next to Marc and led him past the drama room and on toward the chemistry lab. It hurt him that she never looked to see if he was following.

Alex skipped out of third hour and hung out in the boys' restroom, scrolling through his phone searching for the cryptic message he'd received from Selina's father shortly after school started two months ago. Her father, Rudy Langston, was as involved in his kids' lives as Alex's own dad was, though it was mostly by long distance.

Selina had always said her father worked as a traveling robotics technician, spending eight weeks in Tennessee, then home for a short while before driving off to Missouri or some other state where his particular skills were needed. Last year she had found out some of the truth: her father didn't know an actuator from a transducer, but he spoke fluent Arabic, Turkish and some crazy sounding foreign language and worked for the government. She immediately shared the knowledge with Alex. Then she swore him to secrecy.

Alex had known his friend's father his entire life, but the soft-spoken man in no way fell into the category of "men in black," "mission impossible," or "secret agent." Alex was awed by the mysterious Mr. Langston and the shadowy job he held, traveling to who-knows-where out of the country. When he came home last August Alex had stared at him too long and Mr. Langston discerned the breach in confidentiality. Rather than confront Selina, though, Mr. Langston had taken Alex aside, explained a minimum of details, and enlisted Alex as a private source of security for his family. No one would guess that a neighborhood teen knew the phone number and the panic code that, when repeated twice, would bring a squad of armed men to Selina's home.

For Alex, it was already routine to keep an eye out for Selina's well-being. He was fired up to play the hero-guardian and had even started memorizing car license plates whenever an unfamiliar car drove through their neighborhood; but by November he'd grown convinced that Selina, her mom, and her brother were under no threat of harm and that Mr. Langston had merely fed his wild imagination. Classic parental teasing.

He stopped thinking that yesterday after he saw the suspicious box in Coreg's hand, then witnessed Marc spying on Selina. Being disguised as exchange students seemed a ridiculous cover to Alex, but who knew how terrorists would infiltrate America? And they were obviously targeting Selina. Marc hadn't taken his eyes off Selina for an instant in choir. Alex wavered between doubt and suspicion. If someone had a plan to kidnap her, her father must have either ticked off somebody incredibly evil or possessed some phenomenally important information and the bad guys needed Selina as leverage. His proactive imagination flipped through every hostage movie he'd ever seen. Suspicion trumped doubt.

After fifteen minutes of hunting through hundreds of text messages and finding that he'd gone farther than he needed to, Alex realized he no longer had the puzzling message from Mr. Langston on his phone. He squeezed his eyes closed and willed himself to remember the words. The text read like an order, something similar to 'limit contact with' followed by several names. He pounded his fist into a stall door. It swung hard and slammed back, rattling the frame. Then he thought of a possible solution: signing into the computer lab where his friend Niket Patel spent his lunch hour. Niket would know how to hack into the deleted texts and find the message.

❄ ❄ ❄

MARCUM MISSED THE presence of the time-bender during fourth hour, the first class he had without her. The algebra class included, right in the middle, a trip to a noisy, weirdly lit room called a cafeteria where hundreds of these adolescent humans fed themselves vast amounts of beige foods. Marcum took a seat with a friendly female from his class. She invited him to take her dessert after she discovered he had no money to buy a meal.

"What this is?" he asked, sniffing deeply at the cherry pie and inverting his question. It too was covered in a beige blanket of crispness, but at least it boasted a center of rich crimson color.

"You don't have pie in your country? Try it." She smiled and handed him a plastic fork.

Marcum scanned the neighboring students, quickly discerned the customary way to handle the utensil, and scooped up a generous forkful. He placed the not-so-dainty serving on his tongue. His lips closed over the treat and his tongue smashed the flavorful morsel to the roof of his mouth. He couldn't stop himself from releasing a groan. The pie at first tasted tart, causing his mouth to water profusely. He chewed through the crust and berries and found the sweetness even more tantalizing. He'd never eaten anything as wonderful.

"Do you like it?" The girl stared, as did several other students who also snickered at the sounds he made.

"I like," Marcum purred. He took another bite and another and wondered if he betrayed his alien status by consuming this pie incorrectly.

"Here, have mine," a boy to his left said, shoving a blue-centered piece in Marcum's direction.

"Five bucks says he can eat five pieces in ten minutes," another boy said.

Marcum wondered who 'Fivebucks' was and why he would say such a thing, but he thought he'd better show these new algebra friends that it was true. Lesson one in infiltration techniques stressed blending in any way that presented itself.

❄ ❄ ❄

COREG FOUND HIS second day of school to be less exhilarating than the first. Tedious. Nevertheless, he didn't use his pacing to speed up the day. He observed, participated as necessary, and made a few male and female allies. He even skipped out of the class after lunch, persuaded by five guys who insisted he learn a game called basketball. They weren't convinced that Coreg came from a country that knew nothing of the popular sport.

"What do you have on your feet?" Brad, the tallest of the five asked, his voice echoing in the empty auxiliary gym. "Those are awesome. Sports Authority? Dick's?"

"Yeah, man, where'd you get those? Are they custom?"

Coreg answered truthfully, including a click of the tongue on the first unaccented syllable of each Klaqin word, "Tlugmallood Supplies, Outer Plickkentrad, West Glak."

Five pairs of eyes stared.

"Huh. Cool. Well, we'll play three on three. These are the rules." The leader of the group gave a brief summary, grabbed a ball from the bin and moved onto the court. Coreg followed, all his senses on alert. It wouldn't be inconceivable that these humans had gotten him off alone to test him, maybe even kill him. He was suspicious of the shorter male they called Lance whose eyes shone with an abnormal glossiness.

The game began and Coreg caught on quickly to the style of movement, the dribbling of the ball, and guarding an opponent. No one passed him the ball at first. He matched their speed as they jogged up and down the court.

Their shoes squeaked while his footwear gripped and released with imperceptible puffs of air.

The score was ten to six when Brad stole the ball and blasted it toward Coreg. Coreg caught it, analyzed its circumference and weight, dribbled it a couple of times then took aim at the circular band. The ball hit the backboard, but when it failed to sink Coreg mouthed a Klaqin curse. Brad slapped him on the back. Coreg nearly used a Gleezhian underpunch to fend him off, but caught himself in time. He'd seen the others slapping backs and holding their right arms up to slap hands. This wasn't the hostile behavior it was on his planet. He also determined this was not a pre-sacrificial ritual he'd failed to discern. It was, in truth, a game.

The second time the ball came to him he released it like a pro, making it arc over the others' heads and trace a trajectory that matched his mental calculations.

"Three pointer!" Brad sounded incredulous. "Beginner's luck or are you shittin' us that you've never played before?"

"Never played before," Coreg answered. He was the only one not sweating.

Lance started to speak, but a shrill whistle caught them all by surprise.

"Oh, crap, we're busted. It's Coach."

"Do that again," the old man said.

One of the boys dribbled the ball twice before bouncing it toward Coreg who had moved closer to the free throw line. Coreg caught the ball, glanced at the net, then turned and faced the farther goal. With no hesitation he aimed and shot the ball. It covered the sixty foot distance like a bullet and dropped neatly through the rim. It was, quite literally, in his DNA to exceed all expectations.

The coach laughed. "I heard we had a couple of tall transferees. I'm sure I can find a spot for you on the Panthers. What's your name?"

Coreg wasn't sure he needed to go this deeply into covert infiltration, but at least a dozen swooning females had commented on his height and asked him if he played ball. Perhaps a place on this team would translate into an advantage with the time-bender. His left ear curled.

"I am Coreg."

❄ ❄ ❄

ALEX AND HIS friend Niket sat together in a corner booth and worked quietly on Alex's phone records. It was a simple task for Niket to locate the specific text Alex was searching for. It began as Alex had remembered and read: Limit contact with Ludlum, Fleming, and Conrad.

"What's so important about that?" Niket asked, leaning back and balancing his hulking frame on two legs of the chair.

"I don't know. Selina's father sent it to me. I think it's a warning." Alex cracked his knuckles and glanced around the room. He took a chance on revealing more than he should. "I think they're the names of government spies."

The expression on Niket's face, a cross between incredulity and pity, stumped Alex. Niket's Indian accent ratcheted up a notch as he spoke, "Dude, these aren't spies, these are the guys who wrote the books on spies. These are famous authors."

"What?" Alex frowned at the names. So it *was* a prank. A good one. He should be laughing. *Ha. Ha.* But the feeling in his gut held him back from letting go of the mystery of Marc and Coreg. "Yeah, okay, so they're authors. Um, I got another question for you, mastermind. Can you get into the school's system and check out a couple of new exchange students?"

"Piece of cake, bro." Niket smiled and sat forward, blocking the screen from the media center administrator across the room.

Alex couldn't follow the keystrokes even though Niket's fingers didn't fly over the keyboard as fast as hackers were portrayed on television. Still, he typed quickly, and within five minutes he got through the firewall and started scrolling through personal student information.

"That's funny," Niket murmured.

"What?" Alex leaned forward, cracking one knuckle and then another.

"Not much info here. Usually these blanks are all filled in."

Not one for pondering, Alex jumped to the conclusion that made sense: these guys truly were foreign exchange students; if they'd been undercover agents or terrorists then the paperwork would have been flawless. He didn't mean to sigh like a girl, or to lapse into silent reflection, but something else puzzled him: how to keep those two Romeos away from Selina.

"Hey, dude," Niket scraped his chair back as he closed out the open windows and shut down the computer, "you gonna go out for basketball again or keep us whiz kids company at chess club?"

Alex started to answer with a shake of his head; he'd decided last week to give basketball another try. Last year he sat on the bench. A lot. There were twelve on the team and he was eleventh. But right this minute, thinking about Selina, he was torn between going out for the team again—he hadn't practiced much—or sticking with chess. It was Tuesday. Selina's mom didn't work a shift at the hospital on Tuesdays so she'd be home for Buddy. He and Selina usually stayed after to play chess. She hadn't mentioned chess this morning on the bus and he forgot to tell her he planned on going to tryouts. "I don't know." He had mixed thoughts on it now.

"Man, you got a couple of class periods to decide. I think you should go out for ball again. You've grown a few inches. We lost six seniors last year and only three guys moved into their spots. You'll get more game time."

"Yeah, I suppose."

"Come on, dude, you gotta represent the nerds." His sing-song lilt and earnest plea earned a positive response from Alex.

"Yeah, okay, I'll try out."

"Great. That gives me a better opportunity with a certain girl." Niket smirked. Alex punched him in the arm. Hard.

CHAPTER 9
#MotorMouth

OH. MY. GOSH. I was starting to sound like Mingzhu. Emoji: heart pulse. Heart-throbbing crush. On Marc. We had the same third hour class, too: Chemistry. Mr. James assigned Marc to the table three rows behind me. I couldn't see him for the entire hour, and that sucked because the hour dragged on and on, but I could feel that undeniable physical chemistry all the same—*hello hormones*.

I usually see Alex between all but my last two classes. Today, however, he disappeared after choir and I guided Marc to third hour by myself, showed him where his fourth hour was, and afterward took him to fifth hour History. We had that class together, too, but not Spanish. So out of the whole day we had all except two classes together. Incredible. This was destined to be the best school year ever. He still spoke to me in two word sentences; I, however, made up for his silences. Well, in my limited way; but I maintained eye contact and that was a milestone for me. I felt encouraged that he hadn't found anything to ridicule me about. Yet.

After History I showed him where his last class was and then sprinted to Spanish. I totally forgot about the other exchange student, Coreg, until I reached the room and saw that Señora Vargas had reassigned him to a new desk she'd requisitioned. Hooray. The creep was now on the other side of the room, out of my line of vision. Poor Mingzhu would have to do her drooling sideways.

Señora took roll and then went right into Spanish, *"Atención, clase. Vamos al laboratorio de lenguas."*

Double hooray. I loved the language lab. Everybody picked up their stuff and we filed out of the room to go down the hall to the new zillion-dollar addition to the language wing. Mingzhu held me back with a whisper, "Hey, there's always one empty seat in the lab next to you. Trade with me today so I can sit next to Coreg."

I saw no harm in that, in fact I thought I'd make it official by asking Señora to permanently change our seats. I entered the lab and went straight to her raised platform where she sat behind three monitors and an array of keyboards and controls.

"En español," she said before I got two words out.

Caramba. I should have asked Mingzhu how to phrase my request. "Um, *¿puedo cambiar asientos con Elisa?"*

She rattled off an answer that started with no, I couldn't change seats with Mingzhu—Spanish name *Elisa*—and continued with, to the best of my understanding, an explanation of why she wanted a good student like me next to the new kid. Unbelievable. Why me? I wasn't nearly as good a student as Mingzhu.

I shook my head at Mingzhu and she totally deflated. I went and sat down as directed, but made sure to grumble about it under my breath, making use of the few Spanish expletives I'd learned. The albino giant, however, seemed pleased to find me in booth number thirteen. Lucky me. I hunched forward a little, protecting my miniscule boobs from his gaze.

"*Hola*, Coreg," I didn't look directly at him. I took a moment to formulate all I'd need to say and droned through my instructions as if I were tutoring Buddy. "Log in with your first and last name and use your mom's maiden name as your password. Put the headset on and adjust the volume. She records everything we say so if she doesn't listen to you now, she can check it later. Got it?"

I made eye contact. Big mistake. Coreg gave me a smile that flipped my stomach. I felt bad for thinking of him as an albino or a giant. He was amazingly handsome and the whitish hair didn't freak me out as much today. It seemed familiar in fact. He reminded me of somebody ... somebody good. His skin didn't appear as sallow anymore. Those light colored eyes bore through me in the same way that Marc's had and I thought I'd never breathe again if I didn't look away. I noticed he wore the same shirt as yesterday, but he smelled wonderful. Okay, my breathing worked again. And there was a good chance that my chest started expanding. I uncorked a fairly high-caliber stare of my own. All my senses abandoned my prior thumbs-down evaluation, refuting that negative assessment and now acknowledging his total awesomeness. Somehow he pulled a smile out of the depths of my previous disgust.

My cheek muscles twitched. I was frozen in a stomach-knotting stare down. I had no power to ignore him. When he dropped his gaze my heart thudded to the bottom of my stomach and I stifled a hiccup.

"This is right?" Coreg asked. He moved two fingers off the keyboard. I looked at his screen and choked back a laugh. He'd typed "Coreg Klaqin" with the password "yormothersmadename." Not the best speller.

"Yeah," I pulled my cheeks into obedience, "that'll work." We both reached for our headsets at the same time.

I gave him the cold shoulder the rest of the hour which, amazingly, dragged by forever while his body heat radiated my way.

❄ ❄ ❄

COREG WAS CERTAIN of persuading the time-bender to walk away from the school with him, believing that he could simply take her hand before she got on the bus and lead her away. He had seen males holding females' hands at various opportunities throughout the day, no different than the courting rituals on his own planet. Taking a female's hand instantly made her submissive, he had no doubt about that.

He'd also seen couples kissing in the halls, which had disturbed him. Though not an unusual activity on his planet between mating individuals—older ones like his parents—he'd rarely seen it practiced in public. These humans obviously enjoyed it and flaunted the enjoyment as well.

Coreg laughed inwardly at the crudeness of the language lab, the small screens, the simple headsets, and the distraction of having thirty youths learning at the same rate. On his planet they'd perfected language learning "cabs," individual booths with surround sound and surround screens that gave a concentrated full body experience to increase input and retention.

Though tempted to speed up the time in this crude lab, Coreg did not use his pacing skill. He allowed the time-bender to display her own talent for bending the time and lengthening its limits without interruption, which permitted him to study her.

The abundance of hair that before had hidden her ears and the sides of her face was held in place under the top band of the headset. A few strands escaped. From time to time she passed her fingers along the side of her head as if to tuck those loose hairs behind her ear, but each time the black headphones thwarted the habit. He determined from her first returned smile that she was nervous to be so close to him. She exhibited affected mannerisms that he knew from study and experience were designed to hide sensory responses. Interesting, he thought.

The mouthpiece that she adjusted multiple times kept slipping down to touch her chin. Coreg stifled his own smiles, spoke softly into his microphone, and repeated the

Spanish lesson. The language was easier than English, but he continued to think in English, planning the special words of seduction he'd need to keep her calm on their trek to his ship.

❄ ❄ ❄

A BOMB EXPLODED on my heart and in my brain today, scrambling my emotions, confusing my thoughts, and turning my life into a soap opera. I was pretty psyched that Marc had four classes with me. I'm sure I hyperventilated myself into an oxygen high. For the first time ever I was making a "connection" with someone—*butterflies!*—and I dared to anticipate a romantic relationship in my future. Maybe hooking up with the hottest guy to walk into this school would earn me a little respect and a lot less harassment. One could hope.

Then ... Spanish class. Holy crap. Talk about a soap opera triangle. I didn't see that coming. Coreg ... crap ... Coreg. This had to be some tremendously involved hoax to humiliate me.

The closest thing I had to a friend, not counting Alex, was Mingzhu. And here I was betraying her because of my sudden interest in Coreg; she claimed him first after all. Oh brother, I'd sunk to the lowest of the low—*drop head, shrink to nothing*—with no moral standards, no redeeming personal qualities. I was toe jam, bug spit, and snake poop.

I couldn't wait for the final bell to ring. I always loved the language lab activities, the short video clips of native speakers, the questions, and the games at the end; I loved speaking into the mic and hearing myself clearly in my headset. But not today. Today I didn't like it at all. I cowered like an abused dog, squeaked like a chew toy, and reddened like a boiled lobster. I kept rewinding the dialogues because concentrating was impossible with Coreg's deep velvet voice repeating his lines a mere twelve inches away. My mic picked him up clearly; he was in my head. And so close to me.

When I couldn't stand the prickly heat any longer I chanced a look his way. His eyes met mine; his pupils dilated and his mouth closed in mid-answer then turned up in an inquisitive smile. He covered his mic to whisper to me and that's when I noticed his hand. He wore on his thumb the same stylized ring that Marc had: three silver bolts soldered together and engraved with hieroglyphics. I didn't respond to whatever he said because the center of one of the markings started to glow red then faded out. What a dorky mood ring. I looked back at his eyes; his irises had returned to their full rainbow.

"Your ring," I whispered, "is exactly like Marc Marcum's. Do you know him?"

Coreg pulled his headset down to his neck. His ears stuck out. I swear they moved. "What?"

I glanced at Señora; she'd probably excuse Coreg for breaking protocol, but I didn't want to get caught with my earphones off. "Never mind," I mouthed. I scooted my chair away from him and leaned forward so I'd be hidden from his view by the side panels of my booth. My mind started whirling around crazy conspiracy theories. Maybe Marc and Coreg were both undercover spies and maybe it had to do with me ... because of my dad's job. I needed to talk to Alex; he was the only person who knew the real reason why my dad kept leaving us for months at a time.

I squeezed my eyes closed. Stupid. I was being stupid. And paranoid. Marc and Coreg looked older, but then that wasn't unusual for foreign exchange students. I'd heard most of them finished their schooling first before they came here. And government agencies wouldn't employ two outrageously good-looking guys to go undercover in a high school. Silly idea.

I got hold of my crazy thoughts for a second and started to convince myself that it was a coincidence that they had the same ring. It was probably some gamer's device. I remembered Alex used to wear a ring that went to one of his online video games.

But why was Alex so ticked yesterday when Coreg approached us? 'You didn't see what I saw,' he'd said. Maybe now I *have* seen what he saw. And I had a strong reaction to it, too. It didn't make any sense, but I grew a little calmer knowing I could talk to Alex about it after school. Good old Alex.

Good old chase-after-the-bad-guy Alex, who thought Marc was spying on me. I didn't know what to think.

"Hic—"

Ay, caramba, I missed the whole last dialogue and there were only five minutes left of class. I circled random answers and hung my headset on the hook. I pushed my chair back and glanced at Coreg's paper; it was blank. He caught me staring and smiled. I suppose I melted again. There seemed no way to shield myself against that magnetic pull. Or those distracting butterflies. The fluorescent lights struck sparks in his hair and the infinitesimal stubble of his beard, wreathing his head in silver glitter.

"Too hard?"

"No," he said, "too easy."

I wanted to get out of the language lab without saying another word to Coreg. The bell rang and the usual chaos made it easy to slip past him. Mingzhu pulled me aside at the door and gave me the "look," that somber stare-down that said she'd seen the flirting.

"It's not what you think," I lied, forcing a smile. Her eyes, pale gray and wet as dew drops, flickered toward the ceiling, then rested with strained loyalty on the tense face before her—mine.

And then Coreg cut in between us—*did he push her?*—and took one of my hands so that I had to shift my books up against my chest. He pulled me away—didn't say a word! Maybe he didn't see Mingzhu. Yeah, that had to be it, he was totally tuned in to me. *Me.* And I left him speechless. *Dream on.*

My mouth started spouting a fountain of words all on its own, probably not comprehensible words, more like embarrassed grunts and tongue-tied blubbering, but at that moment my brain definitely did not connect to my lips. His hand on mine short-circuited everything. I heard Mingzhu snap a sarcastic *gracias* after us and I pulled my hand away.

"You can't do that," I said, trying to sound a little miffed, but not enough to discourage him. His amazing eyes found mine and my shoulders loosened, my whole body responded and I was tempted to let my hand slip back into his. Then I remembered my first impression of him, Alex's coarse reaction to him, and that weird ring. I kept my hands tightly cradling my books.

"Do what?"

Oh, he sounded so innocent, so smooth. What was wrong with me? I was having the best day of my life. If a guy, a really handsome, tall, blond guy—*take a breath and reason it out*—wanted to hold my hand, why should I get all huffy and uncool?

"The hand-holding. I... we... it's not what we do here... so soon after meeting, I mean. Maybe in your country... uh..." We moved through the crowded hallway at a snail's pace, went down the up staircase—everybody did after sixth hour—and headed toward my locker. I wanted to see how many girls noticed me, the screw-up, getting walked to her locker by the new hot guy, but I couldn't lift my eyes. For the few seconds my brain switched gears, I wavered between my original creepy assessment of him and this new feeling. Apparently my body, with an assortment of unused social gears, had its own physical opinion: reckless optimism. And those butterflies were stretching their wings, ready to migrate.

Coreg bent nearer as we walked, giving his silky words less distance to travel, and whispered, "I am sorry."

I glanced at him. Crap. I wished I had left my hand in his. I smiled. I probably laughed, too. Probably one of those inane girl giggles that so irritate me. With his white hair, hunky face and dark-lashed, unblinking eyes, he strongly resembled the hero on the cover of a romance novel. My face could scarcely grow redder; for sure the back of my neck flamed crimson as the shush-shush of feminine whispers followed us down the hall.

When we got ten feet from my locker I noticed Marc standing there and I was definitely glad I wasn't holding Coreg's hand, but the social implications overwhelmed me.

CHAPTER 10
#DazedAndConfused

MARCUM STOOD AT his locker with an armload of books. He had no intention of leaving such valuable intelligence locked in the flimsy blue metal cage. He would ask Selina—he meant the time-bender, he had to stop thinking of her too personally—he'd ask the time-bender for help with the homework as a way to lure her away. The words to woo her to his spaceship were poised on his tongue, but he was going to lose focus with all the attention he was receiving from several passing students. They flung multiple idiomatic salutations his way. Friendly species. They were quickly growing on him.

"Catchya later, Marc," a girl who'd been at his lunch table called.

"*Ehk* ... Later," Marcum echoed, reflecting on the marvelous pies. He had eaten two red, two blue, and one called apple.

"Don't forget to do the math homework," another girl called, a slim female much taller than Sel—the time-bender.

"Homework." Marcum nodded. He dropped the books onto the floor of the locker so he could check something he had on his arm; putting ink to skin was a clever reminder system he'd learned from a male in one of his classes.

"Hey, dude, you should come on down to the gym for B-ball tryouts." A lanky boy from an earlier class slapped him on the back as he went around Marcum to open the locker on the other side.

Marcum sprang into a defensive pose then relaxed and repeated the last word under his breath. What the Gleezhe was a tryout? And where on earth was the time-bender? A chill went up his vertebrae as he imagined Coreg whisking her out of the building right under his nose.

The chill reversed course as he spotted Coreg coming down the hallway, the time-bender at his side, smiling and laughing, as she had with him all morning long.

What the—!

"Oh my gosh, Marc, how'd your last class go?" She hopped to his side, fumbled with her lock, and thrust her books onto the top shelf. She gave off a new scent, the blue cast to her skin was gone, and her cheeks were pink, but he stopped staring and tuned in instead to Coreg's attitude. He read the victory smirk for what it was, and kept his own mouth tightly closed.

"Well?" Selina held her locker door open, her elbow sticking outward. Touching elbows was a common greeting on Klaqin. Without thinking Marcum nudged her. She didn't seem to notice, but for him it changed everything. The touch felt electric even through the material.

He shuddered as he mulled over an answer. His rehearsed statement would no longer make sense; he thought as quickly as he could, well aware of Coreg's cold stare.

"Good. Classes good." He flicked his eyes between Coreg and Selina.

"Oh," Selina began, "do you two know each other? Marc this is Coreg. Coreg ... Marc."

Both stood statue still. Selina broke the awkward standoff. "So, uh, I'm meeting someone for chess club. See you tomorrow." She closed her locker, ducked around Coreg and headed further into the building instead of toward the exit.

Marcum grabbed Coreg's arm as he was about to turn after her. He uttered two words, total gibberish to anyone standing nearby, but effective in halting Coreg's pursuit.

"Use English," Coreg hissed.

Marcum stuttered, "You felt it too? Now? It was the very opposite of your time-pacing."

"I know," Coreg said. "And she can resist. I had her by the hand and she got away."

Marcum twisted his thumb ring and surveilled the emptying hall. "Do you know where chess club is? Should we go?"

"You can. I doubt you'll do better than I did at taking her. Besides, I've learned a new competition. It's called basketball and one of their leaders expects me to join their team today."

Marcum studied Coreg's face, assessing why Coreg would let him have a shot alone at the time-bender and why he would put this mission on hold to join a team. "Interesting. I'll go with you."

❄ ❄ ❄

ALEX LET OUT his breath. He felt bad spying on Selina from the side of the vending machine. But not that bad. He intended to meet her at her locker, as usual, but when he spotted Marc waiting there he moved out of sight.

She looked amazing coming down the hallway. Glowing. He had no idea how a girl could do that. She had smiles for both of those foreign dudes. A flirty attitude, so not like her. Why couldn't she see how phony those two were?

Alex wanted to punch the side of the candy ma-chine. He settled instead for clenching his teeth and his fists. Watching Selina respond to other guys the way she did was like sandpaper on his soul.

Hell.

This was taking forever. *Go on, guys, get away from her. Find your own lockers. Catch a ride. Leave her alone.*

At last Selina moved off, skirting around the blond dude and leaving both guys staring after her. She was headed for chess club, no doubt. Alex was glad to see her go alone. Something still bothered him about the guys though; he decided to follow these dickheads and skip tryouts.

They didn't move at first. Both stood in front of Selina's locker and exchanged a few words. Alex wondered if they were speaking in English or not. A couple seconds later they turned and started coming toward him. When they passed the vending machine they both pivoted their heads his way, their eyes registering something between surprise and suspicion, but neither of them spoke. They took up half the hallway with their football-worthy physiques and NBA height. Alex was considered tall, but these two had a couple inches on him.

He trailed them toward the gymnasium, mocking himself inwardly for his earlier conclusion that these foreigners might have been terrorists or, at the very least, kidnappers. They were awkward, didn't blend in, and most importantly, let themselves be seen together. Where was the top-secret skill in that?

When they found the entrance to the locker room, Alex groaned. If they were as athletic as they were tall, he'd be sitting the bench again this year. He should stick to chess club.

❄ ❄ ❄

SECOND COMMANDER DACE'S premonition was on target. The result of the report he gave at the council meeting was as predictable as their two moons passing at noon. As he suspected, the First Commanders voted to send Dace himself, armed and accompanied by two Third Commanders, to retrieve the AWOL youths, Coreg and Marcum. The explicit order was for Dace to ensure that if the youths had indeed located a time-bender, every effort should be made, would be made, to capture it. Or him. Or her. Regrettably, the lesser of the Fifth Commanders, Marcum, was expendable if need be.

Dace clucked his tongue twice and bowed before the First Commanders, not disclosing his belief that Marcum possessed a superior ability. He left the council room and immediately began his preparations. He had a modern ship at his disposal, though it would be a tight squeeze for five and almost impossible for six. Unfortunately one of the Third Commanders assigned as his time-pacer was semi-reliable, performing sporadically under pressure. Regardless, Dace had made a promise to Coreg's parents, and to Marcum's, that both boys would be found and returned. But he couldn't promise leniency unless they'd captured a time-bender, if such a being even existed.

There was an urgency to his mission since the Gleezhians had doubled their campaign in the star region closest to Klaqin. Two ships had broken through Klaqin defenses and directly attacked the planet, leaving multiple scars by way of demolished cities before being brought down by a young team of Fourth Commanders.

CHAPTER 11
#FootInMouth

NIKET AND SIX other nerds were turning several of the desks around when I got to Mr. Farr's classroom. Chess boards straddled the ones that faced each other. I was on such a high from having two guys—let's face it they were stud-muffins—show me more than a little interest, that I caught everybody by surprise with my announcement:

"I am a-vai-la-ble," I said, swinging my hips to each syllable. Totally out of character for me. A whistle and a cheer went up from a few and I tried not to giggle too insanely as I lowered myself into the first empty seat. *Cue embarrassed blushing*. I instantly resumed my more timid persona, eager to avoid any more interaction. "I meant, uh, I meant that Alex isn't here yet so ... anyone? Anyone want to play with me first?" Oh, that was so not coming out right. I frowned at the door willing Alex to enter, but the traitor wouldn't materialize. Some best friend he was.

Niket slid into the desk opposite me and smiled widely. "You're mine tonight. Alex went to tryouts."

I'm sure my face fell. Alex never said a word to me. In fact, last week he made it pretty clear that he was too out of shape and too out of practice to make the basketball team.

I glanced at Niket's dark face to see if he was kidding or not. He was not. I lost half the exhilaration, but none of the embarrassment, as I skipped from Niket's ogling eyes to Daniel, Bryan, Tushar, Bala, Rick, and Quinn. I played chess because Alex played chess. He loved it and he wanted me to love it. It had been a huge social risk for me to join the club, but I did it for Alex. I wasn't bad, I beat him maybe thirty percent of the time, but I didn't have Alex's passion for it. And I especially hadn't been fond of competing against the other guys, though they were as limited on eye contact and social interaction as I was. All of them except Bala used memorized openings; Bala was a berserker, which Alex explained meant he made rash moves and attacked erratically. Not fun for me. I didn't mind being paired against Shena, the only other girl, but she was a no-show so far.

I wondered if Coreg or Marc played. Maybe chess was a national thing in their countries. Maybe if I hurried I could catch up to them and invite them to come here. I knew that Coreg cut across the back field ... no, by the time I went back for my coat he'd be out of sight. Wait, what was I thinking? I never made that kind of social advance.

Niket still stared at me, a polite smile crisping up the edges of his lips. Not exactly creepy, but not comfort-able either. I glanced at the others again. Something was off. Everyone looked like they were in suspended animation. Nobody moved, like they were waiting for me to make another suggestive offer and put my foot in my mouth again. I braced myself for embarrassment and humiliation, something that so far I'd avoided with this group. The air around us grew stale as if someone had bewitched the room.

I interrupted the spell and got up. "Hic—! Uh, excuse me. I'm going to go watch tryouts and cheer Alex on."

I broke seven hearts with that announcement. Not. All eyes fell to their rooks and knights, all except Niket's. His eyes narrowed and he spoke in that tinted accent of his, "Wish him luck. Tell him he was both right and wrong to listen to me."

I nodded; Niket is always saying weird stuff. I think he spends too much time alone. I headed to the door and for the second time in one day I ran smack into a chest. I would have been so embarrassed if it had been the chess club sponsor, Mr. Farr, but no, this chest was definitely teenage male.

Of course it was Alex, as though my thoughts had summoned him—nothing new. He caught me by the shoulders before I completely smashed my nose. He left his hands on my arms as he asked, "Hey, where's the fire?"

I stepped back and he dropped his hands. "Niket said you were trying out."

"I was going to, now I'm not."

I glanced behind him and watched a couple of hand-holding kids head for the stairs. Everybody was in a relationship except me. I looked at Alex. "Why not?"

He shrugged his shoulders. "Changed my mind. Your new friends are gonna make the team. I didn't feel like warming the bench another season."

"My new friends? You mean Coreg and Marc?"

One eyebrow flicked up. "How many new friends have you made this week?" Alex's tone made me feel like a traitor, but I ignored the implication, well, except to give him one of my cold stares. Alex lowered his voice, "Sorry."

"You should go and try out." I flipped my hand through my hair and took a step farther out into the hallway. Okay, so I guess I *was* in a sorta, kinda relationship. Not quite what I had in mind, but there was an unspoken friends-to-the-end commitment here. "Better to have tried and failed than never to have tried at all." I grabbed his forearm. "Come on."

"You're gonna drag me to tryouts?" Alex laughed, finishing his hoot with a couple of bars from the Rocky movie theme.

"What are friends for? Besides, I'm not going back in there. Niket wants more than my queen." I mimicked Niket's inappropriate laugh.

❄ ❄ ❄

I THOUGHT THAT tryouts went especially long. The session turned into a show as Marcum mirrored Coreg's incredible skills, dribbling, passing, and shooting. He must have practiced this sport all his life. I watched from the top of the stands where I sat on the periphery of several gawking spectators, mostly girls who were stuffing their faces with vending machine nutrition. They gasped in utter awe at the physical abilities of those two; so did I. But I found myself wishing Alex would step it up. It became pretty clear that he was probably right in supposing he'd see little court time with the addition of Marc and Coreg on the Panthers.

When a couple of kids near me began to speculate about who the new guys were and whether they were wearing yoga pants or running tights, I exposed myself to their possible mockery and joined the conversation.

"The blond is Coreg and the black-haired guy is Marc. They're super nice and they're exchange students." *News alert: I was interacting socially and ... Coreg elbowed a guard then tripped another player. Not so nice.*

"I can't believe they're not wearing something more comfortable, more loose-fitting," a geeky, freckle-faced girl said. She was obviously a sophomore who didn't know any better than to talk to an outcast like me.

Somebody else added, "Who cares? They look like Adonis and Apollo."

"They could be Olympic stars the way they jump and shoot," Jamie Michaelson said. He was a pimply faced junior who'd shown up at chess club once and he was in choir last year though of course I'd never spoken to him. He snapped some pictures and wrote in a notebook. "I think they're from the university. This has gotta be a prank."

I watched him tap his pen. "What do you mean? Why would college guys come here, take classes, and go out for basketball? That's crazy." I shouldn't have added that; he'd mock me for sure.

He glowered at me, a telltale sign of scorn spreading fast across his face. "Maybe it's an initiation prank. Rush week for a fraternity. The college is only eight miles away."

I mulled that over and gambled a response he'd no doubt reject. "No, no way. They disbanded the fraternities after some problems a couple years ago."

"Yeah, and then they went underground." *See? Shoot the weird girl. Shoot her now.*

But I considered what he said. They did have those identical rings. They seemed older, cooler. Those accents—they could be fake. I studied the back of Jamie's head and then his narrow and homely face as the guys on the court dribbled and passed and ran to the other end. Jamie had a tapered jaw making him look like a trust-worthy collie. He had switched from choir to yearbook staff. Probably wrote for the school blog, too.

I took a big breath. "Jamie, are you making this up for a story?"

"I don't make anything up. I'm only saying they're awfully good and they just happened to enroll right now, in November, and they're like ten feet tall and way better than our guys. Makes me wonder."

Hmm—*thought bubble over head*—I started to wonder, too.

❄ ❄ ❄

COREG STRODE OUT of the building with Marcum.

"Did you see who sat in the terraced seats?"

Marcum clucked his tongue. "Of course. Did I not outscore you in observation and retention exams? Every time?" He expected Coreg to debate that point as there were few areas where Marcum held bragging rights over Coreg.

Coreg ignored the comment. "She left with that hovering male. He's watching out for her. He's her guardian, I suspect."

Marcum fussed with the zipper on the pink coat and responded, "Did you see his eyes? The left one has amber pigment in the iris."

Coreg shook his head. "Why would I notice? Everyone has amber pigment. I'm trying to make the point that he could be trouble when I, not you, convince her to come to my ship."

Marcum gave up on the zipper and held the coat closed against the chilling wind. "For us, yes, amber is the common denominator, but here I haven't seen another person with that eye coloring. Sel—the time-bender has brown eyes. That seems pretty common. I've seen a lot of green and blue, too. Nobody has commented on my eyes. Has anyone said anything to you?"

Coreg again shook his head. He frowned then. "They see differently than we do."

"That's the conclusion I came to, but you're missing *my* point. Her guardian, Alex, is more than trouble. He may have some other special ability we haven't counted on. Something we haven't even thought of."

Coreg scoffed at Marcum's conclusion, but Marcum decided to pay a visit to the time-bender that night. Though it disconcerted him to have each day end with so many hours without the sun, he saw the advantage of the darkness. By morning, when Coreg walked into class and no Selina sat there, he and his prize would be a good light year or two away. He hoped.

❄ ❄ ❄

"I'VE GOT A PIE ready to put in the oven if you want to come over after supper, Alex," my mom said. She always included Alex.

"Thanks, Mrs. Langston. That sounds great." He hopped out of the mini-van, but not before doing a clumsy mitten hand shake with Buddy and softly singing a made up song about pie. He whacked the back of my seat, too, his usual form of farewell, though this time he added, "Talk to ya later, Selina," which meant he would probably call later with some excuse I'd have to relay to my mom. He wasn't keen on her pies. Too sweet, he once told me.

We drove around the block and pulled into our garage. For some reason known only to him, Buddy decided to throw a fit as soon as the engine turned off. My mom tried to get his seat belt unbuckled, but he fought her so hard she threw her hands up in exasperation. By the time I got around to the driver's side she was in tears and Buddy was yelling for "Alekth." He'd kicked off both his boots and was ready to throw his mittens out the door.

"I'll take care of him, Mom. You go in and preheat the oven. I love your pies."

"Thanks, honey. He's been acting out so much while your dad's been gone. He should be home for Thanksgiving. Christmas for sure."

She hit the garage door button before she closed the door into the house. I took a deep breath and grumbled along with the motor above my head. "Okay, Buddy, okay. Did you hear what mom said? Daddy's going to be home for Christmas. And what happens right after Christmas?"

He started throwing his head from side to side and shouting "No, no, no!" He held one hand over the belt buckle and waved me away with the other. "Alekth do it."

"Come on, Buddy, I'm not going to ask Alex to come over here to unbuckle you from your seat. Now, who has birthdays right after Christmas? Who gets more presents?"

That got his attention. "We do. Thelina and Buddy. Pwethenth."

"That's right. We get presents. Lots of presents. Let me unbuckle you and we'll go in and make a list of what we want."

His mood changed in an instant. I unsnapped him, grabbed his boots and mittens, and helped him jump down. He walked sock-footed through the snow tracks behind the car, but that seemed a small price to pay for ending his tantrum in record time.

The house smelled wonderful. Crock pot wonderful. The apple pie would soon add a new flavorful scent.

Ninety minutes later we'd finished dinner and the pie was cool enough to serve. Mom was cutting the first slice when I heard my name being called at the front door. Mom gave me a raised eyebrow and I shrugged. I was equally baffled as to who would stand and yell, but not knock or ring the bell.

"You better see who it is, but check before you open the door. I hate how dark it is already; it's not even six thirty." Mom went back to serving Buddy the first piece.

I put my eye to the peephole and flicked on the porch light at the same time. The figure on the porch twisted in the yellow glow and I cringed when I realized it was Marc. I defied my natural inclinations and didn't give myself time to think of what to say, or imagine how embarrassed I was going to be, I simply opened the door and pulled him inside.

The foyer was completely out of view of the kitchen, but I was nervous that my mom would peek around the corner and see this giant wearing her ski jacket. Not even Buddy had told her about our stormy night visitor.

"Why didn't you knock?"

"Knock?" His eyes pierced right through to my soul.

Knock? I'll tell you what knocked. My knees knocked. How? Could? This? Be? I thought that Coreg gave me goosebumps, but Marc gave me goose mountains.

I yelled over my shoulder toward the kitchen, “It’s somebody from school.”

“Invite them in for pie,” Mom called back.

“Pie?” Marc’s face brightened. He started shrugging off the jacket.

“Here, let me take that.” I stuffed it in the closet then pointed at his footwear. “Better take those off, too. My mother is fussy.”

Marc smiled, nodded, and said, “Fussy,” like his mother was the same way. He was a man of few words, for sure.

He followed me into the kitchen and I made introductions, hoping to high heaven that my mom wouldn’t comment on his health or try to take his pulse or his temperature like she did with Alex. Thankfully, she didn’t. Marc pronounced ‘hello’ right—he had lost his accent pretty fast. Mom dished him up an extra-large piece with two scoops of ice cream and Marc said he was thankful in the most endearing way. My mom instantly fell for him. But Buddy wouldn’t acknowledge him. I was glad he didn’t make any remarks about his odor this time, because frankly, I thought he smelled slightly like wet dog. He obviously hadn’t showered after tryouts. My knees stopped knocking, my breathing evened out, and my heart beat only ten or so extra beats per minute.

“You kids can have the kitchen,” Mom said. She helped Buddy out to the family room and I took the bar stool at the counter next to Marc. I snuck a thousand little glances at him. For one eerie second he seemed to turn to wax and then his skin pixelated for an instant. I switched my focus to his hand and then back to his face—normal now. I must not have been getting enough oxygen to my brain.

“So?” I prompted him for a reason why he’d show up on my doorstep, calling my name.

“So?” He took a bite of pie and closed his eyes brief-ly.

“Why are you here?”

“For pie.”

I laughed, but only to cover the needles of suspicion that poked my ribs. "How did you know we were having pie? Are you spying on us?" Probably not the most welcoming thing to say. *Start turning hot pink.* I thought of what Alex said about the spying. I so wanted it not to be true.

"I came because I want you to see my—" he took some ice cream and his eyebrows shot upward, "—my ship."

"Your ship?" I realized I could look at him without that peculiar knot in my stomach I always had when I expected criticism or rejection.

"Yes. Will you come? It is a short walk from here."

He took two more mouthfuls while I began eating my pie. I thought about it. Go see his ship? In November? In the snow? Why would an exchange student have a ship? More suspicions fought for my attention. The yearbook kid. What he said. About fraternity pranks. Go see a ship? Yeah, right.

But what I said was, "Right now?"

He shook his head. "Finish pie first." He muttered something else as he rolled a forkful of fruit and crust around his tongue. I was too shy and too polite to ask for a translation.

I watched him put another piece in his mouth. His manly, masculine mouth. I hadn't noticed before how strong his jaw was. Square. Marine-like.

And his eyes. He'd look at me—and I could hold his gaze!—and I swear he admired me, made me feel beautiful, needing no words. He fell pretty short on words anyway, so I soaked up the unspoken flattery. Of course, it might have been that he was wondering why I sometimes blanched blue, like I couldn't get enough oxygen, and other times I blushed as pink as a baby. I had no idea what color I'd turned now. Unaffected by my sudden change of complexion, he went on eating.

I guess a little ice cream melted and dribbled off my bottom lip then because he reached a thumb toward my face and caught the drip. I got a closer view of his thumb ring as his hand moved back. Greek letters? I knew maybe three: alpha, omega, and pi. None of those on the ring looked familiar. Fraternity prank? I honestly didn't care.

I yelled toward the family room, "Mom! I'm going for a walk with Marc."

CHAPTER 12
#KissMyLips

MARCUM SAVORED THE last bite. What a wonderful food pie was. He eyed the two remaining pieces.

The time-bender slipped off the stool and moved behind him. "I'll get our coats. Do I need boots?" she asked.

"Boots?" He looked down at his bare feet and noticed tiny spikes protruding through the floor around his toes, as if the wood had produced thorns.

"Yeah, the sidewalks are shoveled, but, oh, never mind. I'll wear shoes."

She stopped and looked up at him. Then she did it again: she slowed the movement of time down to a standstill. Marcum marveled at how she governed the ability so effortlessly. He knew the mathematics behind Coreg's time-pacing, but the equation would not allow for negative numbers, making time-bending an unproven theory on Klaqin.

He stared at her, studied her eyes, admired her mouth and leaned an inch closer to her face. What would it be like to press his own lips gently against hers? Would she taste like pie?

He wasn't breathing. He wasn't thinking in English. He wasn't thinking at all. He leaned another inch closer and closed his eyes. He breathed in through his nose and filled his lungs with all her scents. He didn't know these aromas, but analyzed each fragrance as coming from a different source on her body: her hair, her clothes, and, of course, her mouth.

"What's the matter?" The time-bender stepped back, made a funny little gasp, and resumed the steady tramp of time. She raised her eyebrows at him.

"Matter?"

"Yeah, I thought you were going to pass out and fall forward or something."

"I am fine." Marcum recovered. "I want to show you my ship."

The time-bender—no, he wouldn't call her anything but Selina—Selina smiled and nodded, turned and led him to the foyer, and plucked out two coats from the closet.

❄ ❄ ❄

ALEX CUT THROUGH the snowy backyards intending to come up to the Langstons' deck and trigger the motion detector lights. Instead he stopped several yards short and stared at the scene through the kitchen window. Selina sat perched on a stool next to that foreign guy he was beginning to think of as Superman. He was eating pie. Alex's slice of pie.

He pounded one ungloved hand into the other, took an icy breath and cracked his knuckles before pulling out his phone to text Selina. But before he pressed send he glanced up and saw them, faces inches apart, in a frozen stare down of some sort. He couldn't stand the thought of that dude, any dude, so close to her. He hated what he saw, but he couldn't look away. *Don't let him kiss her,* he prayed. *Move away from him, Selina. Move. Move now.* He saw Marc touch Selina's face. Classic pre-kiss move. Alex set his jaw and imagined Selina moving off her seat and then, as if by magic or the pure force of his will, she did. The giant Superman followed her toward the front door, out of his line of sight. Alex stepped back, pocketed his phone, rubbed at his nose, then moved to the side of the garage and listened.

❄ ❄ ❄

HO. LY. CRAP! THAT was crazy. If I didn't know better I'd swear Marc was as innocent about kissing as I was. Wait. I don't know better. Maybe it's all an act. Part of the fraternity prank or rush or whatever.

Either way that was the longest stretch of time I ever experienced. I was sure he meant to kiss me. I wanted him to kiss me.

I know what that says about me. I hardly know him—*exclamation point*. He leaned back and time started again, without my having noticed it had stopped.

I handed him my mom's coat and pulled on mine. We both put on our shoes. His were more like boots than shoes and struck me as ten times more expensive than anything Alex wears—a funny little fact to file away. I patted my pants pocket to make sure I had my phone. I'd want a picture of this so-called ship.

I left the front door unlocked and closed it behind us. "Which way?" Marc pointed left, but we had to walk right and then down the driveway first before we headed that way, toward the open field and the woods behind it. I used to play in those woods, even in the winter. When I was twelve, Alex made a tree fort there in an attempt to create a small enclosed space he could handle. He was claustrophobic and mostly I teased him about it. Those were fun times. *Cue heroine: snap back to present.*

Marc kept squinting at me as we made our way over clumps of snow, where hand shovels and snow plows crossed paths. I felt tingly all over. But not from the cold. Still, I should have worn a hat and scarf.

❄ ❄ ❄

ALEX HEARD SELINA ask, "Which way?"

He didn't need to debate with himself whether or not to follow them. That kid was basically a stranger. Selina's dad wanted him to keep an eye out for her safety. Heck, forget her dad, Alex himself wanted to be sure she was safe. If anything ever happened to her he'd quit school, run away, become a hermit. Or more likely, if anything happened to Selina he'd wither up and die.

❄ ❄ ❄

"COLD?" MARC READ my mind. "It's not far." We crossed the road and he indicated a well-trodden narrow path. It wasn't too dark to follow it. He took the lead. The snow was different here, a hard surface crust compressed beneath our feet with a soft crunching noise.

"So," I said to his back, "how did tryouts go?" I thought trying to start a real conversation might elicit more than one-word sentences from him.

"We made the team."

"You and Coreg? How'd you find out? Alex wasn't told anything."

He spoke over his shoulder. "The man, the coach, told us. He shook our hands. It's a contract."

"What?" Something got lost in the translation.

"We are on the team," he repeated.

That was weird, but I decided not to pursue it. The woods closed around us and it became harder to see the white path. I kept a hand out to push away the sharp branches, some of which snapped in two as we passed. Dead leaves blew round my ankles and I stomped them into the snow. Drips from overhanging pine boughs splatted on my head.

"Here." Marc stopped and faced me. For one thrilling pulse of time I thought he had brought me to this private, mom-proof, romantic spot to fold me into his arms and give me that first to-the-moon-and-back kiss I so desperately wanted.

But no.

"Here," he said, "is my ship."

He raised his arm and waved it across the area like a model on The Price is Right revealing a showcase of prizes. Granules of ice crusted his brows and lashes, and his face was wet with melted snow. Momentarily disoriented, I reached out—totally unlike me—to touch him. His shoulder shook under my hand and I pulled it back.

"Um, where?" I only saw a huge mound of snow. I didn't remember a hill being in the middle of the woods. The air shimmered as if it were reflecting through a dozen carnival fun mirrors.

The hill trembled and I jumped ten feet. Stupid me, I should have jumped into his arms. Colored lights sparkled beneath the mound as something pushed outward and opened, sending a blossom of snowflakes my way. "What's happening?" Something sounded like boulders rolling muted underwater.

"My ship." Marc waved his hand again.

I'm sure my jaw dropped and my chin reached all the way down to a freezing pile of snow at my feet.

"It's warm inside." His voice was little more than a hoarse crackle. He cleared his throat and tried again. "Warmer."

He ducked in and I could do nothing else but shut the gaping hole in my face and follow.

The interior put Alex's plywood and cardboard tree fort to serious shame.

"What is this place?" I kept my jaw at chin height this time, but I was in total awe.

"My ship."

"Your ship? Like a science project?" I looked from the sparkling walls to the array of square buttons, labeled with those funny hieroglyphics, to the reflective surface on the ceiling where a ton of various sized levers hung down, too high for me to reach. I saw a single seat, which apparently was custom molded to someone's spine and bottom. Off to the side there was a round hatch, like what I'd expect to see on a submarine. I took everything in slowly, quietly, without any explanation from Marc. He didn't acknowledge my question—maybe I insulted him—so I asked, "Is this how you got here from your country? Is this an airplane? Because, wow, it looks like a video game chamber." The outside door had been slowly closing like a throat constricting and now it gave a final whoosh and lip smack. The distant traffic sounds ceased and if the air stirred at all it made no sound here.

"Video game chamber."

I couldn't tell from his tone if he was confirming my guess or mocking it. I had questions: one, why would he bury an elaborate, obviously expensive vehicle or machine or whatever this was—*his ship!*—under the snow in the woods? And two, was he inching closer to me? It was pretty cramped in here. Close quarters. Warm.

"Show me," I said. His face loomed a few inches above mine, close enough I could see a facial tic make his ears quiver. I wanted to close my eyes *and please oh please let something good happen*, but I kept my eyes focused on his. It turned out to be one of those long moments again, when I imagined time standing still and the world passing me by. It should have been awkward, but I grew quite comfortable in the way Marc held my gaze. Except he wouldn't act. *Come on, guy, get it over with. We're alone and—*

"I will show you. Sit there."

Why does this happen to me? The spell evaporated with the tiniest of gasps. I moved to the chair, sat down, and found it to be as comfortable as I thought it would be. A silly boy could probably sit here for days and play stupid video games. A helmet hung hooked onto the wall next to several angular-shaped accessories. Guns, probably, and wireless gaming controls. Marc touched some of the levers on the ceiling and I swear the seat tightened around me. This was going to be a Disney-like experience, no doubt. I only hoped the game wasn't going to be a shoot-up-the-lizard-aliens sort of game. Or any kind of war game. I kept my eyes glued to the larger screen in front of me and ignored the smaller monitor near the floor. Several lights began blinking and the walls started shimmering. I swear they were moving, too. Had to be some sophisticated mechanics here. My seat vibrated. Marc pressed his shoes into indentations in the floor I hadn't noticed before. He held onto one of the levers and pulled another.

"Feels like we're going up in an elevator," I said. Nothing like a plane, I thought, more like a spaceship. That would be cool. Then something happened. I felt like I was pushed into the seat by an all-encompassing force. I couldn't swallow; my stomach pressed against my bladder; my hands stuck to my thighs. Then the feeling passed and I shook it off as nerves.

The screen brightened, but there must have been a glitch in the computer, all I saw were streaking lines of colors. Then armrests sprang up from the floor and I put my elbows on them. And there they were, of course, the joysticks, right at the ends of the armrests. Three knobby levers shuddered up into place. Yeah, perfect. Triggers, bomb drops, explosives. Every boy's dream.

❄ ❄ ❄

MARCUM HID HIS elation from Selina. Despite her repeated displays of time control he had managed to get her to come willingly to his ship. He'd won the bet with Coreg. More importantly he could return to Klaqin with the ultimate prize. His euphoria felt as beautiful as Selina's face and as sweet as her mother's pie. His mind flashed on those last two pieces. Then he thought of how close he'd gotten to Selina's lips. Had she slowed time on purpose to help him decide? Decide what? The compassionate side of him questioned his moral duty. Should he take off, fly her out of this atmosphere, and kidnap her? What would she do? What would she think? Maybe his conscience wanted to tell him something else. Maybe he should let her decide for herself.

He worked the levers, flew the ship, slipped through the troposphere and entered the stratosphere more slowly than he should have.

"What game is this?" Selina asked.

"This?" Marcum didn't know the English equivalents for the atmospheric layers. "We are going to the moon."

"Awesome. Are we going to shoot little green men?"

"Green men?" Marcum's stomach caught in his rib cage. How did she know? Had Coreg shown her his arms? The skin that hadn't been exposed to the sun's rays? Holy Gleezhe. He glanced at the screen she stared at. Sure enough. Coreg's sleek, narrow vessel barreled toward them through the mesosphere. Coreg would latch on, use his time-pacing ability and take them straight home.

Home. Selina would miss her home. She didn't even say good-bye to her mother. He couldn't steal her away so abruptly.

"Selina! Use the anti-flames." Marcum shifted his craft's trajectory. "The nearest levers on both sides." He centered the angle to compensate for not being in the control seat. It would have been so much easier to do it himself. She was bound to fail. He hoped he had the correct

English words. “Put your fingers around the controls and squeeze.”

“Like this?” She got off a round that scattered above Coreg.

“Take your time,” Marcum said, hoping she understood that she needed to slow things down and take more careful aim.

Bursts of anti-flames met Coreg’s repulsion jets. Both ships automatically engaged. Marcum wouldn’t be able to evade Coreg for more than a few seconds now.

“I’ve got this!” Selina took her time. Aimed. Shot. Pushed. Repelled. Shot. Shot. Shot. Marcum felt seconds disappear into eternity. He mentally kicked himself for not closing in on that kiss earlier. He would have figured out his feelings then. He would never have left Earth without her permission.

In protracted motion, Coreg veered away.

“He never retreats,” Marcum whispered.

“Who?”

“Coreg.”

“We’re playing against Coreg? He’s online? Oh wow, and I beat him?”

Marcum smiled. “You didn’t beat him. He’s injured.” Marcum realigned his course to head for the moon. “He’ll have to land on Earth again and lard up his bio-metals.”

“How long will that take? I’m ready for round two. This is a lot like a game Alex has.”

❄ ❄ ❄

ALEX STOOD UNDER the first clump of trees in the snowy woods, not fifty feet from where he’d built a secret hideaway, a tree fort where he and Selina had challenged each other at board games on endless summer days. There was no way she'd take that anemic looking Marc there. She would never betray their friendship that way. Besides, he'd seen Marc leading her.

A sudden blast of heated air pulsed over his head and he ducked involuntarily. He couldn't believe his eyes. What was that? A flying white bus? The pine branches overhead obscured his view.

He had a bad feeling. "Selina!" He raced down the path, tripped, took a heavy fall and scraped against a thorny bush. He rose, pulled out his cell phone and turned on the flashlight app to follow the footprints further into the woods. "Selina!" he called again. The trail ended in a space where mounds of snow had spread into exotic patterns, swirled neatly over the last footprints. An old oak tree lay crushed against a stand of pines, their boughs petting its trunk and covering the bits of nailed plywood that poked through at odd angles. "What the—" Alex didn't care about the old fort, but he did care about Selina. A lot. He crooked his head skyward again, but not even the stars shone through the early winter clouds.

CHAPTER 13
#GamesWithThrones

"WELL, THAT WAS fun," I lied. I'd probably never understand the appeal of shooting blips off the screen. Give me Sims Pets or Zelda or even Candy Crush. But, whatever, at any rate Marc was opening up with longer sentences—kind of like me—though his accent returned thicker than before. "So, game over? What now?" I looked from the screen to Marc. He still stretched between the floor and the overhead controls like a wedged stick. Well, not a stick. He might be tall and thin, but he had this muscular vibe going on. His jacket swung open and his chest was there for me to gawk at. He was really ripped. I dropped my eyes fast when he caught me staring.

"We keep going to the moon. With your permission."

"With my permission? Well, if you ask like that—" I almost declined, but I checked the screen again and the most awesome view of the moon started to enlarge. Maybe this game would let you colonize it. Something peaceful. I thought I better say yes so I could stay in this nice tight, possibly romantic space which, by the way, had grown a tad more humid. And stinky. That oily garage odor oozed from the walls, the ceiling, and the floors. "What's that awful smell?"

"I am used to it. It is the bio-metals. They work hard to keep this vessel from burning up. We are traveling at tremendous speeds."

"Right." My stomach did a little flip-flop and the apple pie threatened to come back up. "Hey, I'm getting sick to my stomach. Can you turn off the special effects? The simulated movement?"

"Simulated movement? I don't know what that is." Marc's hair spiked out away from his face, floating, some of it wavered in front of his eyes and I wondered if the smell had made me high and caused me to see in slow motion. Weird. Then I saw the glow of the screen twinkle off the wall behind him. He lifted his gaze, flipped his head back, and pulled two more levers. My seat tightened around me even more—extending upward like a throne—and I felt the movement smooth out, like when you're tubing through rough water and then you go around a bend and everything is silky smooth.

"Yeah, that's better. I have a tendency to get car sick on long rides."

"We are two hundred thirty thousand miles from Earth. A very long ride. The moon looks good, yes?"

I glanced at the screen. Huh. This set-up had some pathetic graphics. I expected flashy colors, but I guess simple black and white made it more true to life. "The moon looks like it should, I guess." I wanted a picture of this, but no way could I get into my back pocket with this hugging chair gripping my cheeks. "Can you loosen this seat?"

"That would not be safe for you."

All right, so maybe my math skills aren't too great and I'd been ignoring how certain things didn't add up. "Marc. I want to get up. Please." I softened my jaw, tried for the innocent, congenial smile that worked on my dad, Buddy, Alex, and my male teachers, not to mention Niket. And I waited.

Marc pushed something into the ceiling and the chair released me. And when I say released, I mean gently launched me into the cramped cabin as if I were a limp party balloon. I floated upward, light as chocolate mousse.

The only reason I didn't totally freak out was the expression on Marc's face. You would've thought fairies were tickling his feet. As for me, I'm not ticklish—this was scaring my toenails off.

"Uh, what's happening?" I began flailing my arms and kicking my legs, but felt no resistance. It wasn't at all like swimming.

"You have no weight in outer space."

"Yeah, I get that. But I can't believe it. I thought this was a game." My panic turned to anger. "I want to go back. Right now." I floated into the ceiling, scared to death that I'd touch a lever that would open a door and suck us out into oblivion. No way did I want to be freeze-dried space litter, orbiting the moon for eternity. My fingers found some empty space around the levers, where I could touch the ceiling, and I managed to balance my upper body, but my legs were on a slow-motion course toward Marc's torso. To top it off I started to hiccup nonstop. Weightless hiccups tend to change directions repeatedly. Crap. I used all the strength in my core to adjust myself. If I could push off at the right angle I'd be able to descend toward the chair or at the very least wedge myself in the tighter space near the round hatch door. The hiccups increased.

"You are very good," Marc said. "Push lightly and grab the chair with your legs."

Easier said than done.

"What is this sound you make?"

"Hiccups," I said as another peculiar sound squeaked past my vocal cords. Nothing worse could happen to scare them out of me now. I hoped. I must have looked and sounded crazy judging by Marc's laughter. I bungled my first attempt by touching the chair with my feet too soon. Instant direction reversal. But I'm a quick learner, just ask Alex how I did when I attended his twelfth birthday party as the only girl. Martial arts themed. Ha! Got it.

"Hold yourself in," Marc said. I did, the hiccups stopped, and the helpful chair rewarded me with a comforting hug. My phone was still stuck in my pocket, so of course I totally missed my chance for a unique selfie.

"I guess you weren't kidding when you called this a ship. How does an exchange student get a spaceship?" I forced the words out, trying to cover my absolute terror with calm banter.

"I am not this exchange student." His laughter ceased, leaving no trace anywhere on his face, replaced with a seriousness that left no doubt as to his honesty. "I will tell you the truth."

I wasn't cold. I still had my jacket zipped up. But I started to shiver as if a very localized earthquake had begun in my chest and vibrated its way to my very frightened, orange and black polished toenails. The truth, as Marc told it, was exceptionally chilling. I listened as we vaulted around the dark side of the moon and headed back to my precious home. To say that time stood still would not be an exaggeration.

❄ ❄ ❄

COREG LANDED ROUGHLY, miles and miles from his intended site. He blew out every ounce of frustration and anger with a dozen Klaqin curses and a fist through the viewing screen. When the bio-metals failed to reform the screen he punched it again. Unquestionably Marcum had used the time-bender against him. Every time he paced she would bend, though it must have been Marcum who fired at him. Fine. Revenge it would be. It would take a day or so to treat the bio-metals, then he'd follow them. He assumed they were headed to Klaqin. He could pass them or lock on to them. Certainly he'd be able to convince Marcum to let him pace them home. He would concede the win, act contrite, and grovel if he had to. The time-bender would be his in the end. He had, after all, received the radio report that morning. There was a search ship headed to Earth. It shouldn't be a problem to meet them en route.

He tried his communication device.

"Marcum," he said, following the name with a string of Klaqin expletives. When he heard no response he turned up the receiver's volume. He caught the time-bender's voice, then Marcum's laughter, followed by his command to the time-bender to hold herself in. "Marcum!" Five more tries and still no response came. Marcum must not have been wearing his helmet and hadn't switched the comm over to the wall unit. The *Galaxer*'s communication system was starkly inferior. Then Coreg heard the soft words of Fifth Commander Marcum giving the Earth girl way too much information.

❄ ❄ ❄

WITH THE EARTH in the viewing screen, more realistic than a thousand classic movie shots, I loosened my grip on the armrests, but kept my fingers well away from those joysticks. I had a crimp in my neck from gawking up at Marc as he made one momentous revelation after another. He described Klaqin, its forever sunny days, steady temperatures, single government, and his service in a military space corp. I experienced a psychological calm and numbness as he spoke in shaky, uneven chunks of English. His voice wavered as he revealed the tyranny on his planet, the despotism and something else about their population. I didn't think he meant that their species was dying out, but that was how he phrased it.

He continued with more choppy descriptions about the ship we were on—not his favorite choice because of its age—his training maneuvers with Coreg, how they escaped getting banished twice—which I totally didn't understand—and their rivalry. He made earth-shattering facts seem like ordinary and pleasant conversation. Well, as pleasant as it can be with the speaker faltering over words and the listener hanging on those words with her mouth open.

I'll admit to being gullible. Yeah, like every teenager takes a joy ride past the county lines—in his case past the space alley. Sure, there'd be consequences—my head bobbed with the slow rhythm of his confessions—but he intended to return with something that would make him a hero. Cool. He smiled and I believed every accented word. Undoubtedly I'd gone beyond being mesmerized; I sat in shock.

"So ... how old are you?" That was the best question I could come up with because, in the recesses of my mind, I was blacking out thoughts of his head splitting apart and a slime-dripping alien face erupting through it.

"I am not old. I am a Fifth Commander. It is the first thing you become when you are no longer a child." Ah, a child, a human child, Marc was human; I wanted to believe that fact. According to him there were humans on many planets out there.

"So, you're like my age." I probably wasn't going to get an answer that matched up to an equivalent earth age. One thing was for sure: he was definitely not a college freshman. This was no prank. The pauses between his astonishing disclosures stretched out as the Earth got closer, or rather we got closer to the Earth. It wasn't fast enough for me. I clung to supreme thankfulness that he was taking me home and not to some galaxy far, far away.

After an uncomfortable silence he answered, "I am like your age. Yes."

Okay, so I smiled back. I wished on a star for a boyfriend and if this was what the stars provided, I could handle that. The stars knew best. *Cue the fairy god-mother—wave wand.*

Then he asked me a question I couldn't quite process ... *willingly ... help them fight* ... I quickly said no.

Marc did a bunch of lever pulling then and my stomach dropped. It didn't come back up. I didn't even feel the landing. Somehow I knew he'd set this ship in the same spot in the woods. Maybe by morning I'd be able to convince myself this was all a dream, forget the crisis and disbelief, and make a slow quivering return to reality.

"We have more time now," Marc said. I thought that sounded a bit cryptic and I suddenly feared he meant more time to get romantic. But that wasn't what he meant, because he followed that statement with, "Now that Coreg is grounded we have to wait until his ship is repaired. I will come to your learning center. I will play basketball." His licked his lips. "I will eat more pie."

He slipped his feet from the indentations in the floor which sprang up to make the surface flat again. My seat, that tight throne, released me, this time without a liftoff, and I rose to face him. Marcum reached around me and snatched the helmet from where it hung.

He put it on. "Coreg?" He lurched into a language like nothing I'd ever heard before. Klingon, I thought with a chill, or rather Klaqin. There was no mistaking he was having an argument. His facial expressions went through multiple distortions.

"Is he okay?"

"He is far away. He is ... angry."

"I'm so sorry." I stepped a little closer. Maybe Coreg could hear me. "I'm sorry, Coreg."

Marc spoke a short utterance, removed the helmet, and tossed it onto the chair.

"How far away is he?" I imagined him stranded on the moon.

"Too far to go on foot. I will walk you home and then fly to him."

Okay, so we'd ended date night. Uh, I took it pretty well, all things considered. I couldn't wait to tell Alex. He'd never believe me. I pulled out my phone but kept it behind my back. I thought I might sneak a few pictures in case Marc didn't allow it.

"So, uh, can I tell anyone about your ship?" Swipe, click, tilt, click. "Or is this our secret?" Click, up, down, click. I palmed it, turned and wiggled it in front of his nose. "May I take pictures?" My phone rang then, startling us both.

"No. No one can know." Marc said. "Not yet."

Well, the 'not yet' part at least seemed semi-reassuring. I didn't have a speck of guilt for already having taken some shots. I hoped they weren't all of my butt. I answered my phone. It was Alex.

"I'm okay ... yes, I'm sure ... hold on a second." I muted the phone and asked Marc again, "Please, can I tell Alex? He's super loyal. He won't tell." I considered batting my eyelashes, but what if that equaled some alien gesture that would start something I couldn't finish?

I watched Marc's Adam's apple rise and fall as he swallowed. A human trait. He blinked a couple times. More humanness.

"Selina ..." He breathed out slowly and his hands came up along my shoulders. Oh, no. I wasn't sure how I felt if there might be a kiss now. Marc leaned in and my heart puddled into my shoes. Alien—human—hot alien— "Selina," his hands grasped me gently, "please, not yet."

The longest cycle of time froze over, twice, and then I realized he didn't mean 'not yet' to a kiss, he meant 'not yet' to telling Alex. Oops, Alex. I unmuted the phone and told him I'd call him right back.

Marc's hands were no longer on my sleeves. The door opened and he stepped out first. I scarcely noticed the cold air, but I was aware that something was off. The shadows were faint, the twilight had faded and there was no depth to what I could see. I checked my phone again and nearly slipped as I stepped into the snow.

"What! It's after midnight! How did it get so late?" I looked at Marc, the blank expression on his face faked innocence. The door shrank to nothing, the light diminished, and my head swirled in disbelief as the ship vibrated and sank into a totally cartoonish shape. I've never done drugs, but if I did, I'd expect it to be like this. Things changing shape, feelings of euphoria, feelings of panic and fear. The urge to vomit.

After midnight. And on a school night. I was so dead.

Marc hurried me down the path. He'd resumed being a man—alien—of few words. The November wind rattled through the tree branches like the passing of a deer's ghost. Panic battled against my nausea.

"Holy crap," I said when we got to my street. A cop car sat parked in my driveway. Now I was going to throw up. "Um, maybe you better, uh, fly away. You know?"

He frowned at me. I could at least make out that expression. Definitely human.

"Honest, Marc. Go. Those are cops."

"Cops?"

"Police. I'm so late my mom called the police."

"I can fight them. I have weapons."

"Fight them? Are you crazy?"

"I am trained to fight the star cannibals, the Gleezhians. I will win."

"No, uh-uh. I am totally against violence of any kind. No fighting, please. If you want to keep your spaceship a secret you better take off and quick."

He nodded. "Quick." After that single word he turned and disappeared into the cold darkness. Huh, I told a space warrior to cool it and he did. Weird. I watched him hurry away, mumbling some unintelligible gibberish into his hand. Really weird.

I walked slowly home, pushing down the anxiety and dread.

My phone chirped. Alex again.

"Sorry," I said, no need for a hello.

"Where are you? Your mom called the police. I can see two uniformed officers standing in front of the family room window right now."

"I know. I'm almost to my house trying to figure out how to sneak in and be asleep already."

"Where have you been?"

I didn't answer.

"Selina, tell me."

"You wouldn't believe me, but I might have pictures to prove it." A sudden thrill rushed up my middle, a delayed reaction to an incredible evening. And I knew that I was going to tell Alex everything. I didn't exactly promise Marc I wouldn't. Alex was my best friend and that was that.

"But you're all right?"

"Yeah, I'm fine. For now. I really don't want to face the music. My mom is obviously freaked out. And with the cops there ... oh, brother, this will not be good."

"You'll survive. She'll be so happy that you're safe. Do you have a good excuse ready? You can always say that that Marc Marcum dude kidnapped you. I wouldn't mind if he were deported."

Alex's jealous feelings did more to calm me down than I would have imagined. The panic was gone. Good old Alex. Then I saw movement at my house; the front door opened. I moved up the Wilsons' driveway and hid behind their van, whispering to Alex what was happening. I stayed super still as the cop car backed out and drove away.

"Okay, I'm going in. Wish me luck."

"Luck."

I hung up and moved to the sidewalk. It occurred to me then that Alex had guessed what had happened: I *had* been kidnapped. I tilted my head toward the sky. No stars. Then a dark shape hovered above me and disappeared. Marc's ship. Un-freaking-believable.

CHAPTER 14
#LateLateShow

IT WASN'T THE first time I'd lain in bed at 3 a.m. and talked to Alex with my head under the blanket. I needed to unload after the dreadfully upsetting scene with my mom. She was seconds away from calling my dad when I opened the front door. I'd never seen my mother cry so miserably. She thought I'd been kidnapped or lay frozen in a ditch somewhere. Where had I gone? Who was that boy? Where was my phone? Why didn't I answer my phone?

Gee, mom, I wanted to say, maybe because there aren't any cell phone towers on the moon yet. If I'd said that, she would have thought I was sassing her. In this case lying seemed preferable to sassing. I told her we walked all the way to the twenty-four hour diner and sat at a booth talking about Marc's life. I apologized a million times and said we lost track of time and I didn't know why her calls didn't come through. Sheesh, that turned into an hour lecture I sure didn't need.

Alex agreed with me that I had to lie. I told him how my mom sent me to bed with a *we'll-talk-about-this-more-in-the-morning* threat. We both knew that meant I'd be grounded.

While I still had access to my phone I sent Alex the pictures and I told him everything. Well, not the physical attraction part and not me shooting at Coreg's ship, but everything about the weightlessness, the trip around the moon, and some of what Marc told me about his planet and the Gleezhians.

"Tell me again what he said about their sun," Alex whispered. "I'm still a little suspicious that this is all made up."

"You don't believe me? Alex, I told you: I was floating. Floa—Ting! You can't get zero gravity in a homemade, college prank, science project or whatever."

"Drugs, maybe?"

"I didn't take any drugs."

"Maybe he slipped something into your pie."

"How did you know we had pie together?" Silence on his end. I couldn't imagine he'd fallen asleep. "Alex, were you spying? Hey, you were all over Marc for watching me from the Wilsons' house. Well?"

"Selina, you know I have to watch over you. I lov—uh, well, hey, I wasn't intentionally spying. I was coming for my slice of your mother's pie. She invited me, remember? And I saw you guys in the kitchen and then I saw you take off with him up the street and then I saw, well, I saw something weird, but it wasn't a spaceship." He had to be out of breath after that explanation, and so was I because of what he almost said.

"Did you look at those pictures? It's a spaceship. I was weightless."

"Well, actually the pictures are a little dark and blurry and at funny angles. They could be photo-shopped."

"When did I have time to do that? Come on. You have to admit they look like a video gamer's control panel or a jet fighter's cockpit, right?"

"Uh, sure."

"He sounded super adamant that I not tell you, at least not yet, so don't give away at school that you know anything. Okay?"

"Yeah, okay, but ... the sun, tell me what he said about the sun, because my dad used to tell me a bedtime story years ago that started on a cloudless planet that always faced the sun and it was attacked by star cannibals. Sounds like the same story. Maybe Marc Marcum has heard it, too."

That stopped me. I hadn't yet told Alex how Marc described the Gleezhians and if his old bedtime story matched what Marc told me about the Gleezhians' hands then I'd have to reevaluate my perceptions. I asked him a question that he'd surely answer wrong: "Did your dad describe these monsters? Anything special about them?"

"They had six fingers, like claws, on each hand."

Oh, oh, either I just got teensy chills or there were bugs in bed with me. "Oh, crap, Alex, he said Gleezhians have six-fingered hands. Now I'm not sure anymore ... maybe I was drugged. I got nauseated and I had the hiccups bad. You know that happens to me when I take medicine. And more time passed than I experienced. Five or six hours."

"Selina, do you *really* believe you went to the moon and back that fast?"

"Well, the ship had some kind of living metals that kept it cool at super speeds."

"Did you see these living metals?"

"I smelled them." That sounded unconvincing even to my ears. Time to change the subject with a fake laugh.

I didn't want to talk science anymore. What I wanted to do was lie there and relive a few of the moments I had alone with Marc. Yes, I overlooked the alien thing and convinced myself he was human. Was he shy? Was he inexperienced? Should I make the first move next time? These were all questions I should have been able to discuss with my best friend if my best friend were a girl, or if my best friend were a boy who wasn't in love with me. Emoji: grimacing face.

"Can you get him to take you to the ship tomorrow? But don't get on it again. I'll follow more closely."

"So you're assuming I won't be grounded?"

"Oh, right. Well, then, I'll try to get up early and go check out the woods before we catch the bus."

“You won’t find anything. He had to fly off to help Coreg.”

“That’s convenient. I’ll bet it was one of those tricked out vans and his flying was just speeding down slippery roads.”

“I’m going to sleep now, Alex. Thanks for listening, even if you don’t believe me.”

“Well, whatever happened, I’m glad you’re home safe and nothing happened. ’Night.”

❄ ❄ ❄

“SO, I GUESS I won. *Ehk*. Again,” Marcum said when he entered Coreg’s narrower cabin and started helping him with repairs.

Coreg glared at him. “I don’t think so. Are we on Klaqin? Have you handed her over to a First Commander?” *Did I get my reward?* he thought.

Marcum shook his head in disgust. “Maybe your English is bad. We made an oath, Coreg. I said whoever gets her to come willingly onto his ship wins. I said it in English. I made the oath in Klaqin. Do you not remember?”

Fifth Commander Coreg glowered at Fifth Commander Marcum and wished they were beyond the exosphere where he wouldn’t restrain from firing more than anti-flames at Marcum. He’d blast that old ship and Marcum along with it into that freezing vacuum and not feel a minute’s regret. He ignored Marcum’s question and said, “New bet. You won’t win this one. We take turns and you can even go first. Here’s the thing: there are derelict satellites orbiting the next planet, the big red one. We’ll set a time limit, real time, and you and the time-bender have to shoot out as many as you can using her bending ability as if you were fighting the Gleezhians. Then I’ll take her and do the same, but with no time-pacing on my part. Something tells me she'll work harder for me than for you. Is it a bet?"

Marcum clucked his tongue. He'd submitted to Coreg's schemes regularly on Klaqin. Nothing ever turned out as planned. But he swore by the same oath as before anyway, realizing it meant nothing to Coreg. He felt sorry for his friend for a minute, then tucked that burdensome compassion down as far as it would go in his conscience. Coreg was hiding something and he wasn't quite sure how to get him to reveal it except to continue acting as if they were equals on this illicit mission to Earth. He knew Coreg was a liar. He knew he had no intention of fulfilling the challenge to disintegrate space debris. And he knew that Coreg intended to use his turn to steal away with Selina, leaving Marcum behind with a tired and slow ship that might never finish the trip. He'd have to stay on Earth and blend in for real. His heart sank when he realized he wouldn't mind that at all if Selina were here.

He needed a tricky scheme, something that Coreg would invent if he were in Marcum's position. He was good at infiltration tactics, he had done it alongside Coreg, and the first thing he learned—the hard way—was to determine an escape route. As he helped Coreg with repairs he studied the sleeker ship's cargo bay, weapons bay, safety pod, and supply compartments.

❄ ❄ ❄

ENGLISH CLASS, MUSIC, chemistry, but no aliens—or rather, humans—from other planets. I moped all morning. I was tempted to put my head down on my arm and get one of those red-marked foreheads that shouts *you loser, you slept in class,* but I managed to stay awake, especially in choir where singing doesn't give you any other option. I didn't hold out a speck of hope that Marc would show up for history. I figured it was my fault anyway for wrecking Coreg's ship, make that gaming console, and I was sorry that Marc had to spend all day helping him fix it.

Then, miracle of miracles, Marc strolled into history a couple seconds before the tardy bell. I sat up straighter, smiled, almost winked, and my heart rate skyrocketed, or I should say moonrocketed.

It was real. All the blurry excited illusion of last night rushed back completely clear. Alex had tried to talk me out of the unbelievable and I almost bought it. But as soon as I saw Marc's awesome physique, that shiny blue-black hair, his hands—hey, they looked tanner—and that incredible smile, I mentally catapulted back to the ship, the spaceship, remembering every vivid detail. His eyes met mine and it was jet propulsion, hold on to my heart. Whew.

I couldn't wait for class to end so I could talk to him. For once the hour didn't drag.

He waited for me at the door when the bell rang.

"Hi."

"Hellew."

I laughed at his renewed accent and thought of a thousand questions I wanted to ask him: How did he learn English? Did everyone on Klaqin know about Earth? Why hadn't they made official contact? Or had they? Were there others living among us?

Oh, my gosh, this opened up a ton of possibilities. My mind buzzed all over the place. I even wondered if my dad's super-secret job had any connection to outer space.

Five minutes between classes was all I had now. I needed to make them count.

"Did you get Coreg's, uh, vehicle fixed?"

"Yes."

"And he's all right?"

"He is here."

"Good. I'll apologize in Spanish class."

"Selina."

"Yeah?"

"I would be pleased to take you to the next planet."

"To Mars?" I looked around to make sure no one was listening. We were walking in a crowd, but there was so much noise I could pretty much count on no eavesdroppers, and people ignored me anyway. "It'll have to be after Thanksgiving. I'm grounded until then." *What the heck did I agree to?*

"Grounded?"

"Oh, that means I can't leave the house except to come to school. I can talk on the phone though, thank goodness."

"Phone?"

"Oh, you don't have a phone, do you?" I glanced at the people we passed. Letting the world know that a teenager didn't have his own phone was the same as saying he came from another planet. Oops.

I saw Mingzhu coming toward me then, eyes wide. Oh, fudge. She hadn't seen Marc before now and I knew what she must be thinking. I hated like heck to cut this short, but if I had any hope of saving my only girlfriend relationship I'd need two minutes to explain—make that lie.

"I'll see you later, Marc," I said and I saw the sweetest hurt look in his eyes, but he turned away and headed to his last class while I grabbed Mingzhu's arm and faked a giggle.

She wasn't fooled. "So, why are all the hot guys gravitating to you all of a sudden? New perfume? Pheromones? Are you wearing Victoria's Secret stuff? You can have that brunette, give me the blond." Her tone breathed arctic cold.

"I don't know," I said. "Maybe—" and then Coreg came up behind us both and butted in.

"*Hola, chicas,*" he said and that made me wonder how many languages they'd learned. Maybe their brains were bigger than ours or they used a hundred percent instead of only ten.

"*Hola*, Coreg," Mingzhu cooed.

"Hi, everything okay?" I wanted to say I was sorry, but not with Mingzhu there.

"Yes, I mean *sí*."

We entered the Spanish classroom and I didn't get another chance to speak to him. I started getting weird sensations five minutes in. *Cue the eerie sci-fi music—Alex would know what to hum.* It got harder and harder to pay attention to Señora.

❄ ❄ ❄

COREG KEPT AN eye on the time-bender throughout class, short as it was due to his time-pacing. His gift to manipulate time outshone hers; he tested her every time she looked his way. Eye contact. Pace forward. Wait. Watch her head turn. Smirk.

The funny thing was he had more trouble control-ling the pacing when he caught the time-bender's friend Mingzhu staring at him. He had to break eye contact to start the pacing. Incredible. Another time-bender right under his nose? And could she in fact be a stronger specimen than the other one? He tested the theory, looking her way more frequently, then pretending to be interested in the colorful *sombrero, poncho* and *piñata* that decorated the far wall.

Stare. Try to pace. Fail.

Stare. Pace. Lose the pace. Look away.

What? What if the whole planet produced a multitude of girls who slowed down time? The logical conclusion was to harvest all the girls the Klaqin military could take back. He imagined himself in charge of the entire fleet, pacing them across the universe with as many as their cargo bays would hold and returning to Klaqin. He wasn't stupid. He knew his government would want to create a hybrid time manipulator. Perhaps he'd be required to mate with them all. An exciting thought.

The bell rang and Mingzhu got between him and Selina. He had planned on a different outcome, but he was adaptable. He left the classroom with the somewhat pretty Mingzhu, walking in step with her, and turning in the direction she headed.

"I will walk with you," he said, first in English and then in Chinese, charming the new possible time-bender into a beaming smile.

❄ ❄ ❄

COREG KEPT GIVING me that perverted leer all through class. Creepy alien! Just as I thought at first. And then I saw him try it on Mingzhu. She, of course, fell for it. They left Spanish class practically entwined with each other.

I reached my locker where Alex leaned, arms crossed.

"What? Aren't you going to basketball? I saw your name on the roster posted in the lunch room."

"Yeah, I'm going. Not that I'll get any game time with those ... you-know-whats ... on the team. I'm here to make sure you get safely on the bus. No more abductions."

"Sweet. Thanks, but you don't have to worry." I pulled all of my textbooks out of my locker, even the ones I didn't have written homework for, and loaded up my backpack, careful not to crush the emergency candy bars at the bottom. Being grounded meant my grades were going to go up.

"Oh, shit."

"Alex!"

"Sorry, but here comes your new boyfriend."

I twisted fast and looked. Marc ambled our way, still halfway down the hall. Then I saw Coreg come around the corner. Swearing was probably in order, but I was trying not to get into the habit.

"Listen," Alex lowered his voice and I turned to him, "I'm not moving. I won't give away that I know what they are, but—"

I raised my eyebrows. "So now you believe me?" His nod was barely perceptible; I'd never seen his lips so tightly pressed together. Then my skin tingled and I knew who stood behind me.

"Hellew, Selina."

"Hi, Marc."

"Hey, dude," Alex sounded louder than he needed to be, "missed you in choir. Skipping school already?"

"Skipping?"

I dropped my bag to the floor. "Skipping means being absent without permission. It's not skipping if you were sick. Were you sick?"

"Sick? Yes."

I almost chuckled at his easy lie. Coreg joined us then.

"So," I said, "how do you like Mingzhu? She's a super nice girl."

Coreg's expression clouded over. "I thought she was like you, but she is not. You are much ... better."

His words hung in the air. It sounded like a compliment, but maybe it was a cryptic puzzle. I started getting three different vibes from these guys. On one hand, Marc exuded a puppy-dog, tail-wagging, happy-to-see-you impression. On the other hand, Coreg oozed suspiciousness and I felt more than a smidgeon of distrust toward him. And if I had a third hand, that's where Alex came in. He projected all those things: happy to see me, suspicious of Coreg, and distrustful of Marc. The moment drew out longer and more awkward. The silence was excruciating. I didn't want to respond to Coreg's weird compliment. Marc had lapsed from one and two word utterances to none. Somebody had to say something or—

"You better run, Selina, or you'll miss the bus."

"Right. See you all tomorrow. Have fun at practice!" Good save, Alex. I love that guy. I swallowed a hiccup, hoisted my backpack up and took off.

CHAPTER 15
#CliffsNotes

ALL THREE BOYS watched Selina until she went around the corner. Marcum expected Coreg to speak first, but Selina's protector spoke instead, urging them not to be late for practice.

As an intergalactic warrior-in-training, Marcum had participated in sports, though they were more blood-oriented than this simple game of putting a ball through a hoop. But while he matched steps with Coreg and Alex and headed toward the gymnasium, he realized that he'd trade his spaceship in a heartbeat to be a carefree young human, play this game, eat those pies, and pledge whatever allegiance necessary to get to know Selina the way that Alex did.

"Hey, Marc, what's that in your back pocket?" Alex asked as they reached the locker room.

Marcum pulled out his tattered copy of *Romeo and Juliet* and showed Alex the cover.

"Shakespeare?"

"Shakespeare," Marcum repeated. "It is hard."

Alex snorted. "You should get CliffsNotes."

"Who is Cliff? Does he play basketball?"

Alex let loose a loud laughing *no* and the other boys in the locker room stared at them. Marcum realized his blunder. The second thing he learned in infiltration tactics was never to admit you didn't know what something was, or in this case who. Opinions trumped knowledge. He should have said *Cliff is unreliable* or *Cliff is stupid.* He riffled through the pages and glanced up to see Alex studying his face. Their eyes locked and an unmistakable electricity flowed between them. He switched his gaze to Coreg; his comrade's eyes gave away nothing. Marcum had little time to recover. He struggled for an acceptable way to continue the conversation, but not reveal his ignorance. He needed to befriend Alex.

He decided to share the humiliation. "Coreg, have you read this?"

Coreg grabbed the book, turned a few pages, and flung it back. "It doesn't appear to be your English. What is it?"

Marcum smirked at Coreg's similar mistake. Per-haps the Earth boy would consider them merely ignorant foreigners.

Alex bent to lace his shoes and said, "That is probably one of the greatest English plays ever written by the greatest author who ever lived. *Everybody* knows that." He stood up, almost as tall as the aliens, and added, "You both should read it. It's a tragedy. Romeo and Juliet are *star-crossed* lovers. That *never* works out. They both *die* in the end."

❄ ❄ ❄

"I DO NOT TRUST Alex." Coreg said in Klaqin as he and Marcum trooped away from the school after practice. Most of the snow from the storm had turned to slush, but their shoes repelled the moisture.

"He is jealous."

"Then he will make trouble."

"He has extremely strong feelings for Sel—for the time-bender."

"I thought there might be another time-bender in one of my classes, but she deceived me. Selina is the only one.

You can say her name, Marcum. I know you too have strong feelings for her."

Marcum stepped over an icy puddle and ignored Coreg's correct assessment. "She is grounded."

"Do you mean she can't fly?"

"It's some sort of punishment, so yes she can't fly. We'll have to wait a few weeks before we can test her bending ability around the red planet."

"Marcum, I should tell you I've heard from Second Commander Dace. We can't wait. There is a search party coming after us. We'll have to forget about the bet. Take me to her house tonight and we'll capture her." He chuckled. "Having regular periods of darkness will work to our advantage."

Marcum discerned a spike in his own heart rate.

They reached the end of the parking lot and a dark blue SUV careened around the corner, passed them, then stopped and backed up. The driver rolled down his window and shouted at Coreg. "Hey! That's my son's jacket, you a-hole." The door opened and a hefty man got out and started around the car. A young man sat in the passenger's seat, a grin stuck roundly on his face.

Coreg did a quick calculation of the situation. Empty parking lot. Uninvolved cars flowing steadily past. No human traffic around. He and Marcum could take down the man and then his son and not even require the weapons they'd left in their ships.

"You should be ashamed of yourselves," the man yelled. Then he gestured at Marcum's pink ski jacket. "I suppose you stole yours from a girl, you little creep."

He was five steps away from reaching Coreg when Marcum stepped in front of him and spoke in halting English, "We are exchange students. No coats. New friends help us. Please, Coreg, return the coat to our new friends."

The man stopped abruptly and looked over at his son. "What? You told me a white-haired bully stole it from you in the bathroom. Come on, Jason, what are you trying to pull? Did you lend it to him?"

Marcum yanked on Coreg's sleeve while the man's attention was turned to his son. Coreg slipped his arms out of the coat, mumbling menacing words at Marcum. He threw the coat forward and the man closed the distance, snatched the jacket, and backed away, a string of unrecognizable words escaping his lips. The man acted confused and embarrassed, but he returned to his car, pushed the jacket at his son, and did a U-turn to leave the campus.

"Give me your coat, Marcum, you Gleezhian momma's boy. Why did you not want to fight him with me? Did you forget you are genetically enhanced to be brave?"

"Coreg," Marcum answered calmly as he succeeded in zipping the pink jacket up, "did you forget rule three?"

❄ ❄ ❄

COREG SNICKERED TO himself. Both spaceships sat parked side by side in the woods where Marcum had originally landed. The camouflage worked better on Coreg's repaired vessel; Marcum's old ship appeared mottled and pixelated. Coreg was glad to get out of the cold. On the way back from the school they had jogged along the route to help him stay warm. He didn't hide the annoyance he had with Marcum and kept giving him furious looks. And that paid off, he thought, because Marcum's expression changed as they passed one particular dwelling on the street before the woods.

He took a ration of his liquid nourishment and sorted through his tools. Forget about jackets, and school, and basketball. He was done with all that. He would break into the time-bender's place by himself and take her.

❄ ❄ ❄

MARCUM WONDERED IF Coreg caught him involuntarily scoping out Selina's house. Probably not. Coreg had exhibited numerous faults in his tactics. Maybe the only thing Coreg was good at was time-pacing.

And lying.

Marcum fed his bio-metals some of the galactic lard, a smelly brew of refined organic compounds, complex polymers, and oily preservatives, not to mention the required human ingredients. Then he checked his communications. Nothing. He tried multiple times to reach the supposed rescue ship, Second Commander Dace, or anyone that used the usual inter-galactic frequencies, Earth not included. Was there in fact a search and rescue unit or was that another of Coreg's lies?

He added extra lard to the bio-metals around the transponder then demodulated the output for his transmitter. His devices were literally light years ahead of anything they had on Earth, though the humans' use of phones intrigued him. He briefly considered leaving his ship and going in search of one in order to contact Selina.

He let his breath out in stages. Selina.

His eyes settled on the communication controls and he decided to try his hand at hacking into Earth's phone system.

❄ ❄ ❄

"EASY, BUDDY, WAIT." My brother enjoyed getting on my nerves. "Mom called and has to cover for another nurse for half a shift. Let me get dinner ready and then we'll play a game. You've watched enough TV. Turn it off."

Buddy pitched a fit. A leg kicking, loud yelling, floor pounding fit. Sheesh. You'd think the world had ended or something. Any change to his routine and World War III erupted. I gave him a box of crackers to shut him up.

Sure, Mom, I can get dinner. No problem. Buddy's fine. Yeah, I'll turn off his cartoons and make him do the next set of lessons. Yeah, I know it's his bath night. I can handle it. He won't freak out. Right. Right. Right.

I tried not to sound peeved on the phone. I couldn't afford to sound anything but sweet and sorry—*polish up the fake attitude*—if I wanted the grounding to get shortened. I hadn't been grounded more than half a dozen times my whole life. As a matter of fact I'd never been grounded when my dad was out of town. I guess I tried harder to follow rules and be helpful when he was gone.

Still ... it wasn't fair I got this punishment for taking a walk with Marc. Of course I couldn't say *hey, he took me to his spaceship and then we went to the moon, so don't blame me for missing curfew.*

Ouch. The pan was hot. Mac and cheese the hard way. Buddy insisted I not make the microwave kind so ...

I heard a noise then. Oh my gosh, it would be so *not cool* if Marcum showed up at the front door again. I hoped he knew not to come over. I checked the time on the stove. For sure he'd be finished with practice by now. I wondered what he ate for dinner. And if he could fly off to Paris to get it.

I heard it again. The front door. The handle.

I turned the flame off, put the spoon down on the counter top, and started toward the door.

"Where you going?" Buddy followed right on my heels.

"Shh, I think somebody's here."

"Who'th here?"

"I don't know. Shh."

We crept to the foyer. Well, I crept and Buddy grabbed my waistband and tried to slide sock-footed behind me.

I put my eye to the peephole.

"Me look." Buddy started bouncing up and down.

I saw no one out there so I lifted Buddy and helped him get his eye to the hole.

"Gwampa Too-lek," he said.

I dropped him to the floor, untwisted the deadbolt and flung open the door expecting to see that white-haired, champion teller of tall tales, Grandpa Turlek. He never remembered the code to our lock even though he used to babysit us a few years ago.

But it wasn't our fun, story-concocting grandfather.

My jaw dropped to see a slimmer white-haired person bent forward who I startled into jumping back.

"Coreg! What are you doing here?"

"Who'th that?" Buddy yelled. He started pulling on me, trying to climb up my body, but he'd grown too big for that anymore.

"Come in, come in." I moved Buddy out of the way and hurried to shut the door behind a shivering, wet Coreg. I should have been scared to let another alien into my house, but it wasn't like he was a stranger, and his eyes drew me in and erased whatever hesitation and fear I might have had. I ignored the sixth sense feeling that made me wonder why he'd been examining the door lock, and wrote his action off to curiosity. Buddy went into a fit of wailing, repeating his question louder and louder.

Coreg bent low again and faced Buddy eye to eye. Coreg matched Buddy's screaming by saying his own name in a low growl. Then, out of the blue, utter silence reigned. Coreg must have told Buddy his name and that he was a friend of mine a hundred times, yet it echoed in my head in a second's length. Weird. And Buddy's cheek blossomed red as if someone had pinched him hard.

"So ..." I waited for his explanation. I figured Marc must have told him where I lived.

"You shot me. You hit my spaceship."

"I'm so, so sorry."

Buddy resumed his persistent bouncing. He smiled and recited *Selina shot Cork's spaceship* several times which must have sounded like gibberish with all the s's lisped.

"Buddy, you didn't turn the TV off, did you? Go do that, please." I knew he'd get distracted and plant himself on the floor two feet from the screen and forget about Coreg, or Cork, as he'd called him.

A moment later I stood alone with the beautiful—sometimes creepy—alien in the foyer and tried not to drift into those eyes. I never understood how some girls went hot then cold on a guy in a matter of minutes, but I seemed to be having the same trouble coming to a conclusion on how I felt toward Coreg. Hot, then cold. Right now things were heading in the hot direction and the minutes were stretching longer than they should.

"Will you come up in my ship? It is much newer and better than Marcum's."

"Uh, sure."

"Now."

"Sorry, I can't go anywhere now, even if I wasn't grounded, but I am, like for two weeks, can you believe it, and anyway I have to watch my brother, so ..." My brain kept disconnecting from my mouth, but I was quite proud of my new ability to hold a grip on a conversation, rambling or not.

"He is small. He can come."

Oh, now wouldn't that get me an award for sister-of-the-year. I could hear my mother now: *You took him where? In what? With an alien?*

Suddenly we were at the end of my street, Buddy between us, and I struggled to slow things down as Coreg pulled us toward the path into the woods. Oh. My. Gosh! When had we gotten our coats on? How had this happened so fast?

CHAPTER 16
#Kidnapped

COREG KNEW HE had to keep the time-bender and the child moving and not give her a chance to combat his pacing by slowing things down as she had in her house. She had tempted him. It was exhilarating, better than any challenge he'd faced to date, and he acted on it without weighing all outcomes.

The child he regarded as expendable. He'd get the time-bender into the ship and leave the boy outside. He should certainly be able to find his way home, though he judged him to be an odd little thing. It occurred to Coreg then that perhaps the child had unusual abilities of his own. Change of plan. He'd take the child, too. The ship had several cargo bays, and there was also a little space next to the lard processor.

That quick brainstorm made him lose his concentration. The time-bender stopped in the road, ready to speak, maybe scream. He gritted his teeth and paced them on toward the ship. In what seemed like a second he had them at the door, inside, stowed. And then he took a breath to release his time-paced tension.

He donned the helmet, partially blocking the sounds his unhappy captives were making.

He spoke into the helmet comm, "Marcum. Are you there?"

No answer. He was either taking a single necessary hour of sleep or out collecting data as Coreg had suggested to him. Perfect.

Coreg settled into the chair, tightened it, and did his customary pre-flight check of the systems: measured the lard levels, released the camouflage, checked the immediate air space, made visual and audio assessments, and brought up the controls. His hands hovered, ready to start what would be the equivalent of an engine, yet was something much more advanced. But his hands stayed poised.

Coreg tried to swear aloud, but nothing came out. He stood frozen. Frozen in time. That exasperating little time-bender did it again, she managed to bend time from her cramped cell. At least it gave him time to think.

Think, think. How could he get her to comply and stop this manipulation? Of course, it would be easy. The human touch. A special human touch that involved nothing more than two sets of lips. Yes.

He relaxed into the sluggish interlude and moved as slowly as time allowed, aiming to pull her out of the enclosure and change her mind about going with him.

❄ ❄ ❄

I DON'T KNOW why it rattled around in my head, but something my mother once said about exercising made me perk up. It wasn't speed or distance, she told me when I mocked her for her long, slow walks around the neighborhood, but *time* that mattered. Time! *Cue the heroine*—me—*who slowly figures out something big*.

I was stuck in some kind of semi-dark tomb without Buddy, who I faintly heard whimpering somewhere—which was making me furious—and I was reflecting on time. All my life the moments that were the best were either gone too fast or lived in slow motion. I needed that slow motion right then to figure out what to do. I absolutely hated Coreg. Alien jerk! Giant brute!

There had to be a way to open this hatch from the inside. If only I could see better. Uf! Coreg, I hate you. Multi-lingual monster.

I'd allowed myself a single stupid second of heart-fluttering excitement for him in my foyer. And to think I seriously considered kissing him. Blond beast. Freakin' freak.

"Buddy, it's okay," I yelled at the walls. The walls. I wondered if they were made of the same bio-metals that Marc had explained. I was on my knees so I put my hands out to the sides and touched everywhere. Holy cow, Alex would freak out in this claustrophobic cranny. Okay, okay, so this was close to the size of Buddy's indoor pop-up tent. I could stay curled up and sleep all the way to Klaqin or Gleezhe or the moon or maybe work my way through the walls. Hadn't Marc said the bio-metals could be manipulated?

Time. I envisioned unrolling the minutes and turning them into elastic.

Coreg, that creepy kidnapper, did something with time. And what about my trip around the moon? Time withdrew its properties then. Maybe it had something to do with these spaceships. Maybe they were time capsules, or time machines, or space transporters that moved outside of normal time constraints. Holy cow.

I didn't hear Buddy.

The hiccups started then and I bumped my head. Ha, lucky me, it was the latch to open the round door. I crawled through and spotted Coreg immediately. The creep.

"Hey!" I straightened up and took two steps toward him. His arms dropped to the armrests and he turned and tried, unsuccessfully I might add, to smile sweetly at me. I hiccupped again.

"Where's my brother? Get him out right now," I said, anger and panic packed like twin fireballs under my lungs.

Coreg removed his helmet and spoke slowly, as if I didn't understand English. "Selina. You are so beautiful."

Give me a break. Like I'm going to fall for that now? I. Don't. Think. So. Jerk.

"My brother?" I felt oddly in control. That time theory stuff slowly rolled around in my head like pinballs in molasses. I bristled with anger and with a power—*cue the Eureka moment*—that all of a sudden I knew I had. "I can slow down time," I said, knowing, and not just wishing, that it was true. "And you can speed it up. That's how you got us out here."

"Of course. That is why Marcum and I came to Earth. To find you. You are a time-bender."

"A what?" I guess that scared the hiccups out of me because they stopped. I've been called a lot of things, but never that.

"You can bend time down to its slowest movement. I am a time-pacer. I can speed it up."

"Right." I've heard of ideas so complicated they make your head swim, but this called for a life jacket or at the very least Buddy's floaties because my head wasn't only swimming, it was drowning. I stuck my hand in my pocket, got my phone, and took my own sweet time-bending time to carefully text Alex: HELP. COME TO WOODS.

I hoped my time-bending was limited to the immediate vicinity and Alex would not be slowed down. Uh-oh. If they were in the middle of dinner his mother wouldn't let him out.

Maybe six feet separated me from Coreg, and he had the advantage of being much bigger and stronger, and of course he was male, and if he used his pacing or whatever-he-called-it, then I'd find myself in big trouble.

I kept my eyes on the goon and thought I'd better make a bargain. "So ... you and Marc are here because I'm a time-bender, huh? Were you going to kidnap me and use me against the star cannibals?" Whoa, saying that gave me a thrill. And power. All this time I thought I suffered from APD, an avoidance personality disorder. But this? Not cool. No way would I ever be part of a war even on Earth, let alone any intergalactic confrontations. That wasn't me. I almost went to a peace march last year. I wrote a paper defending conscientious objectors. I didn't even kill spiders.

"Yes," Coreg said. "With you we could take better aim, raise our accuracy to one hundred percent."

"All right, then. Sounds reasonable. But my brother stays on Earth." Yup, I held bargaining chips with aliens. I was lying and not even trembling. It felt like someone was plowing a huge weight against my chest, slowing my breathing and my heart too. How long I could keep up this bending stuff was anybody's guess. So far Coreg hadn't made a move to grab me again, but just because time was creeping along didn't mean he couldn't move. I was ready.

❄ ❄ ❄

ALEX WAS OUTSIDE, taking his second-best friend, his dog Baxter, for a walk. The old boxer was slow, half-blind, but loyal and eager to please. When Alex got Selina's text he urged Baxter into a run. There was no leash to pull him along, but the devoted dog did his best to stick to his master's heels.

Alex came to the end of the path and told Baxter to sit and stay. The poor old thing obeyed, but alternately growled and whined.

"What the—" Alex stared at the two large shapes taking up the middle section of the woods. One ship, the size of a double-decker bus seemed to be lying on its side. The other, of a smaller diameter and with a silky smooth sheathing, lay with its nose end pointed at Alex. He sucked in a breath of cold air and gave Baxter the hand signal to heel. He bent close to the dog's head and tussled him under the ears, calming himself as well as assuring the dog that nothing threatened them. Yet.

Even though the ships weren't enormous, snuggled into the clearing as they were, they gave the impression of colossal machines. Alex rose. "Selina!"

Baxter perked his ears at her name and began sniffing in circles. There were plenty of footprints around, some small enough to be Selina's. Baxter headed for the sleeker spaceship.

"Find Selina, Baxter," Alex urged. The dog pawed around a spot a third of the way down from the front of the ship, sat down in the snow and woofed.

"Hey! Marc! You in there?"

"No. I am out here. Hellew."

Alex turned as quickly as Baxter did, grabbed the dog's collar, and held him tightly as he barked once and growled a canine curse at the tall intruder.

"Where's Selina? I got a text that she needed help."

Marcum's face contorted and he took quick strides toward them, his eyes never leaving the dog's menacing fangs. He looped around them and touched both hands to two dimples in the ship's side. A portion of the side opened, revealing Selina facing Coreg who was inches away from grabbing both of her wrists.

"Lay off her!" Alex released the dog and jumped up into the cabin. Baxter lunged for Marcum, but Marcum vaulted toward Coreg.

❄ ❄ ❄

MY HEART DROPPED through the floor. One second I was contemplating my options and the next instant Coreg was in my personal space and there was nothing pleasing about that. His hands gripping my arms made me squeak like a startled mouse, a natural consequence, I suppose, of trying to scream with a decelerated heart in my mouth. I held my breath and stared him down. Or rather up, he was *so* tall. He exerted a rippling force that pummeled the air around us, but did nothing to my skin other than to make it crawl. I fought back, one hiccup at a time, and gained some weight and potency in this battle of wills. My dad always said I had a stubborn streak. I heard him tell the doctors my days on Earth might be numbered but I'd live longer than they projected. I could be obstinate. That worked for me. And look, I was doing something totally radical for me: making steady eye contact.

Magic adrenaline, that's what I had. And passion. Though this passion reeked of resentment, and, um, maybe some fear. I repelled him with double the scorn and a couple more hiccups. I felt his thumbs lighten up and his grip falter. That invisible weight was lifting from my chest.

The side of the ship slid open then, distracting me, and before I could comprehend the speed at which it happened, Marcum had pushed Coreg into his chair, Alex had his arms around me, and sweet old Baxter started pawing at a low interior handle.

"Are you all right?" Alex's voice came out hoarse. I looked up into his eyes and let all my important organs—heart, lungs, stomach—find their way back to their rightful positions. I got control of the time around me again. Even though they were Alex's arms wrapped around me and not Marc's I had to admit I enjoyed the rescued-princess feel of it. I took longer than necessary to consider how serious his green eyes glowed, how the tiny little laugh lines around his mouth accented his lips, and how he smelled like fresh-from-the-shower manliness.

But Alex was Alex. I released my hold on time and he released me when I wiggled, nodding toward Baxter.

"Is he in there, boy?" I glared over at Coreg and knelt down. "It's okay, Buddy, I'll get you out." Marc still had Coreg in a martial arts hold which apparently kept him from using his special ability. Alex pulled Baxter back and made him sit while I opened the hatch and peered inside. I laughed, not a funny, joking laugh, just a short gulp of relief. Buddy was sound asleep, his glasses cocked all wonky across his adorable face.

"Help me pull him out."

Alex burrowed half his body in—despite the suffocating feeling he must have had to do that—and scooped his arms under Buddy's back and legs. I put one hand under Buddy's head and the other under his arm and together we bumped him up and over and out.

"Wake up, Bud, we're going home."

It took some jostling to get him to come awake enough to stand him up. Alex lifted him up and draped him over his shoulder and Buddy, in his typical innocence, fell again into limp slumbering. That was good; this would all be a dream to him. Mom would never know.

With a free hand Alex took my arm and moved me toward the opening, keeping himself between me and the aliens and commanding Baxter to heel. He let loose with threats and more than a few vile expressions which I imagined weren't on Marc and Coreg's vocabulary list.

I had a sudden absurd wish that I was a dragon. It would have been so cool to breathe fire and flame on Coreg. Instead I huffed a threatening sigh and my harmless white breath vanished into the cold.

I looked back when we stepped out and my heart clutched a little to see Coreg's eyes closed and his head bent funny like Marc had broken his neck. He was as inert as a marionette whose strings had been severed. Marcum's countenance was not as mellow; his eyes were popping and his neck cords strained making a tremor visible from chin to chest. I didn't want to be the reason for somebody's death. The pathetic look Marc gave me in that instant, while Baxter growled at him and slowly followed us out, made one of my recently repositioned organs thump a little harder. I saw him swing a hand toward the wall and then the door contracted and what little light the opening had given to our departure disappeared.

CHAPTER 17
#ChocolateLover

ALEX CARRIED BUDDY upstairs and helped me get him into pajamas. Best friend ever. He was more concerned about us than about leaving Baxter outside in the cold. We walked out of Buddy's room and headed for the stairs. He asked how we got ourselves into that situation, but I gave him a sad face and shrugged my shoulders. I heard Baxter whine a couple of times and then he scratched at the door.

"Oh, poor Baxter," I said. "But you know how my mom feels about animals in the house." We came down the stairs side by side.

"I can stay until your mom gets home. No problem." Alex had the most peculiar look on his face. Tight muscles twitched at the corners of his mouth, but he wasn't even close to smiling. We stood at the front door. I didn't want him to stay and I didn't want him to leave. I was so confused. Spaceships! Twice I'd been abducted!

"You can go. I'm okay," I said, smoothing my hair as if neatness proved that point.

"You sure?"

I nodded my head.

"Do not open this door again, Selina." He'd never spoken to me so forcefully before.

He pointed at the security code box without saying a word and then tapped the deadbolt before leaving. Okay, message received. I locked the door behind him and turned the alarm system on. I stood at the door for the longest time before I walked zombie-style into the kitchen switching every light on along the way. I threw out the cold macaroni and cheese and ate a bowl of cereal. My mind was an empty box. I tried hard to make sense of everything, but coherent thoughts remained outside the box. I left all the lights on and went up to my room.

My chocolate stash beckoned me so I obediently opened a dozen Hershey's kisses and lined them up on my bedside table, made a wad of the foil, and unsuccessfully shot for the waste paper basket. I sniffed the first piece of chocolate and let the wonderful scent relax me. Talk about stress. I had started crying halfway home and Alex took one hand off Buddy's back and reached for my hand. Not that holding hands with my best friend meant anything. It couldn't. Alex was Alex. I was interested in Marc. But feeling the warmth through his fingers did help the tears stop; it was as comforting as an old teddy bear and a fluffy blanket.

I popped the chocolate into my mouth and held it there. My thoughts fluttered all over the place. What a night. I tried to remember what Coreg said about time-bending.

Time-bender, my foot. What was that all about? Nobody could manipulate time. Perception yes, maybe through drugs or adrenaline, but not time. I must have imagined it all. Like I could be a super-hero. Right. More like a teenage cry-baby.

The chocolate melted and I let the obligatory groan escape my throat and savored the silky sweet satisfaction. It settled my soul.

Then I had another. And another.

When I got to number six I hiccupped. Wait. Hiccups? Was I unconsciously controlling the time?

Time-bender, huh?

I needed to test it. I unwrapped another one, balled the foil, took aim, and ... slowly ... slowly ... a perfect arc. Success. Yes, I could see how that could be an advantage.

What if I worked for the good guys and snuck in where the bad guys were and slowed stuff down, then if Coreg speeded things up around the good guys they'd swoop in and—

Wait. If Marcum killed Coreg ... no, I didn't want anything to do with good guy, bad guy stuff anyway. And if Coreg was alive and breathing—if aliens breathed—he wanted to take me as a prisoner. So, no way was any of this going any further. Maybe I should stick to unconsciously slowing down time in history class, the dentist's office, and when Alex aimed from the free throw line. And making my life last past my teen years.

But what about Marc? Did Marc have any special ability? Other than make me get flustered, that is. Crap, my empty box of a brain was filling up fast with nonsense.

I ate another chocolate. I ate them all.

By the time I finished I was too charged up to sleep. Too confused. I wondered if Alex had ever been aware of my time-bending.

And then it happened again. Another vision. Clear as day. Me running from a small spaceship to a giant Star Trek worthy one. The sun high but a cloud of mist pricking at my hands and face. And scores of brilliant starships lasering down to land behind a glittering monster of a castle. I was taking long strides, bouncing on the earth ... only I knew it wasn't Earth.

❄ ❄ ❄

MARCUM WAS MORTIFIED. Technically what he did to Coreg violated his classification, but with no one other than Earth beings as witnesses it would be his word against Coreg's; and though he was usually as truthful as he was fearless and compassionate, he'd lie if Coreg reported him.

He had acted with impetuous unrestraint and it confused him how quickly he had gone to Selina's defense.

Before the ship's door opened he suspected Coreg's deceit and as soon as he saw Selina inches from his rival commander's grasp, he correctly assessed the most efficient course of action that would satisfy Selina, her guardian, the guardian's animal, and himself: he caught Coreg in a Gleezhian choke hold, one that would render his friend unable to fight back. Unconscious in five one-hundredths of a time unit.

As soon as the door closed he released the hold he had on Coreg. Blood, basic human blood that held the same salts and proteins across the galaxy, flowed freely to Coreg's brain. He awakened.

"Hey!" Coreg leaped up, yelled at Marcum and moved into a defensive stance. But he was wobbly. Marcum pushed him to the floor and began a tirade, something he would never be able to do with as much force and fluidity in English, but in Klaqin he verbally pinned Coreg down.

"Are you done?" Coreg spat back, making no effort to rise.

"No. You can forget your little plot to steal away home with her and leave me exiled here. She's not going anywhere with *you*. If *I* can convince her to come and help us, then fine, *I'll* be her pilot and *you* can pace us to Klaqin. But she's not getting on *this* ship again for any reason."

Coreg pressed his hands onto the floor and pushed himself up. "You nearly killed me. I won't forget that."

"You weren't even close to dying. I should have torn off your head and made you swallow it." He made a throaty challenge sound then calmed considerably. "Now, concerning the search and rescue ... I didn't get any signals from anywhere out there, but then my *Galaxer* is old. Bring them up on the *Intimidator*'s screen. I want to talk to the Second Commander."

❄ ❄ ❄

SECOND COMMANDER DACE scowled at Third Commander Enrimmon whose time-pacing had been spotty at best. Enrimmon had peaked early and made Third sooner than he should have due to the great losses the Klaqin military had endured, but his performance on this venture proved him to be a most frustrating member of the crew. Dace silently cursed the First Commanders who'd voted to send him and these two Thirds after Coreg, Marcum, and the prospective time-bender. Perhaps he'd fallen victim to a conspiracy to eliminate him from important campaigns. Perhaps they never expected him to reach the under-developed planet. He'd seen no evidence of advancement in the inadequate intelligence reports he scanned daily. And the higher-ups couldn't possibly know his ulterior motives. Why were they wasting time on language and culture courses for a civilization so far out of their empire? It offended practical reasoning. Unless. Unless the star cannibals had their eye on something valuable on that planet.

Dace stood at the controls and urged Enrimmon to try harder. "Come on. Pace it, you sorry excuse for a Third."

"Second Commander," the other Third, the one seated at the screen, called out, "we're getting comm waves from Coreg's *Intimidator* again. I'll bring it up."

"Go ahead, Lektur. Stand down, Enrimmon. Let's see what the Fifth Commander has to say."

The screen centered on Marcum's face and his voice came through the speaker. "Second Commander Dace, this is Fifth Commander Marcum."

"Marcum. What's the matter with your face? You've burned to brown."

"Sir, the sun here changes our skin. Fifth Commander Coreg is experiencing the same phenomenon."

"Where is Coreg? Why are you calling from his *Intimidator*?"

"Sir, my *Galaxer* is experiencing communication deterioration. The bio-metals are low on humanoid proteins."

"You seem to be having a number of experiences, Marcum. Have you experienced any time-bending?" Dace blended his impatience with sarcasm.

"Yes, sir, I have. The time-bender is here on Earth, as I determined."

"As *you* determined?" He huffed. "Yes, Fifth Commander, I've been informed of that. Why haven't you captured her yet? Coreg should be halfway here to meet us. We need his pacing—" he narrowed his eyes at Enrimmon "—to shorten our return to Klaqin. There are battles raging over the moons. The sooner we get her mated to Coreg, the sooner we can raise a breed of pacer-benders."

Marcum blanched at Dace's last statement. "Sir, I've asked her. She doesn't want to come."

Dace's yellow face darkened to orange. "You've *asked* her? *Asked?* Fifth Commander Marcum, you don't *ask*. You take! Let me talk to Fifth Commander Coreg. "

While Coreg took a turn at fielding Dace's questions and commands, Marcum moved out of view and glanced around for the tiny hydraulic bleed lever. If Coreg's ship was not a total redesign then he'd find a small fire extinguisher button directly beneath the lever. He found it and pushed it in. The ship would not take off until someone reset the button and Coreg would most likely overlook the easy fix and waste time, days maybe, tearing apart the systems, the stabilizers, the detection circuits, the bio-metals, and the analyzers.

He made his exit from the ship before Coreg signed off with Dace.

He loped up the path, easily finding the way, even in the dark. Snow began to fall, heavy and wet. Selina's house sat a short way ahead with no sign of Alex or his animal guarding the front. He slowed and studied the windows. There were lights on in the first and second levels. He stopped and listened then moved stealthily to the back of the house, peeking in first floor windows and glancing at the neighbors' houses, checking for animals, wondering if Alex had left, or if he remained inside.

The thought of mating Selina off to Coreg disgusted him. A successful pregnancy, made quicker with Coreg's concentrated pacing, would lead to subsequent matings, probably a state-sanctioned alliance or marriage of some sort, and Marcum would never see her again.

He shuddered at the thought of Selina succumbing to the coercion and being plunged into the endless day and chaos of his warring planet, forced to procreate, forced to bend time. Life appeared to be better on Earth. But he was torn; was it more noble, more compassionate to betray her to save his planet—*possibly* save his planet, did it even deserve saving? Or should he betray the Commanders and everyone on Klaqin to keep Selina for himself?

❄ ❄ ❄

I COULDN'T CONVINCE myself that I was a superhero, but neither could I shake the certainty that I was in a freakin' category of my own. Emoji: confused face.

After all, my brother was special in one way, why couldn't I be special in another?

I looked out my bedroom window at Alex's house. His window was dark, but since my alarm clock said eight thirty I imagined him sitting there watching my backyard, lights out. In case he was, I waved. A second later he turned on his desk lamp so I'd see him and he waved back. He grabbed a pillow and made like he was having a pillow fight with an invisible attacker. I rocked at the waist, pretending to give his performance huge belly laughs. I closed my blinds then and turned off my light. His vigilance saddened me. Poor guy, unrequited love and all that. But hey I couldn't tell my heart who to fall for. Either there was chemistry or there wasn't. He couldn't make me fall for him.

My being grounded didn't mean I couldn't watch television—I assumed—so I tiptoed downstairs. I expected my mom to be home in an hour and she'd watch with me. She preferred the shows about medical oddities to unwind. They bored me, but maybe that was what I needed to get my brain back to reality.

As I entered the family room I stopped before I switched on the lamp. Something caught my attention outside. Snowflakes. Crap, not another early November snowstorm. I flicked the light on and the black windows reflected a sorry imitation of me. Not a superhero.

A hard knock on the front door startled me. Sounded like Alex's fist, though. He's a one knock kind of guy and he could have run over here that fast.

I raced through the house and slid to an Olympic stop. *Do not open this door again, Selina.* If it was Alex, he was testing me. Had to be Alex.

The peephole told me something different. Double crap and a half, it was Marc!

I ignored Alex's admonition, swung the door open, and cringed when our security system's thirty second alarm warning started its panicked whine. Marc's eyes widened. "What is that?"

"That, my alien friend, is my house. It's on the threshold, pun intended, of blowing up if you don't give me a good reason why you're here. In thirty seconds or less." Huh, maybe my special time-bending ability came with a bad-ass attitude, too. So not me, but I might as well go with it. I concentrated on holding time to a near stand-still and seeing if I could delay the alarm's inevitable ten-seconds-left squeal.

Marc stared at me. He probably didn't understand puns. He kept staring. There were snowflakes caked on his eyebrows. The tingle started in my toes. Mmm, I held on to that feeling. A little knock in the knees. Butterflies in the belly. Up to the heart. Uh, huh. Slow tick, slower tock. Marc didn't say a thing and the alarm didn't squeal.

"Oh, for Pete's sake, you're going to turn into a snowman. Come on in." I moved out of the way and punched in my birthdate to disarm the security system. I reset it. Not that I didn't trust Marc, I did, but if Coreg was alive he might have followed him. "Coreg's alive, right?"

"He is fine."

"He scared the heck out of me. Out of us. My little brother freaked out to the point that he passed out."

"Passed out?"

"Yeah, like what you did to Coreg. Why did you do that?"

Marc's eyes wouldn't meet mine and I consciously slowed things down again so I could verbalize my anxiety. I had so many questions. But they all went out of my mind when Marc answered.

"Alex is one of us."

Right. Right. *A little less time bending here, please.* Alex is an alien? Sure, like I haven't known him all my life. "No way."

Marc stood there not meeting my eyes, melted snow stringing his hair into clumps, his shoulders hunched a little bit forward. I took his stance to mean I'd caught him in a lie.

He lifted his eyes and whispered, "Pie?"

So now he changed the subject and decided to beg for food. Adorable. I swung my arm out in the direction of the kitchen. "After you." I followed with a whole shopping cart full of emotions that I wanted to ram into the back of his legs. Why did he have to be so cute? And now with one word he made me smile. Pie. The urge to laugh overtook the previous urge. His shoes resonated on the floor, two squeaks to every ten beats of my heart.

We sat next to each other on stools at the counter and he got two bites into the pie before he spoke again. Small talk, very small, a question about dogs and other pets. He told me he liked animals, called them weedix or something like that. Hard to tell with his mouth full.

"I am ... what is the word? ... dependent ... on the pie."

"Addicted, you mean. Yeah, I see that."

"You are not eating your piece?"

I hadn't lifted my fork even. Probably not the best idea to eat it after all that chocolate. "You can have it if you want. I have a different addiction."

"What?"

"Chocolate."

"There is so much to learn here."

He'd already learned a lot. He handled a fork with ease; he'd navigated a large high school and charmed students and teachers alike, switching between enchanting accent and perfect pronunciation; and he certainly knew how to make a less than ordinary girl feel extraordinary.

"Marc?" I probably said his name with a sigh. He looked amazing. As always. Even with his hair in melting snowman style. "Can you keep Coreg away from me? Send him into outer space or something?"

He stopped eating then and looked so deeply into my eyes that I involuntarily held my breath and made myself bend time for one endless minute.

Then I hiccupped and he answered, "I have a plan. Will you trust me?"

How could I say anything but "Sure," as I leaned a smidgen closer and prayed that my chocolate breath had not turned sour.

Marc set his fork down. I silently cheered that the stools we sat on didn't have wheels or mine would've been spinning. My brain urged me to turn from the waist to face him full on, but I'd tucked my feet behind the lower bar of the stool and I couldn't safely balance and all of a sudden confusion overwhelmed me. He placed both hands on the counter and shifted on his stool—that's what I wanted to do—and then he leaned to within two inches of my face. I swear. I. Could. Not. Stop. This. Now.

But then he drew back and said, "There is another ship coming. They will take you if Coreg doesn't."

❄ ❄ ❄

ALEX PUNCHED IN all but the last digit of the number that Selina's father had given him. He hesitated, ready with the panic code that might or might not bring a squad of armed men to Selina's aid. He looked at her window again. Dark.

Then the family room light downstairs came on. Maybe her mom got home. Good. He took a deep breath and let himself relax. Baxter made a low plaintive sound and lay down next to Alex's bed. If the dog was satisfied, so was Alex.

He heard his dad come down the hall and stop at his door. "Going to bed so soon, son?"

"Not yet." He cleared the number and set the phone down. "Hey, dad."

"Yeah?"

"Remember that thing you showed me once a long time ago? That brown and gray box in the garage?"

"I didn't show it to you, Alex. You found it. Snooping through my things." His father stepped into the room. He had the same good looks, tall frame, and dark brown hair as Alex, but wrinkles, a bad back, and gray sideburns emphasized the age difference. The white glow of the ceiling light enhanced the amber in his eyes.

"What was it? Because I saw a kid at school with the same thing."

Mr. Rimmon pressed the door closed behind him with a hard click. "Son, we need to talk."

CHAPTER 18
#BedtimeBookClub

NATE RIMMON SAT on the edge of Alex's bed. What he had to say reminded Alex of bedtime stories from a dozen years ago. Only this one chilled him far more. And it wasn't a story.

"That gray and brown box isn't a box at all. It's a weapon. A deadly weapon. I used it in training. And then I used it to kill ... to save my life. To escape." He took a slower breath. "I wasn't born on Earth. My history, that whole background story your mother believes about me surviving an accident, the head injury, loss of memory, all that, it was mostly fiction that allowed me to become part of ... of a necessary existence."

Alex scrunched his face up and pulled his chin down. "Are you kidding me, Dad?"

"Listen, son, I was born on the planet Klaqin. It exists, a planet that always faces its sun, so it's always daytime, like I told you in those stories when you were little. My parents worked in food production, deep underground where the earliest cities existed. We weren't poor, but we didn't have much compared to those whose sons and daughters went into the military. I had two younger brothers. All three of us wanted to join as soon as we finished our early education."

"School?" Suspicions began to tease Alex's heart rate, but his inner voice kept repeating *it's a joke, it's a joke.*

Mr. Rimmon faked a laugh. "School is universal, quite literally. We learned things children shouldn't have to know. There were wars going on. Interplanetary wars. So we studied weaponry and science and how to annihilate whole cities. Those six-fingered monsters, the villains of my stories, were real. They were who we were fighting; they were evil."

"Yeah, right, ha, ha."

"I'm not kidding, son, I'm deadly serious. I always knew there'd be a day when I'd have to tell you the truth. That day has come."

"Okay, so how did you get here?" Alex held his skepticism in check, still sure his dad was pulling his leg.

"Easy, not so fast. I've had the burden of this secret for too many years. Let me tell this my way. I want you to understand completely because if you've seen a Klaqin weapon it means there's an invasion imminent and I have a lot of questions to ask you. I want your head in the right place, with everything in context, so your answers include all the smallest details."

Alex fidgeted as a chill shot up his spine. He reached for Baxter's head and began petting him a little too fast. "Okay, Dad."

"My parents, my brothers, everyone on my planet had skin in varying shades like on Earth, but also shades of yellow or green or sometimes pale blue. That probably had something to do with our sun. I browned up as soon as I was exposed to Earth's sun and I lost my green tint." He cleared his throat, trying to get comfortable in his tale. "Anyway, back on Klaqin, I left the shadowless farm region where we were belittled and called 'sunnies' in order to enroll into military training. I said goodbye to my parents and brothers and never saw them again. I did well. I learned about the Gleezhians' planet,"—Alex's hair stood on end at the mention of Gleezhians—"their colonies, and their culture, and prepared infiltrations. On my fourth training exercise into space a small group of us was captured. They confiscated our weapons, clothing, and food and took us on board their ship. I had a knack for figuring out their language so I soon became important to them as a way for them to learn ours. I had to cooperate. Six others were captured with me, but one by one the Gleezhians executed them and ... I believed ... ate them. True to their nickname: *star cannibals*."

"That's awful." Alex surprised himself, he was actually starting to believe this was real. He moved to the floor and sat with his arms flung around Baxter. The old dog laid his nose upon Alex's thigh, but kept his ears cocked, in case he should be called upon to render support in some other way.

"Yeah, the only thing worse is when it's your turn. They marched me past our confiscated weapons a number of times—they hadn't figured out how to use them—but I, being naked, had no way to grab one and conceal it. That last time, when I was sure they were planning on turning me into lunch, I took a chance and grabbed—"

"The gray and brown box."

"Right. It's called an arc-gun. I spread it quickly into an arc, twirled, and fired."

"So you killed them all? You got away?" Alex's heart beat fast and his mouth went dry.

"Right. After I double checked that I'd killed all my guards, I explored the ship and vaporized every other Gleezhian I encountered. It was awful, but I figured I was disabling their vessel and doing my part in the war." He paused.

"So then?"

"There was no way I could figure out how to fly the ship or use the communications to call for help. I spent a long time, maybe a month, trying."

"How could you survive for a month?"

"I found my clothes, my comm ring, and the rations they confiscated from us, liquids formulated for long space travel. That was what I was in for, because the ship drifted. One day an inter-ship jet arrived and tried to dock, but, with no Gleezhian to operate the doors from inside, that wasn't going to happen. He flew alongside the ship for hours until he finally did something militant. He blew himself and his jet to kingdom come. The force of that knocked something loose, alarms sounded, and a recorded voice gave commands to exit. I figured out that much. It also helped that a few pod bay doors automatically opened. What did I have to lose? I grabbed the arc-gun and jumped into an escape pod to take my chances."

"And it sent you to Earth."

"I don't even remember the trip. I might have ... uh, never mind. An automatic dispenser released a gas that put me out for the duration. Must have been a long time. I don't know. I was pretty skinny and hungry when I woke up. And a pretty rude awakening it was. Sea sick. I ended up floating in a deserted bay of Lake Superior. The hatch popped open and the pod sank. I didn't. I made it to shore with the arc-gun. Even though it was summer I nearly froze from the swim. Some hikers found me. Gave me some dry clothes. Ignored the arc-gun, because, well, it looks like a box. They took me to a hospital and left me."

"Where you met Mom. But why haven't you ever told her the truth?" Alex licked his lips, felt some of his panic begin to dissipate and something between calm trust and measured disbelief take over.

"I don't know. I was overwhelmed, I guess. Later it was easier to keep lying. And then, well, you came along. She loves you. You love her. What if she couldn't love you if she knew you were half alien?"

"I'm half alien? But I'm like everybody else. So are you, Dad."

"Son, I agree. You're like any other boy." Nate Rimmon sighed. "When you were born the doctor thought you were jaundiced because your skin had a yellow tinge. He told the nurse to get a blood sample, but I wouldn't let them prick your heel for blood. I couldn't chance that. I kept the nurses away and the first chance I got, when your mom took a nap, I held you up at the window. It took less than five minutes in the sunshine for you to lose that color. When the doctor came to the recovery room a couple hours later he apologized for making a hasty judgment. You were normal. You *are* normal."

"This is a lot to take in," Alex said, his face buried in Baxter's neck. The possible bright spot was that maybe Selina would find him more attractive now. She hadn't backed off of crushing on Marc after she found out his pedigree. He mumbled into Baxter's fur, "Selina's going to freak out when I tell her."

"No, son, you can't tell anyone."

"But Dad," he lifted his head and rubbed his nose, "she told me a bigger secret than this. There are two exchange students at school, they're the ones ... from your planet ... um, one of them is who I saw with an arc-gun. And Selina knows they're from outer space. She's been in their space ships. So have I."

"What!" Mr. Rimmon stood up, groaned as he straightened, and ordered, "Where? Show me!"

❄ ❄ ❄

MY EARS RANG right down to my toes, reverberating Marc's crazy-bad proclamation that more aliens were coming to get me. *Ladies and gentlemen, starring in her own personal roller coaster ride of a nightmare—cue the stage manager—I give you Selina Langston, boy-crazy, date-deprived, alien-attracting, time-bending high school outcast.*

I may have stumbled a bit as my feet hit the floor and my butt slid off the stool because Marc's hands flew to both my elbows and kept me steady.

Body contact. That was what I'd been craving and now that it finally was taking place I wanted to shake him off and run away. Talk about expecting milk chocolate and biting into a bitter baking bar.

"My plan. I will hide you." Marc loosened his grip, but kept his hands on me. My stomach tumbled and all I thought of was what to tell Alex. That moment, that exact instant, the floodgates burst. And I'm not talking about crying; I'd cried a little on the walk home, when I came down emotionally from the trauma of Coreg abducting Buddy and me. But this was different. This was accepting a reality that up until that minute I'd pushed to the back of my mind and buried. I'd stepped through a door that not only closed and locked behind me, but also disappeared, like the door on that alien spaceship.

I stared at Marc's eyes. Something glimmered behind that shine. I imagined that I saw death in those eyes as clearly as if the devil had painted a skull and crossbones on his pupils.

"How will you hide me? Why would they come all this way and give up? Wouldn't they start a war with our planet? Holy crap." My mind started working at a much greater speed than possible. I spit out seven or eight more questions, rattled them off my tongue maniac-style, and didn't give Marc a second to answer. He pulled me into his chest in a bear hug and wrapped me tightly in his arms. I trembled, but still I didn't cry; those particular floodgates remained shut.

"Selina," he whispered. One hand came up to my head and stroked my hair. "Your name means heaven. I will take you there."

The roller coaster plunged off the track with that statement. Too cheesy. Bad timing. I pushed away and thankfully heard the garage door rumbling open. "My mom's home. You have to leave." Worrying about being in more trouble with my mom was ridiculous in light of everything else, but worrying came as a relief. Yet it didn't stop the new fun-house ride of possibilities that kept spinning around in my head. But ... no time to figure it out now, Mom was home.

I rushed Marc out the family room door, closed it, turned the TV volume up and settled myself in front of it before my mom entered the house. I heard her footsteps reach the kitchen as I changed channels and tried to sink down further into the cushions.

"Selina? Get in here and take care of your dirty dish."

❄ ❄ ❄

NATE AND ALEX Rimmon rushed with long strides. The wind whipped the snow; visibility was bad. They jumped over patches of slush. When they reached the woods the protection of the trees limited the weather's impact. Alex found the trail and led his father straight to where they had once, five years ago, worked together to build a tree fort.

"Wow," was all Mr. Rimmon said as they stopped several yards from Coreg's ship. The ship's camouflage system had either failed or someone disabled it. They both shined their flashlights across the mammoth form.

Alex shined his light along the human and dog foot-prints in the snow that led to and from the door. He had no idea where the door started or how to make it open. Whether anyone lingered inside—Coreg, dead or alive, or Marc—was another question.

His father held the arc-gun in his other hand, ready. Alex kept checking behind him, expecting Marc to appear again.

Mr. Rimmon shook his head and motioned his son to circle around the vessel with him. The second ship, Mar-cum's, was fifty percent larger. The camouflage system was working sporadically making the outline of the ship hard to discern but not completely hiding the massive size. Rimmon began to nod; he recognized this type of ship, even in the dark, even in intermittent disguise. He shined his light where the snow was most trampled, then walked to that spot and reached out a trembling hand, touched two spots and stepped aside as an opening blossomed in the hull.

"Dad," Alex's voice held fear and awe, "what are you doing?"

A low light inside revealed an empty cabin. "Come on, son." He stepped up and in and Alex followed. The door closed up behind them like flower petals. Father and son let out identical breathy whistles. "You okay, son? It's not too confining for you, is it?"

"I'm okay." He was surprised that the enclosed space didn't feel so restrictive. "It's more impressive than the pictures Selina sent me." His eyes were drawn to a stack of familiar textbooks on the floor. "She said he took her around the moon."

"She traveled in this? To the moon?" He checked the systems, examined a few bio-metals, and ran his hand over the controls.

"Uh, huh. Dad, can you read this stuff?" Alex pointed to the strange symbols.

"I can. It's a much simpler alphabet than English. Fifteen letters. Similar numbering system, based on ten." He audibly sighed.

"Dad?"

His father coughed. "It'd be a dream to fly one again. I'll teach you. It's easier than a car. And you're tall enough to manage."

Alex swung his head around, trying to take in all the levers and buttons, and wondering how this could possibly be easier than a car.

❄ ❄ ❄

THWARTED AGAIN IN another attempt to entice Selina away, Marcum was thoroughly confused about his next step. He circled her house twice before heading to the woods. He heard whispers before he saw two figures. Then he watched two intruders enter his ship. He was pretty sure one of them was Alex. Marcum had no weapons on him, but then he was genetically fearless. He was all thought and planning too. The what-ifs of this situation were endless.

As soon as the door closed he backed away and went to Coreg's ship.

Coreg spat when he saw him. "Hey, get out, sunny."

"Be silent, Coreg, we have a situation. Alex and another man are in my *Galaxer*. Here's what we're going to do."

Marcum explained in a few Klaqin words. The plan was simple. Hover, latch on to the *Galaxer*, and fly away, taking Alex and the other spy to an unpopulated island.

Coreg argued. "Their communication devices—those phones—are connected to satellites. They might call a leader, start an interplanetary incident. It'd be better to go grab her now and the three of us leave together. Implode the *Galaxer* and pace away."

Marcum stared at the control panel. In his fearless pride he hadn't thought it through. Coreg might be partly right. But blowing up the *Galaxer* was not acceptable, nor was being crammed into the *Intimidator* for a long trip.

"Wait," Coreg said. He sat down in the chair and brought up the view from the side cameras. He was stunned by what he saw.

"They're stealing your *Galaxer*. How could they possibly know how to fly it?"

He jumped up to move into standing pilot position, waved Marcum to the co-pilot chair and hurried to put the *Intimidator* to the chase.

But nothing happened.

Marcum didn't know whether to reset the fire extinguisher so Coreg could take off or just allow his true rival, Alex, to lose his way in space. Revealing that he'd disabled the *Intimidator* meant relinquishing his advantage in their power struggle.

"Amazing," Coreg mumbled. He clicked his tongue twice and punched the ceiling. "They've disabled my ship and stolen yours. I'll notify Dace to intercept them." He glanced at Marcum and noticed the hollow look on his face. "Marcum, disembark at once. Bring the time-bender here while I find a way to empower this machine."

Still unsure of his next move, Marcum did as he was told, hoping it was better to let Coreg assume he'd regained authority.

CHAPTER 19
#Stalker

MARCUM'S PREVIOUS FOOTPRINTS were covered with fresh snow, but he tromped around Selina's house in the same path as before, waving the flakes away from his face as if they were gnats. He stopped near the deck and looked into the downstairs room that was lit. He saw two figures reclining on the sofa in the spot where he had sat the night he discovered the time-bender. A rectangular screen on the wall glowed with pictures, very much like the visual screens he and Coreg had on their ships. He observed Selina and her mother intently watching the constantly changing scenes. The good thing was they were not receiving any images of him lurking around the backyard.

He waited. He waited and watched and wondered how far away his ship had flown. The flakes settled on his head, arms, and shoulders. He turned his attention from the screen to Selina's face. Colors and flashes of white strobed against her skin. Her expressions changed. She frowned, spoke to her mother, laughed with her, spoke again, but kept her focus on the bright screen. Marcum began to shiver and to daydream. Maybe Alex was gone forever. He could imagine the two men flying the *Galaxer* back to Klaqin if they were a stranded unit of previous explorers Dace had sent. That might make sense. But they would have taken the time-bender with them.

Marcum stared through the glass and analyzed the situation further. That intriguing girl had scrambled his brain. Maybe all he had to do was convince Coreg to chase after the *Galaxer*. He could lie and tell him Selina was on board. Once Coreg was gone Marcum would be left here ... with Selina. No, it wouldn't work. He knew he was dreaming. A low grunt, a thoughtful *ehk,* escaped his throat.

There was another option though. A spiral twist of Marcum's thumb ring would align the call back signs, making the ship reverse course and return to the woods. Another careful alignment and he could detonate it ... and if the *Intimidator* was still within range then both ships—and both rivals—would cease to exist. He took his eyes off Selina and held his hand up closer to his face. He touched the thumb ring. The symbol indicating his ship still faintly glowed. What would she do if he risked the unthinkable—exploding his own ship—to remain on her planet, to be near her?

And how much did Alex's life mean to her?

Of course if he blew both ships there'd be no way to return to Klaqin, though that thought was less disturbing than the compassion, the concern and the benevolence that surged through his DNA. It was one thing to blow up Gleezhians, quite another to eliminate friendly opponents.

Besides, Second Commander Dace was due to arrive soon. He'd already confirmed the time-bender's existence. Dace would not hesitate to start a war with Earth in order to capture her. They'd find another pacer to breed her with.

Marcum's thoughts went black as the screen in Selina's house blinked off. The two females rose. Selina's mother left first, turning on more lights in the hall and up the stairs, while Selina herself leaned over slowly and touched the lamp on the table, extinguishing it. She was backlit from the hall, silhouetted in the darkened room. He assumed she was staring out here. At him. He didn't move. Didn't blink. Didn't shiver.

Selina turned and the trail of lights went out as she hurried up the stairs. Marcum waited and watched as a light in her room went on. From this angle seeing inside was impossible. Besides, the blinds were closed. He remained perfectly still. Plotting. Planning. Dreaming.

❄ ❄ ❄

I TOTALLY SEIZED up when I thought I saw Marc standing like a snowman a few feet beyond the deck. I had to be imagining it—*cue the dry ice*. I wanted to bend time for a bit to study the illusion, but I held off on that and raced upstairs behind my mom. We said goodnight and she closed her door. I peeked through the blinds half afraid I'd be face to face with a vine-crawling alien ready to jerk open my window. Not that having a hot guy on a Juliet balcony was out of the realm of my fantasies, but one abduction per night was quite enough, thank you. Anyway, there was no face at the glass. There was, however, a tall, snow-covered Marc Marcum in my backyard.

I heard my mom's shower start so I crept downstairs, pulled on a coat and boots, disarmed the security system, and did the bravest thing of my life. I was, after all, grounded, so sneaking out on a school night pretty much defined the ultimate act of courage ... and defiance. And to meet a guy yet. An alien guy. Alex was so going to kill me. Not to mention my mom if she found out.

I tried not to imagine impatient cops pulling up the driveway any second. I couldn't see any advantage to bringing on the hiccups so I hurried around the garage and surprised Marc.

I hissed at him, "What are you still doing here? I thought you left. I saw you walk away. Have you been out here freezing this whole time?" Boy, I was getting pretty smooth at this social stuff.

The porch light from the neighbor's house came on and I grabbed Marc's arm and started walking him toward the street.

"I am not freezing," he said.

"And?"

"And it makes me warm to see you."

Oh, puh-lease. Well, all right, so that did fall into the realm of sweetness. "Marc, I'm going to be in so much trouble. You have to leave."

We reached the end of the driveway and I pointed toward the woods. "Go."

"Alex took my spaceship."

"What?" Now, *that* bordered on the preposterous.

"I told you ... before, when we were eating pie ... Alex is one of us. There must be several Klaqins or Klaqin descendents on this planet. He stole the ship with another man."

I patted my back pocket so fast you'd have thought I was spanking myself. My phone wasn't there. I'd left it to recharge in the kitchen.

"Come. I will show you. My *Galaxer* is gone."

Like I'm falling for that one. No way. "Wait right here." He let me go back into the house. I grabbed my phone and snuck out again, punching in Alex's number before I had the door completely closed.

Out of service area.

Holy crap.

❄ ❄ ❄

"DAD, DAD! NOW what?" Alex fell into the rhythm of flying as if he'd been born on the other side of the galaxy."

"Feel that? The propulsion is smooth. We're at zero gravity. You'll have to push down with your feet. Your shoes are definitely not space worthy." The older Rimmon laughed and slapped his hands over both his ears. "Doesn't matter. You're tall enough." He dropped his hands and let his earlobes continue their spasms.

"How fast are we going?"

"Son, you don't want to know." He slowly raised his hand toward the screen in front of him. The chair squeezed him a little too tightly. It had been designed for a body that hadn't grown heavy on Earth foods. Nate Rimmon had some difficulty piloting from a sitting position, though as a youth he'd preferred that spot for battle. He touched two controls beneath the screen and called his son's attention to the starry scene that glowed before them.

"No way, Dad. No freakin' way." Alex shook his arms out and wiggled his whole body, hyped, ready, and anxious. "Shouldn't we be wearing helmets or spacesuits or something?"

Nate unclipped the helmet at his side and said, "No. The ship is our spacesuit. This helmet is for communication and for brain wave protection when navigating space alleys."

"Space alleys?"

"I have a lot to tell you, son. Once around the moon and then we head home." His laugh bubbled with nostalgia and reverence.

❄ ❄ ❄

"WE HAVE GLEEZHIANS trailing us." Second Commander Dace clucked his tongue on the last word. Enrimmon and Lektur moved quickly into firing position.

Lektur locked on first, but before he fired Enrimmon paced them out of range.

"I had them," Lektur shouted, finishing with the vilest of expletives.

Dace ignored it. "Be ready to re-engage, but, as always, evasion before engagement. You were correct to pace, Enrimmon. Now keep it up."

"Sir," Lektur paused a beat, "we're receiving a transmission from Fifth Commander Coreg."

Dace clucked again. "How fortuitous. Order the *Intimidator* and the *Galaxer* to meet us at these celestial coordinates."

Lektur spoke into his helmet while Enrimmon continued evasion tactics and concentrated on time-pacing.

❄ ❄ ❄

"WHAT IS THAT noise?" Alex held the upper levers steady and nodded toward the helmet. His father put it on and his eyes widened.

In a low whisper laced with disbelief he said, "I haven't heard my native tongue in twenty years." He listened to the message, marveled at its meaning, and then heard Coreg's abrupt reply. He hesitated to respond, wondering if he should, realizing that by taking the *Galaxer* he'd put himself and his son in a position that wasn't only dangerous, it was deadly. Coreg's voice pierced the headset, louder, closer than whoever sent the previous call for assistance. The words were distinct and in English.

"Who are you?" Coreg then repeated the question in Klaqin.

Alex's father took a deep breath and spoke in Klaqin, "I am Fifth Commander Enrimmon." A weak tongue clucking finished the statement.

"You mean *Third* Commander Enrimmon, don't you?"

Nate Rimmon flashed on his days in training, his capture, the flight to Earth, and his assimilation into society. He'd known not a word of English but had given his name, Enrimmon, as a response to the nurse's first question. She'd written N. Rimmon on his chart. After that he'd said *nate*, the Klaqin word for help, and the nurse recorded that as his first name.

"Yes," he said, "Third Commander Enrimmon." Of course he would have been a Second by now, but he was intrigued to be speaking to someone from his planet. "And who are you?"

"This is Fifth Commander Coreg. I'm confused, sir, as to why you've taken the *Galaxer* and left Fifth Commander Marcum and me here in a disabled *Intimidator*. Second Commander Dace is requesting our help in repelling and annihilating a Gleezhian ship."

Nate muted the comm and looked at Alex. "Son, there are Gleezhians out there about to attack another ship. They need help."

"Dad, you spoke ... it was weird. What *was* that?"

"Alex, listen, we've stolen this ship. They should be shooting at us by now but apparently the other ship, the one parked next to this one is grounded, and now there's nobody to help destroy the star cannibals. I'm sorry, son, but I don't see any way to avoid this." He analyzed the look on Alex's face, the fear, the astonishment, and the courage. "We have to help." Inwardly he chuckled. His name meant help, after all. He unmuted the comm and replied to Coreg, his tongue twisting and turning around the almost forgotten words: "Try your best to get the *Intimidator* up, Fifth Commander. Meanwhile we will assist Second Commander Dace. These coordinates are awfully far away. Are you a pacer?"

"Yes, sir."

"Then it shouldn't take you long. Get up here, latch on, and take us both to their aid."

"Yes, sir."

❄ ❄ ❄

I TOTALLY OUTRAN Marc to the woods. Well, I mean for my size, he did reach the path before me, but I took twice as many steps. Definitely not the right time to employ my time-bending.

Alex took his spaceship? Really? He's done some wacky, bizarre things on days that threatened boredom, but those were things designed to get me to laugh. And I always did. But this ... nuh-uh ... way out of character for him. And I didn't believe he was totally over his claustrophobia; the cockpit would be way too suffocating. Besides, he'd never steal anything, not a nickel, not a kiss. Wait, why did I think that?

"See?" Marcum turned as we reached the empty, dark space where his craft had been. The snow swirled, making eddies in the air. Cold. Coldest November ever. I'd have to remember to do more time-bending in June, July, and August, and stretch out the summer.

"Good. You brought her." Coreg's sudden appearance made me forget the cold, the dark, the missing ship, Alex's theft, and ... actually everything. I went into automatic time-bending and stared him down. I analyzed his simple statement. Sounded like Coreg had sent Marc to get me; Coreg was the boss. That didn't make sense. I'd seen Marc take him down. I wanted Marc to have the upper hand. Marc should be the one ordering Coreg around.

Coreg pressed his time-pacing around me, tapping me mentally, hunting for a breach. I guess he found an opening because in an instant the three of us were on his ship and instead of hiccupping I was coughing my lungs out.

"You've hurt her." Marc's concern pleased me. He put one arm around me and held Coreg back with a boxy thing he grabbed off the wall. My seizure stopped and I leaned a little into Marc's side. The door closed up, dis-appearing the same way it had on his ship. Coreg spoke to Marc in a low burst of syllables, none of which were from any language I'd ever be able to learn. Veins popped out on his neck. He reminded me of an albino gorilla ready to do a double chest pound.

Marc answered with words that mimicked Aztec names like Tenochtitlan, Quetzalcoatl, and Tlaloc. Maybe Señora Vargas could make sense of this.

"Speak English," I yelled. "I deserve to know if you're kidnapping me. What's going on, Marc?"

He didn't speak immediately. I watched his lips try to form something coherent and for a moment I thought maybe I'd slowed things down without meaning to, so I relaxed. A tickle of adrenaline worked its way around my middle. I was going to laugh uncontrollably if he said the wrong thing; if he started with *hellew* I'd lose it.

"I was wrong. Alex did not take my ship."

Whew. That was a relief. For maybe a second. Wait, what? I'd been lied to. Now I was trapped. And Alex's phone was out of service. I was right back in the same predicament as before, but at least Buddy was home safe.

Marc kept his arm around me and finished. "Coreg has spoken to someone, a Third Commander, who has abducted Alex and taken the *Galaxer* on a mission to assist in a fight against a Gleezhian ship. The star cannibals."

Me ... speechless. Somebody else abducted Alex? All I imagined was Alex had revealed his incredible video game ability which could be put to use shooting Gleezhians. I'd done it against Coreg. Alex would be way better.

Marc continued as Coreg and I stood mutely giving each other dirty looks. "They cannot reach them in time to help unless we go, latch on, and Coreg paces us there in the fastest way possible."

Coreg spoke, dropping his glare and trying to persuade me with fake niceness. “Once we reach the coordinates we can use your time-bending to take the best aim.”

I thought it through, at normal speed, and asked, “Can I talk to Alex?” I knew they had a speaker in that helmet.

CHAPTER 20
#LostInTranslation

COREG TOSSED THE helmet to Marc who gently placed it on my head. I didn't take my eyes off Coreg though. I shoved back at him, mentally. An invisible force of my own creation held us in a net of time. He pushed time ahead and I pulled it back, so that it kept proceeding at the customary one second intervals though with a tight, compelling edge.

Marcum bent to put his lips near mine and spoke several jarring syllables into the mic near my cheek. I heard a familiar voice respond in short chunks of the same incomprehensible phrases, sort of like the first time I sat in the language lab. Then Alex's steady deep tones began with a tentative, "Hello? Who is this?"

"Alex, are you all right?" I didn't let my sudden surprise veer me away from my time battle with Coreg.

"Selina!" He probably didn't mean to follow my name with a couple of swear words, but I ignored that. "You're in their ship?" he yelled. "Holy crap. Get out of there."

"I can't. Please ... tell me you're all right." I don't know why, but my eyes started leaking like crazy then and my throat closed up so much I couldn't get another word out.

"I'm fine. I'm flying this crazy thing. My dad, uh, my dad is with me. Don't worry. Just get out of there."

The seconds ticked away a hundred times faster as I lost the stand-off with Coreg. In a flash he was wearing the helmet and yelling gibberish at Alex. Then he used English, but not as well as before. He barked a translation of his rant, cursing Alex for grounding his ship.

Marc's hand shot out to the wall and he pushed a button directly under a lever and gave me a look that I couldn't decipher. He spoke to Coreg in that alien tongue, gesturing him to move toward the controls, and then he said in very slow and deliberate English, "Will you come with us, Selina, and use your time-bending along with Coreg's time-pacing to fight against the Gleezhians and save our commanders and your friend Alex?" That was the longest sentence I'd ever heard from him and well, when he put it that way, and with a crinkled brow and sad eyes, I couldn't refuse. I might have gurgled out *sign me up* or something equally trite, but anyway he kept Coreg at bay with that box thing and helped me into a chair very much like the seat on his ship. I wasn't startled when the thing tightened up around me, thankfully not as body-hugging as on the other ship. Marc pulled a drawer out from the wall and sat on it. I guess it wasn't a storage drawer, more of an emergency seat since he pulled out a belt and tightened it around his waist. He never let go of the box and from this angle I scrutinized the business end of it and I knew it was definitely a frightening weapon like a ray gun or beam blaster or photon zapper.

Coreg made a sucky-kissy sound with his mouth and planted himself beside me. I was going to get an awful cramp in my neck if I had to monitor his every move. Thank goodness he put his hands up to surrender right away. Or, I guess because this ship was more compact than Marc's, he was grabbing onto whichever ceiling levers he needed to use to fly this thing.

My stomach flip-flopped at that thought. I succeeded in pulling my phone out super-fast and beat out a text message to my mom: I LOVE YOU. DON'T WORRY.

I did not feel us lift off, but less than five seconds after I pushed 'send' I lost the signal. Then I felt that full body elevator pressure. Outer space, here we come. And more importantly: Alex, here I come.

I could feel an electrifying thrill hit the pit of my stomach, tumble around, and shoot up my spine.

❄ ❄ ❄

ALEX TOSSED THE helmet to his father as soon as Coreg's sputtering tirade filled his ears. His father translated for him. "They're bringing Selina." He frowned. "I'm sorry, son, I guess they've made her a hostage. Don't worry. We'll fight, we'll win, and then we'll negotiate her release." He let out a curious laugh—distinct, formal, and mirthless.

"Tell me what to do, Dad."

"This is going to be a crash course. I hope not literally." Another laugh, this time with some humor. "We're going to switch positions so you can learn these controls, too. This is going to be tricky since we're weight-less. I want you to know as much as possible about flying and shooting in case something happens to me during this, uh, scuffle."

"If something happens to *you*? Dad, if we get hit we'll both be goners."

"Not necessarily, Alex." He swung his right arm toward the closer wall. "These are bio-metals. Something that's unknown on Earth. They can take a hit and distribute the energy without compromising the integrity of the vessel. But occasionally that energy gets redirected outward or inward. Inward is a problem. More than one *Galaxer* has returned to base with a pile of ashes in the seat."

❄ ❄ ❄

MARCUM HELD THE arc-gun lightly in his lap and watched Coreg with a bit of envy as he threaded the sleek

Intimidator through the night sky, dodged a ring of satellites, and flew on toward their objective, the *Galaxer*. There were seas on Klaqin he'd been on once. He'd been entranced by the billows of spray that spread to the sides of the sea boat. Here, though, there were no billows, no spray of visible air curling to the lateral edges of the *Intimidator*, no splash or bounce or rocking motion, and certainly not as strong an odor from the bio-metals that he was used to in the *Galaxer*.

He looked to Selina to see her reaction to the view on the screen. Her presence alone challenged his loyalty. His eyes watered unexpectedly and he turned his head. He had other emotions; he wasn't all fearlessness or all compassion. He lived with guilt; he knew jealousy, shame, anger, and pity. From the moment he met her he'd had a strong response to Selina: attraction, happiness, hope. But now betrayal filled his thoughts. An outrageous plan ripened in his mind: fight the Gleezhians first, then double cross his Commanders, steal Selina and take her and the two in his ship back to Earth. But he needed to know more about the person with Alex. Who was this mysterious Earth dweller who spoke his language, flew his ship, and would fight the star cannibals without hesitation? His puzzlement muddled his thinking.

He spoke softly to Selina. "You will be all right."

"I'm not happy about this," she said, shooting him a hostile look. "Are these armrests going to sprout triggers? Shouldn't you be the person to fire them?"

"You proved yourself proficient on the *Galaxer*. They are the same on the *Intimidator*. You will need to flex between time-bending and firing. Your aim will be infallible."

"Thanks for the pep talk. Now, tell me the truth, what are the odds of us going home in one piece?"

Marcum glanced at Coreg who spoke in English, "You must not miss. I will pace us to an advantageous coordinate. You must not get distracted by their assault. You must bend the time to allow perfect accuracy."

"Perfect accuracy? What's that supposed to mean?" She turned her head back and forth from one to the other. "Is Alex going to be shooting, too?"

"Of course," Coreg said. "We will latch onto the *Galaxer* very soon, so long as you do not display any time-bending in transit. I will pace the two ships together. It is how Marcum and I arrived from twenty light years away."

"Are we pacing now? I don't feel anything. There's no sudden change." Selina looked at Coreg then Marcum.

For an answer Coreg switched on the comm, putting it on speaker so they all could hear.

❄ ❄ ❄

I HAD NO fondness for this—*stomp foot*. I tried not to think how far away we were from my mom, my brother, and my home. But maybe because of the adrenaline—*puff out in-adequate chest*—I felt pretty awesome. I, Selina Marie Langston, little Miss Can't-kill-a-fly, was on my way to blast some six-fingered monsters out of creation. I couldn't decide if I wanted them to fire first so I'd have an excuse for overriding my peaceful principles or if I should blast away without brooding on the fact they were living creatures.

I wished I could see Alex's face.

I asked Coreg, who that very second I silently made my sworn enemy, if we were pacing already. For an answer he turned on a speaker and spoke several of those wild sounds into the air. Equally odd syllables bounced back. Again the voice seemed familiar and it came to me in a brain shattering, heart stopping instant. The voice belonged to Mr. Rimmon. Alex said his dad was with him, but I thought that meant they were both abducted. But if Mr. Rimmon spoke Klaqin ... Oh. My. Gosh. The shivers that prickled up and down my body defied the weightlessness in the cabin. How could he possibly know those words? And then he switched to English.

"Selina, hello."

I spoke into the air, raising my voice like Buddy does from the backseat of the car. "Mr. Rimmon?"

"You'll be fine, Selina."

I swallowed a lump in my throat, but didn't answer. Then I heard Alex. "We have you on the screen." Oh, they had me on the screen. I felt much better. Not.

Marc called out an order of commands to ready them for our docking. Then Coreg called Mr. Rimmon by a Commander title. Yup, way to explode my world. I wanted to yell at Alex, something like *why didn't you tell me your father was an alien?* But then I remembered how I was totally in the dark about my dad's secret work. Alex probably didn't know this whopper of a fact until today.

I whispered at Marc, "Do you need me to slow things down so we can dock?" He looked a little weird. I wondered if I could trust him or if he and Coreg were pulling off a galactic version of good cop/bad cop to manipulate me.

"No," he said. "The bio-metals are brothers."

Whatever that meant. I watched the screen then as Coreg brought us to within inches of Marc's ship's side. Latching on was almost imperceptible. Mr. Rimmon acknowledged the connection and Coreg switched off the comm. I wished he'd left it on.

"Now Coreg will do the time-pacing. Please, Selina, do not bend."

"Okay. I won't. I promise."

So ... he was worried that I might do a little time-bending. Hmm, I had some power, didn't I? I could mess things up at the right, or wrong, moment. I wondered what, if any, was Mr. Rimmon's specialty. And Alex ... my mind raced through a few superpower options: strength, mind-reading, flying, and invisibility. Oh, brother, Alex would love, *love*, that one. My thoughts were zooming right along with the two ships. I thought of other possibilities like super-hearing, seeing through walls, throwing lightning or fire balls, shape changing. Ooh, another one he'd *love*. And then there was magic and healing and time control. Ah, that last power was mine. It would be great if Alex had the opposite ability, time-pacing. Alex would *love* to pace against me.

Quite unexpectedly it hit me what his specialty was ... is.

❄ ❄ ❄

MARCUM REVIEWED HIS plan again. With Coreg's eyes tightly closed in concentrated pacing—this marked the first time Marcum had seen Coreg do it in flight—he thought he might be able to push Selina through the melded hatches and onto his larger ship. His country's scientists claimed the bio-metals were completely stable even during latching and pacing. He believed them, but it was his theory, not theirs, that an injured pilot or galactic warrior could escape through the hatches in flight. He had studied quite a bit more than the basic operations of the *Galaxer*, the *Intimidator*, and several other models, and his innate fearlessness pushed him to try. Even though he'd forgotten to feed his bio-metals the galactic lard when he landed on Earth, they were fine now. He had to risk it; he had to get Selina and himself into the *Galaxer*.

He waved a free hand at Selina and pointed to the hatch where Buddy had been briefly imprisoned. He undid his safety harness and floated sideways toward her, keeping the arc-gun steadily pointed at Coreg whose eyes might spring open in an instant. He loosened her seat and pushed her toward the hatch. Silently and in slow motion, despite the pacing, she drifted in that direction. Her facial expression unveiled a tight blend of fear and trust, or at least he interpreted it that way. He couldn't claim to be an expert on Earth girls.

She didn't kick her feet or use her arms and for an instant Marcum thought maybe a tiny nebula of concentrated carbon dioxide encapsulated her head, disorienting her. He and Coreg were trained in no gravity space breathing, but she was not. He took his eyes off Coreg and air-swam ahead of her, his arms doing the breaststroke at molasses speed, trying to reach the small hatch first.

❄ ❄ ❄

I SEEMED TO exist in a haze of euphoria. Weird. If I had a pulse it was pretty weak. My breathing slowed and grew thin ... inconsequential. Marc undid his seat and floated over to me making outlandish hand signals. He kept that gun thing pointed at Coreg so in my light headed, shallow breathing, anxious state of mind I went with the flow, literally, as he released me from my seat. I floated off like a cloud.

Funny how I silently and slowly analyzed a dozen questions that drifted into my head: Was Marc going to cage me up like Coreg had? Or was he getting me out of harm's way? Was this an escape module that would send me back to Earth? Was he going to kill Coreg? Why would he do that? Didn't we have to fight the Gleezhians? Would Coreg ever open his eyes? Why were the veins popping out of his neck?

Marc went past me and reached the hatch first. I hiccupped.

Crap. I didn't mean to do it. I promised not to do any time-bending, but apparently I lapsed into it. I'm such a rookie.

Coreg's eyes flew open and he shouted. It hurt my ears. Why would sound waves hurt in outer space? Marc yelled back with words that I couldn't understand, but they hurt too. I wished they'd speak Human, I mean English. And at a lower volume.

Coreg lunged for Marc's leg. Pretty hard to do any martial arts in zero gravity, I thought, but obviously not for aliens. I didn't see why Marc didn't shoot him. He must have been bluffing or, more likely, using that thing in this small space could be fatal for us all. Coreg got hold of Marc's ankle and twisted him around toward him. They both rolled themselves into balls, still spitting gymnastic combinations of vowels and consonants and clicks and whistles. And I mean spitting. Small globules of saliva started floating in every direction. Coreg's fighting reminded me of Bala from chess club, the berserker. Coreg made rash moves and attacked erratically, but in weightlessness it was as funny as Bala's name.

I put my hand out onto the hatch that so recently had sealed in my sweet little Buddy and pulled. All I succeeded in doing was to bring my body forward and smack my forehead into said hatch. Turned out to be a good thing though. It knocked some sense into me.

Two against one. Yeah, why not? I launched myself into the fray, my main thought hovering around the idea that nothing would hurt in slow motion, especially if I started bending time to the slowest denominator.

"Selina! Get back!"

Not on your intergalactic life. I'm the time-bender. I pictured Alex rooting for me, confident in my new petite take-no-prisoners-I'm-the-bad-ass-here attitude. He'd most likely have a song title or some lyrics to cheer me on. I was mildly amused at the ridiculousness of our air ballet, but I inserted myself into the dance, ever so slowly. Yeah, I was time-bending. Both of them wanted to avoid banging into me. I succeeded in making Coreg retreat. That's the story I'll tell Alex anyway. Marc grabbed the hem of my coat and somersaulted me out of the way. I lost my concentration and time returned to normal.

Coreg vaulted himself into position, snapping his feet into the floor by my seat. That seat looked instantly attracttive as my stomach finished that somersault. I hoped to Jupiter that I wouldn't release any vomit globules into the cabin.

Marc did some snapping of his own as he pushed his weapon into its holder on the wall. They must have spoken some truce in their mother tongue because they didn't say a word in English about the switch in command. Coreg reverted to pacing and Marc hooked a toe on his seat and reached out to me, grabbed my sleeve, and pulled me to my chair.

"Why don't we talk about what just happened?" I aimed a scowl at Marc not caring if Coreg heard me or not. "What was the deal with taking me to that hatch?"

He leaned toward me, that handsome face not producing any goose flesh under my coat, and whispered, "I meant to help you escape to the other ship, but I failed. You must stay in the *Intimidator* and help us fight the star cannibals."

CHAPTER 21
#StarTrekNotTheMovie

"SO WE'RE NOT even flying this thing now?" Alex took his hand off the lever and held it against the ceiling to keep himself wedged in place.

"No," his dad said, "that Fifth Commander I spoke to, Coreg, fixed his vessel and has reached us, connected our ships, and is now moving us along at time-pacing speeds."

"You mean faster?"

"Look at the screen."

Alex didn't understand what he saw. The visual puzzled him; streaks of mostly white lines angled out from a red centered dot. He couldn't get a feel for speed or distance. A video game would have been easier. Then the scene stopped moving and showed a view that no one but Mr. Spock or Captain Kirk could identify. To Alex it resembled a picture of the Milky Way as seen from an advanced telescope. The screen stayed paused on the scene for a couple of minutes, long enough for Alex to contemplate the enormity of their impulsive act to take this spaceship for a spin. He'd never known his father to do anything brash or remotely irresponsible before, but he was glad they'd done it. If Selina was being held in the adjoining craft, at least he was only yards away instead of light years.

"Are we there? Did we stop moving?"

Mr. Rimmon shook his head. "I don't know what's going on. He must have lost his focus and stopped pacing."

"What's pacing?"

"There's this thing some people on my planet can do. Manipulate time. It's called time-pacing. My grandfather could do it. This Fifth Commander Coreg has the ability. It'll make getting to those coordinates doable. If we didn't pace then we'd never get there in time. If at all." He paused and added, "If you were living on Klaqin, your heart would beat more slowly. Wherever you are, your biology is in sync with the local time. And a minute or an hour wherever you are is a minute or an hour. But a time-pacer can shrink that minute or that hour."

"Look. The screen is a blur again." Alex stared, starting to get a feel for interpreting things, then he thought of something. "Will pacing make us age faster?"

"No, not to my knowledge." Mr. Rimmon donned the helmet. "I'm going to contact the other ship, the one we're going to meet." He began speaking in the strange dialect and Alex listened in utter bafflement.

❄ ❄ ❄

SECOND COMMANDER DACE took over the comm as Nate Rimmon began speaking. "Identify yourself."

"Once upon a time I was Fifth Commander Enrimmon."

"Impossible. Enrimmon is right here doing some intermittent pacing to keep us ahead of the Gleezhians. And he's a *Third* Commander, son of Second Commander Lexal."

Nate was thrilled. Names were sacred, given to one living person at a time. Lexal was his younger brother, and he had made it to Second. And apparently he'd named his son after Nate, believing his older brother had died in the Gleezhian Wars. Lost, but not dead, though his family couldn't have known that. They'd honored him.

"Sir, may I speak to Third Commander Enrimmon?"

"Your real name, Commander?"

He stuttered through an approximation. "Nathan Rimmon. Of Earth."

"Third Commander Enrimmon here."

"Enrimmon, I know your father." He held in the emotion. "Tell me, how did you start pacing? I have someone on board who is of the correct lineage to pace. I need to teach him quickly."

There was no secret to reveal, nothing that anyone could steal. Only a formula to follow. Almost a wish. Enrimmon spelled it out.

"Got it. Thank you, Enrimmon. Good luck and good success in this battle. The *Galaxer* and the *Intimidator* will arrive shortly with an experienced pacer and at least one novice pacer."

"Right," the Third Commander replied, "and a female time-bender. We can certainly use her."

❄ ❄ ❄

"DAD, WHAT WERE you saying to them? That language is totally unreal."

"Son, everything's going to work out great. I have something to explain to you." He spoke fast, stretching Alex's belief, explaining pacing again and adding what he knew of bending, and shocking him with the knowledge of Selina's ability.

"Holy cow, Dad, is she half alien, too?"

"I don't know, Alex, I don't think so. Her eyes aren't like ours."

Alex lapsed into a silence that he didn't break again as his father gave him a more serious lecture on what they had to do and the order they had to do it. Then he asked his son,

"Do you think you can time-pace for me now that I've explained the basics?"

"I'll try." He closed his eyes, thought of Selina, and marked a moment in the future. It was like aiming an arrow at a target.

❄ ❄ ❄

MARC'S WORDS SKITTERED around inside my eardrums: *I must help them fight the star cannibals.* Maybe my reaction was a little off, but I showed my teeth and hissed. An orb of spit splattered on my forehead and another ball of saliva floated off and joined up with their alien slobber. Gross.

Focus, Selina. Fight the star cannibals. Do it and don't act insane ... or unfeminine. I eyed the hatch. If only I'd escaped to Alex's ship.

I spaced out, literally and figuratively, and undoubtedly I was also in shock and denial and definitely anger. I probably needed to skip through these feelings and go straight to acceptance. There was no way off this ship. Emoji: sweat drops. Emoji: big sigh.

Marc looked at Coreg so I did, too. He closed his eyes and paced. I didn't know how much farther we had to travel, but Marc yelled two short syllables and Coreg's eyes sprang open. To accommodate my lack of alien language ability Marc said in English, "Coreg, you have paced twice as much as usual. We are within range of the Gleezhians. See, they are on the screen."

Coreg seemed mystified. They fired looks at one another that made that impression concrete. They couldn't imagine another time-pacer in the area, but I could.

"It was Alex," I giggled. I knew it, I knew it. *Cue wagging finger.*

"She must be right. I told you, Coreg. His eyes. He is one of us. And he can pace."

To say that Coreg acted peeved would not be adequate. Vexed, miffed, annoyed, and riled were better English words.

Coreg switched on the comm as we hovered and yelled out what were obviously Klaqin swear words. I cringed at the sounds. Marc leaned near and translated for me. "Your guard Alex is a pacer. The man confirms it. He promises to restrain him and not let him pace unless something happens to Coreg."

I sure hoped he meant if Coreg got tired. If he meant injury or death, odds were that Marc and I would suffer the same thing. And Alex, too, with the other ship adjoined to ours.

"He is telling them now to prepare for disengagement."

"What's that?"

Marc looked toward the hatch, the tube that might have given me passage to join my ... to join Alex. "He will unlock the connection. We will roll away from the *Galaxer*. Then if he paces it will not affect us."

Great. Roll away. Separate me from my ... from my best friend, my guard, as Marc called him. More like guardian, guardian angel. *Angel.*

I focused on the screen and maybe the emotional high got to me, or the fear, or the staggering trauma of this situation, or the immensity of the universe, or that little blip that signified star cannibals, but whatever, I stared at the infinite scene and hunted for angels. They had to be there. Definitely an angel in the next ship.

We rolled. My hair floated across my eyes and I pushed it aside to see through the ocean of tears in my eyes. The *Intimidator* angled off and Marc's ship, or rather Alex and his dad's ship, gleamed in the corner of the screen and grew smaller.

And then we turned and my angel left my sight. I blinked hard and released a dozen circles of emotional perspiration. Yeah, that's what they were. No way were they tears. Alex wouldn't want me to cry. Be strong, he'd say, you're the best. He'd probably quote some uplifting song lyrics. But whatever our souls were made of, his and mine were the same.

❄ ❄ ❄

"YOU DID IT," Mr. Rimmon said. "I'm so proud of you, son. That was a short pace, but it was enough to double up Coreg's pacing so we're within range." The *Galaxer* rocked and broke away from the other ship. "I'll bet they didn't like that. Figured it out I suppose. Anyway, we don't need them now. They've unfastened themselves."

"We're on our own? Cool." Alex steadied himself, covered his real feelings with bluster and a lie. While they were connected to the other ship he'd worried about Selina, but now, it wasn't worry he felt, but a sense of irrefutable loss. And grief.

He had to stomp out that impression. She was alive. He was alive. His father was with him. He had to trust. He had to believe. He had to have faith. "What do we do now? Wipe out the Gleezhians? How are we armed?"

"Easy does it, Alex. We get into position first. We coordinate with the *Intimidator* and Second Commander Dace's ship."

"Do you know this Dace?"

"I knew of him. Long time ago. And here's something odd: we've got family on that ship. My nephew—your cousin. We have to work this precisely right. Even though it's three Klaqin ships to one Gleezhian starcraft, the starcraft has the advantage."

"Why?"

"It's a pursuer ship. It'll be manned by six experienced warriors, or at least that's how they used to operate. And this old ship only has us. The *Intimidator* has two inexperienced Fifth Commanders, as naive as you. And if Dace called for help, but kept heading this way, I can't imagine how poorly armed his craft must be."

Alex dared to repeat his earlier question, "How are we armed?"

His father examined the readouts. "We have unlimited anti-flames, dozens of freezers, an array of low, medium, and high voltage rockets, and seven defenders."

"In English, please."

"Pretty much we'll act like the defense on the ball court. It'll be up to the *Intimidator* to mount an offense. I hope those boys have the guts to fly in close and fast and then take their time aiming. I suppose that's why they wanted Selina."

A stabbing sensation pierced Alex's heart. He couldn't say anything.

"I'll contact Dace. Don't pace yet. We'll coordinate locations and maneuver into position."

❄ ❄ ❄

WELL, THIS WAS certainly uncharted interstellar space. And not the starless predawn emptiness I'd stared at when I'd stayed up until 3 a.m. on the phone with Alex. I got my silly emotions under control. Not going to be a cry baby. Not again.

Marc put the helmet on and sputtered and babbled directly with someone—Darth Vader or Yoda or Luke Skywalker, for all I knew. Coreg motioned to the screen which displayed planetarium quality star charts with little blips careening around the universe, then he did the decent thing and included me by translating Marc's conference call. Apparently Mr. Rimmon and Alex, the yellow blip, were taking up a defensive position near the rescue ship, green blip, and the commander of that ship had ordered us, center red blip, to lure the Gleezhian craft, blue blip, to a cold planet a ridiculous distance away. Oh, great. A cold planet. I was the only one on this ship wearing a winter coat, but I was ninety-nine percent sure that wasn't going to make a difference.

I started analyzing the outcomes of any plan they came up with, which were basically two: we would win or we would lose. I tapped my fingers along the triggers as Coreg repositioned himself to fly. If we won, for sure they'd take me to Klaqin or Earth. My pessimistic nature told me probably not Earth. I'd brood over that later. The bigger question was: if they took me to Klaqin, would they bring along Mr. Rimmon and Alex, too, or would they be allowed to go home? Probably they would never see home again either. So, if we all had to end up living our lives on a besieged planet warring against star cannibals, would they let Alex and me be together? I'd miss my mom and dad and Buddy and chocolate, but the thought that I could stay best friends with the nicest guy in the universe was massively comforting.

But that was unrealistic. We'd be the aliens on Klaqin and everybody knows what happens to aliens in the end. *Cue puff of smoke.*

I looked from Coreg's perfect profile to Marc's breathtakingly handsome face. Nothing. Nada. I guess I'd run out of thrills. A dark cloud of regret settled over my heart and a string of bad words knotted my tongue. What a fool I was. Last week, in the middle of an early snowstorm I'd made a wish on a star. What idiot didn't know you can't see stars in a snowstorm?

This idiot. I'd wished on a starship not a star. I was paying a big price for that tonight. I had an infinite supply of stars to wish on now, but what was the use? If we won against the Gleezhians today my best hope was to be made into a time-bending slave to fight against them tomorrow. If we lost, well, that was unthinkable. Death, the final frontier.

There was no third option. Win. Or lose.

I accidentally squeezed one of the farthest out triggers then. Oops.

"That was perfect, Selina!" Marc was all smiles—and waving hair. I checked the screen and the blue blip disappeared. I hiccupped and screamed at the same time. What had I done? Wasn't the blue blip the *Galaxer*? Had I obliterated Alex?

"There are more humpbacks," Coreg calmly reported. "This time do not start bending until I say so."

Three more blue blips came on the screen. Holy cow. There were more Gleezhians than they thought. The battle was on. But Alex was okay. He was the yellow blip. I had to keep my blips straight.

CHAPTER 22
#ReadyAimFire

MARCUM SAW HOW quickly Selina engaged in the combat. One moment she seemed to be daydreaming, time-bending effortlessly, stroking the trigger handle, and not paying attention. Then in an instant her hand constricted and the first of the *Intimidator*'s pintsized warheads left the weapons bay on a perfect course to destroy the Gleezhian starcraft. He stifled the pride he felt for her when the missile hit its mark.

But now there were more Gleezhians. He contacted Second Commander Dace who, instead of wasting time praising their quick success, changed his previous order to include all three Klaqin vessels. Together they would triple pace to the cold planet, Azoss. It was their one promising chance of escape.

Marcum repeated the orders to Coreg who argued, “But she took out the starcraft. We can do that three more times. Easier than training exercises.”

“I agree,” Marcum answered, “but we cannot be insubordinate.”

“We can and we will.” Coreg clicked the final syllable and changed to English, “Time-bender, be ready to fire. On my command, bend and take out all three.” He didn’t think he needed to explain which three he meant, though he wondered if her eyes distinguished the shades of the various colors on the screen. Those colors changed based on the craft’s distance.

❄ ❄ ❄

OKAY, THIS WAS too serious. I needed to bury myself in denial. Yeah, good place to be. I didn't want to be a murderer. So what if the Gleezhians had six fingers. That made them special. I was all for special. And humpbacks? What did Coreg mean by that? Some Klaqin prejudice or something? Okay, calm down. Calm down.

Three blips wiggled on the screen. Marc got on the mic and rattled off some weird sounds. His voice sounded stilted, formal. I didn't think he was talking to Alex's dad, probably to his boss, er, general...commander.

Then he had the world's shortest argument with Coreg. Something was up.

Coreg clucked at me. "Time-bender, be ready to fire. On my command, bend and take out all three."

Déjà vu. What if I aimed off center—a tad—and disabled their ships like I did to Coreg when I thought I was playing a video game on Marc's ship? Oh, yeah, way to ease the conscience. Which triggers did I use then? The nearest triggers on both sides? The anti-flames. Right. I yawned. I couldn't help yawning a second time. It had to be so late by now.

The screen changed views in jarring spurts. Coreg paced us to the left, probably not the technical term, and then to the right. If we were on the Gleezhians' screens we must have looked like a flea jumping around the fur of a space doggie. I'd have to share that visual with Alex. On the next paced jump I checked the screen for Alex's blip. What the— All the colors were different. Pink, mauve, lime. Okay, not a problem. Three were lime. Those had to be the bad guys.

"Now, time-bender!"

Coreg's voice made me squeeze off an anti-flame involuntarily. Thank goodness a lime blip disappeared.

Okay, okay, I couldn't make this personal. It wasn't like I'd ever met a Gleezhian. Marc said they were evil cannibals. I needed to keep that thought front and center. Sometimes you have to kill to maintain peace. Sheesh, I argued against that point in that paper I wrote on conscientious objectors.

Focus, focus. We paced up and down and the screen reversed. The blips were bigger, darker colors. Two were beige. Crap. I'd have to take out two this time—*quick mental pause for a crucial decision*—or risk shooting the wrong one next.

"Now, time-bender!"

No, not quite now. Bend, bend. Concentrate, Selina Marie, you can do this, stay steady, steady. Slower. Slower yet. Ignore the orange blip. Ignore the fact that the orange blip disappeared. That wasn't Alex. That couldn't have been Alex. Easy. Aim. Got him. Aim, take your time. Don't think about whether they have a bathroom on board. Don't yawn. *Hic—*

❄ ❄ ❄

ALEX'S FATHER COULD control both the ship and the ship's weaponry from the seat. His long ago training came flooding back. Muscle memory. Instinct. But it did not coordinate well with his son's ambitious spirit and novice skill and that was a problem.

"Did you see that? It looked nothing like in the movies." Alex's fingers tightened on the levers when he saw the devastation on the screen. The *Intimidator*'s missile hit the Gleezhian ship broadside. "Is that all? Is the fight over? We didn't even have to fire?" He relaxed his grip, but that was the wrong thing to do. The *Galaxer* flew in a new direction, sliding through the debris and taking on electrified rubble which clung to the bio-metals on the port side of the craft.

"There are three more," his father called out. He turned the ship's nose to face the newcomers and aimed. He fired a freezer charge followed by a low voltage rocket, but they both went wide, due to Alex's unintended lapse in piloting. "Son, pivot us ninety degrees and keep us steady. Hold on. Watch the screen." They didn't have time on their side like the *Intimidator* did, flexing between pacing and bending, but if he talked Alex through the steps of intermittently pacing and piloting then perhaps he could manage to pull off the more advanced spiral strategy and knock out at least one of the oncoming Gleezhian ships.

"Alex, pace us back to where we were." A moment later, from that position, Nate fired an anti-flame followed by one of the seven defender rockets. He missed. Off by a star. But then their screen displayed an explosion in multiple colors.

"You got him, dad."

"No, son, I didn't shoot that one. Apparently the *Intimidator* found its second mark. She must be time-bending."

"Selina? Selina did that?" Alex shivered.

"Two Gleezhian ships remain. Hopefully these are the last of the pursuers. I don't know why Dace's ship isn't firing." Nate tried the comm. "Nothing. No communication. Must be we caught some debris from the first explosion."

"Dad, why aren't the Gleezhians firing at us?"

"They typically get close, use their freezers, and instead of blasting a crew out of existence, they capture and imprison all on board. I don't know the protocol now, but new procedures were scheduled to take effect after my last flight, when I was captured. If the new rules had been in effect earlier we would have been required to blow our own ships—and ourselves—up."

Alex closed his mouth. The thought of intentionally committing such an awful thing was shocking. To be ordered to do it, unimaginable.

"Here they come. One is going for the Second Commander's ship, one for us. Pace us, Alex. I'll fly."

They watched the screen as one of the Gleezhian ships pursued the rescue ship, fired several anti-flames and followed it with a well-aimed freezer charge. Second Commander Dace's vessel froze mid-flight, hung in space like a forgotten star, and a paralyzing flash of time later imploded.

Alex gasped, stunned. His dad made a similar choked wheeze. Nate had held a tiny seed of hope that he would meet his brother's son, Third Commander Enrimmon. Now no hope of that remained.

A stroke of time later the Gleezhian ship was gone. One enemy remained.

❄ ❄ ❄

I COULD NOT time-bend anymore. Whatever universal clock might be ticking and tocking out here had a will of its own. Or else Coreg time-paced and overrode my efforts to aim and take out the last of the star cannibals. Yeah, that had to be it. Nauseatingly ruthless Coreg. Taking over. I swiveled my head toward Marc to see what he was doing. Maybe he had some weaponry at his control.

He stared at me with sad sweet eyes. I saw no fear in those eyes, no death symbols either, thank goodness.

"What's happening? I can't tell which ship is which. Who's violet? Who's chartreuse?" My voice climbed an octave, as if I'd sucked on a helium-balloon. I was *so* tired.

His face puckered. "Truce?"

"No, *char*treuse. Chartreuse is green. Violet is blue. Which do I shoot next? And where did the orange blip go?" His mistaking chartreuse for truce planted an idea in my head that I'd need to save for later.

So tired. After all this time-bending ... I felt infin-itely exhausted. Maybe we'd been in space for two days. My stomach growled then, most likely it agreed with me.

Marc leaned as far forward as possible and reached the screen with his middle finger. He swiped along the edge and the colors dissolved leaving symbols in their place. Naturally they weren't English letters, not even Roman numerals. That would be too easy. Stupid symbols. Hieroglyphics, like the ones on their thumb rings. If only my phone worked; I wanted to tap out a quick message to Jamie Michaelson and berate him for thinking that Coreg and Marcum were undercover college pranksters.

Way to be totally W. R. O. N. G. These guys were A. L. I. E. N. S. Print that in your school newspaper.

All right, Selina Marie, you are spacing out. Get back on track. I tried and failed to stifle another yawn.

Marc's finger traced the symbol that had a square edge. "That's the *Galaxer*. Don't shoot it. The orange one is gone." His eyes went dead. "Commander Dace and his men followed protocol when the Gleezhians froze their ship." He leaned over and spoke to Coreg. "We must follow the last order."

I tried to process his sentences. Don't shoot the *Galaxer*. Right. Alex was in the *Galaxer*. I studied the hieroglyphics and watched them move around the screen. Wait, maybe we were the ones moving. I was disoriented, and oh so tired, but I struggled to memorize that symbol.

Wait. What was protocol? Was there an invisibility app for these ships? Could that be what happened to the orange blip? Please don't tell me their Commander died. I centered my total attention on the screen. And what was the last order Marc wanted us to follow?

"Time-bender. Release!" Coreg's exasperated shout startled me. I swallowed a hiccup.

"They're dangerously close," Marc yelled. I was thankful he spoke in English, yet scared I was doing something wrong. He bellowed at Coreg, "Pace us away."

The symbols showed the Gleezhians directly between us and Alex. If Coreg commanded me to shoot now and I missed—

I loosened my hands. No way could I shoot in that direction. Not a chance.

❄ ❄ ❄

MARCUM WATCHED SELINA fix her beautiful brown eyes on the moving symbols. He didn't know her alternate word for green, but when he repeated the last syllable of that word and inadvertently said *truce* he was struck by an unlikely idea. They were in a tight spot. The Second Commander had evaporated. He couldn't raise the *Galaxer* on the comm though he could see them trying an outdated spiral move. Doubling up on pacing with Alex, the novice pacer, seemed to be the best option to get them out of range and off to Azoss where they might hide out and regroup, but without the comm he doubted the *Galaxer* would hover in place long enough to latch up. Signaling a truce to the Gleezhians might be the best alternative.

"Coreg, I can't communicate with the *Galaxer*. And—"

The ship's systems seized up, from screen to controls to bio-metals. Marcum spoke the obvious to Coreg in their native language and repeated for Selina, "We've been hit by their freezer charges."

❄ ❄ ❄

I SHIVERED AT the word freezer. "What does that mean? Are we going to blow up?"

"Maybe. They can take their time and either we follow protocol and self-destruct when the bio-metals reboot or they come in closer and ..."

"And what? Burn us up?"

"They might. They would in a battle closer to home, but here, so far ..."

I wasn't time-bending, but the length of his pause kept stretching. "Spit it out, Marc."

"They might board us instead. They might be hungry."

Of course my stomach picked that moment to growl again.

CHAPTER 23
#RocketMan

"WHY AREN'T THEY moving?" Alex took a step toward the screen and almost floated away. He pushed his right foot down and held his place.

"They took a freezer charge head on." Nate evaluated his options and spoke low and slow, "Alex. Pace us right to their side. As close as when we were latched. Do it now."

In a controlled panic, with a prayer and a wish unuttered, Alex did as his father told him. He had a sixth sense for handling the *Galaxer*, but his flying was imperfect, his pacing slower than it should have been. Still, his chess and video game skills, along with a healthy amount of fear, helped him guide the ship into position.

Nate fired off two freezer charges and followed with a high voltage rocket.

❄ ❄ ❄

FOR A SECOND I thought my stomach growls were launching rockets at the enemy. Both blips were gone from the screen. Both blips! Where was Alex?

Coreg and Marc were silent. Stunned, I guess. A sickly smell began oozing from the walls. I assumed that the biometals were rebooting. Either that or we were in a slow-motion implosion and, thanks to my incredible time-bending on an empty stomach and no sleep, we were going to die in three, two and a half, two, one and a half, one ...

"Try the comm, Marcum." Coreg floated his hand in a lazy ballerina arc toward the helmet. Marc slipped it on. Who was he going to call? We were all alone in the middle of ... of absolutely nowhere.

That's when I lost it. I doubled over and wrapped my arms around my head, pressed my eyes into my knees and tried not to ball my lungs out. *Alex, oh Alex! You were always there for me. Even when I shoved you away. I know you loved me. Unconditionally. How could I have been so mean ... so thoughtless ... so selfish ...*

I'd give anything to get you back because ... because ...

Marc yelled over my sobbing, "Their comm is working again. Third Commander Enrimmon, can you hear me?"

Two voices spilled from the speakers. I popped my head up. First I heard Mr. Rimmon: "Are you all right?" And then Alex: "Selina, are you okay?"

I sniveled out an answer as well as I could. "Yes ... yes, where are you? I thought you ..." I choked up again.

There was a worried discussion then between Coreg and Marc and Mr. Rimmon, sometimes with words that neither Alex or I understood, but the bottom line was they'd taken out the enemy and latched onto us. I knew Alex heard my sniffles and I imagined him somewhere out there rubbing his nose, too, and I finally remembered why he always had that habit of putting his hand to his nose. I'd stupidly forgotten. The tree fort. A secret handshake. A secret signal. *Rub your nose if you still like me.* I couldn't suck in enough air and then things went black.

❄ ❄ ❄

I WOKE UP, whether minutes or hours later I didn't know, but nobody's hair floated any more, though mine hung forward over my eyes as I leaned sideways over the armrest; the triggers had retracted. Marc knelt next to me and pushed my hair back, more compassion in his eyes than could fill the galaxy. What was he so sorry about? Hadn't we won the battle? Maybe the war?

Something was different. There was no more weightlessness for one thing, but something else was off. I figured we must have landed and I hoped that meant I'd simply passed out from fatigue and stress and slept the whole long way to Earth. Coreg must have paced us there with no interference from my uncontrolled time-bending.

Now fully awake, the dizzy relief that Alex was alive reanimated me and I wanted to giggle. I asked, in my best non-lisping imitation of Buddy, "Are we there yet?"

Coreg snarled at me. "Where do you think we are, time-bender?"

"Home, I hope. I'm starving."

"We're at the same coordinates we were when you started to cry like a child. Marcum, give her some liquid."

Well, that stung, but at least the offer of sustenance minimized his cutting remark. Marc produced a bottle of something and I was too thirsty to ask what it was. I sucked down a couple of thick gulps and passed it back. I didn't love the taste, but I instantly felt better. I directed a question to Marc, "Why aren't we weightless?"

"We had to employ the artificial gravity in order to feed the bio-metals. We are latched onto the *Galaxer* now. We must use the passageway, board the *Galaxer* and do the same there so both ships will make the trip ... home." He leaned closer to whisper, "I have made a choice."

Could I guess what choice he made that required hiding his words from Coreg with a whisper? Best case scenario: he would pilot me, Alex, and Alex's dad back to Earth—home—then latch onto the *Intimidator* for their long journey to Klaqin. Worst case scenario: we were all going cross-galaxy to Klaqin—*his* home. Or—maybe he whispered because his choice was too crazy or frightening to speak aloud. Some other choice like oh, hey, we're going to land on that cold planet and start a new society. Or we're splitting off from your best friend—he's going back, but you're coming with us.

Coreg snapped a command at Marc. Marc rose, stood nose to nose with him, and sputtered and clicked their funny language in short riled bursts. Coreg spurted equally short answers back at him. I was used to not being included at school, pretty common when I'd spent all of middle school being teased worse than if we'd been in Special Ed classes, but this went beyond rude. I suspected that Coreg heard Marc's whispered secret and knew what his "choice" was.

❄ ❄ ❄

COREG CHANGED HIS demeanor and stopped the argument. He glanced at the confused time-bender and tried to force a smile. He continued speaking to Marcum in a less threatening tone, though still using their native language. "So, you would betray your oath, your government, your family, and your planet? I do not understand."

Coreg's altered manner didn't fool Marcum. "I only ask for time. You must return, report the loss of Second Commander Dace and his crew, and assure the leaders that I will return ... someday ... with a willing time-bender."

"But how could you possibly do twenty light years in that old bucket? And without a pacer like me?"

"I will train Alex and bring him with us."

Coreg's laughter filled the small cabin with humorless noise. "And you propose to fly the *Galaxer* to Earth now with all four of you on board?"

"Yes."

Marcum didn't mistake for submission the false frown that spread across Coreg's face. Coreg clucked his tongue. "But why not bring them all to Klaqin right now? Why go to Earth at all?"

"It would not be best for her. Selina ... the time-bender ... is sensitive to Alex's well-being. She nearly died a while ago." It hurt Marcum to say it, but his compassionate nature demanded that he acknowledge the bond he knew existed between Selina and Alex.

Coreg breathed out heavily and gestured toward the hatch. "All right. Go feed the bio's and bring me what's left of the galactic lard. Then you can take the time-bender back to Earth."

"I am not stupid. You will pace away with her as soon as I enter the *Galaxer*. You go through the hatch first and send the man here ... as insurance ... and protection for Selina."

"The man? Are you afraid if Alex comes over he'll pace away with your prize? You do know, Marcum, that you cannot win her for yourself." Coreg snickered.

Marcum cast a forlorn look at Selina. "That may be so."

❄ ❄ ❄

IF I HAD a better imagination I might think that Coreg and Marc were fighting over me, what with all the emotionally charged glances they were throwing at me, waving their hands, and raising their voices. I so wished I knew a few words of their complicated language. Last Tuesday or Wednesday I would've been thrilled and excited to have two hotties brawling over me, but right now I forgot my wish to find a boyfriend. That is: *another* boyfriend. Yup, sure as space is forever and memories can't be changed, I already had a boyfriend. Just never realized it. We needed to complete one little obligatory boyfriend-cementing-duty though: a kiss. I was pretty sure Alex would be happy to lock lips with me if they'd leave us alone in one of these spaceships. I needed to figure out a way how.

Get the men in white coats—I was having another break from reality. Why did I keep thinking about kissing Alex?

I wiggled out of the grasp of the chair and inched my way behind Coreg. Good old Marc didn't let on what I was doing. *Mental giggles*. I was going to sneak over to Alex's ship.

Wait. What? My butt still filled the chair. Ho. Ly. Space Cow. Something must have been in that liquid I drank. Prescription cough syrup made me hallucinate—this was the same woozy feeling. Woozy was such a funny word. And blips. Blips, blips, blips.

"Hey. Guys." I worried that nobody except me noticed the colorful blips on the screen. Dozens of them. "Hey!" I thought I was yelling, but maybe I was only dreaming in high volume.

❄ ❄ ❄

"WE HAVE MULTIPLE enemy ships approaching." Nate Rimmon's voice lanced through Coreg and Marcum's argument at the same moment that Selina whispered her warning. Instantly Coreg took his standing pilot position and paced both ships away, hardly giving Marcum enough time to belt himself in.

The cold planet of Azoss would have to serve as a hiding place. Coreg's decision was instant. With any luck the Gleezhians would evaluate the ships' debris that floated in ever-widening circles and determine that all involved in the battle had perished. There was no radioactive signature left by either the *Galaxer* or the *Intimidator*. Hide and wait; it was a good plan—the plan that Second Commander Dace had ordered before his death. All they had to do was monitor the stars, the space alleys, the path to Earth, and wait it out. He and Marcum could manage quite a while on the liquid supplies they had. He imagined that amber-eyed Alex could, too, but he had some doubts about the time-bender. She started acting funny soon after Marcum took the bottle away from her lips. He'd noticed her uncharacteristic behavior while they'd argued. Perhaps it was an allergic reaction.

"Hold steady for landing," Coreg announced. He'd never bumped a landing, not ever, and he wanted the others to notice his skill. They were, in fact, already on the ground of a planet that orbited a dying star. The rarefied atmosphere was cold, but not so cold that it couldn't sustain life.

He cast a glare at Selina. "Thank you for not interfering. If you had fought my pacing they would have seen us. Caught us." He smirked. "And eaten us."

CHAPTER 24
#NotEarth

EATEN US?

THE seat released me and I looked around for a bucket, a helmet, anything to throw up in. "Guys, I'm gonna be sick." Like upchuck, like toss my cookies, like ... oh, how embarrassing. Way to be totally unappealing. But ... wait, I felt better. "Never mind. Where are we now?"

Marcum explained while Coreg did some experimenting, testing the air for poison. Great. We'd flown for a zillion light years, battled cannibals, and now landed on a possibly poisonous planet. If they didn't let me take the tunnel over to the *Galaxer* I might scream. In fact, now that the nausea had passed I sensed some super strength coursing through my veins.

I couldn't remember when I hadn't endured being inferior to everyone else, but now, this was awesome. They wouldn't be able to stop me. Well, Marc wouldn't be able to stop me; I didn't think he would try ... something in his eyes told me he was on my side. He was still explaining the stars and moons and this planet's probable lack of humanoids while I pretended to listen, but all I thought about was how I'd always been reluctant to take risks, how I avoided new situations, how I withered away at potentially distressing circumstances. And now ... bring 'em on.

❄ ❄ ❄

"HOW MANY PLANETS have you been on?" Alex trusted his dad when he told him it was safe to exit the ship. The air tested out as breathable and scanning the perimeter revealed no living creatures.

"This is my fourth. It's pretty exciting, isn't it? You're about to walk on ground that isn't Earth." Nate handed Alex a weapon and made the bio-metals at the door retract.

Alex followed his dad and gingerly held the weapon his father had handed him, snatched from the wall of the ship. He began to hum the first line of a suspense theme, his attention on the barren landscape, too similar to Earth's. Snow covered the ground with a few dark patches all around revealing brown grass. Trees stood at angles in the distance, a few tall ones, but the majority were scrubby. No mountains, but plenty of hills with rocks protruding where the snow had melted. Alex suspected there'd be caves among the outcroppings. They still wore their coats and though the climate was not inviting it was as bearable as a typical February day in Michigan. His father put his hand on the side of the spacecraft and the bio-metals responded, closing the opening. While his father gave him quick instructions Alex couldn't help but be amazed that his lungs worked. His eyes could see far distant mounds of snow—or some other type of white protrusions—and his ears reported every tick and whoosh of the cooling ships which were still latched tightly together.

"You understand how this works?" His dad fingered an identical arc-gun, fanning out the brown and gray box that had been hidden in his garage millions of miles away.

Alex forced his attention onto the object in his hands. "Yeah. I won't have to use it though. We're going to get the jump on Marcum and Coreg...get control...rescue Selina."

"Right. Well, we can forget about the Gleezhians. I don't think they tracked us here. A little rest—," he put a hand on his back and pushed out a kink, "—and a little negotiation and I'll convince the Fifth Commanders to listen to me. We'll send them home in that sleek baby," he nodded toward the *Intimidator* as he positioned himself to cover the door, "and we'll commandeer the *Galaxer* to get to Earth. I'll figure out a way to hide it until the bio-metals starve and the whole thing disintegrates."

"Wait, you mean if we stay here too long these ships will ... will die?" He looked in all directions. They wouldn't exist for long here themselves. Living in caves? Not likely. Alex's heart was pounding in his ears, had been since they'd exited the ship. This place spooked him and he couldn't quite believe he was not on Earth.

"Don't worry, son, trust me." He nodded toward the other ship, indicating they both should be ready when its door opened. Their shadows were long in front of them. Behind them were streaks of blues, yellows, pinks, and purples as this planet's sun set.

❄ ❄ ❄

OKAY, OKAY, OPEN the doors, let's check out this planet and get started with the Adam and Eve thing. Crap. If only Alex's dad wasn't here. That was going to be awkward. Hic—

Oh, I was bending and daydreaming. Coreg was going to be mad. He gave me a look.

"Selina." He hissed my name. I definitely did not top his list. That was okay, he wasn't even on mine. "Do not bend while we are here. Faster is better in these situations."

I wondered how many similar situations he'd been in. Big pants-on-fire liar.

Marc pulled me up to stand face to face with him, my back to the albino liar. Marc's eyes glistened like amber diamonds. He wanted to tell me something. Obviously. He was tongue-tied. Maybe he wanted pie. I opted not to laugh out loud at my private joke, but I laughed on the inside.

"The hatch," was all he said, once again a man of few words. That didn't bother me. I followed him and he went first, crawled into the tunnel, did something that opened the other end, and scooted out.

I. Was. So. Excited. To see Alex. I ducked low, crawled, and pulled myself out the other end and took in the interior of the *Galaxer*. So much roomier and wider. The walls were mocha brown and the ceiling more of a dark chocolate truffle color.

But empty. No Alex. No Mr. Rimmon.

"Hello." I was tempted to say *hellew* in case that would conjure up anyone. I guess I still couldn't think right. I stood up and breathed in through my nose. Alex's scent permeated the space, even stronger than the oily bio-metals. I never realized I knew him by scent as well as sight and sound.

Marc came through the opening like a spring uncoiling. He stood and frowned.

Me—*saucer eyes*. Where in the freakin' universe was Alex? Marc checked cubbyholes, drawers and cupboards and announced that his weapon store had been pilfered, but I ignored him and patted the wall. Somewhere there was a hidden lever or switch or button to open the friggin' door. Where was it? I kicked the wall. Coreg slithered through the hatch like the snake I figured him for and yelled at me. I jumped. Good thing he didn't yell in English. I didn't want to know what the creep said. I wanted to get to Alex. I wiped away some tears that had mysteriously formed on my cheeks. I set my jaw.

"Let me out of here." There. I could be commanding. I time-bent and wobbled the time around us a little, too, to make my point. Slow. Normal. Slow. Normal.

Marc held a hand out to stop Coreg and reached across me. He did something I couldn't quite catch. Without even a creak or a squeak the bio-metals parted and cold air rushed in. I took a cautious look at the foreign landscape—not much different than the Michigan winter I hoped to see again—and jumped out. An unusual rainbow—no, it was a sunset—made the *Intimidator* glow along its edges.

"Alex!" I called his name into the void that boasted *another freakin' planet, for crying out loud!* I didn't want to waste a second. Footprints littered the familiar looking snow and the sunset's rays filled them with colors. Obviously Alex and his dad had jumped down and gone around to our ship. I followed the footprints, head down, focus sharp. I rounded the nose of the other ship and crashed into my favorite male chest.

"This is getting to be a habit," I tried to joke. My relief was totally pushing me into the classic hysteria that I so wanted to avoid. I didn't want to be a crybaby. One look from Alex—we were going to be totally alone for all of a second until the others followed—and I knew I had to employ my newly found skill. I stretched that second as long as possible, staring into my best friend's eyes. It didn't matter how many millions of miles from Earth we were; it didn't matter if Coreg and Marcum wanted to fight over me; it didn't matter if the Gleezhians tracked us here where the ground under my feet felt both hard and spongy at the same time. It only mattered that I should stay still and let his eyes tell me, soul to soul, what filled his heart ... and communicate the very same feelings. I rubbed my nose.

❄ ❄ ❄

NATE RIMMON SUSPECTED an ambush when no one exited the *Intimidator* and he heard Selina's shrill call. He stayed where he was as Alex rushed back to meet Selina. When no one appeared from the other direction he came around the front of the *Intimidator* and stopped behind his son. He had watched Alex and Selina grow up together. Like most born on Klaqin he'd been genetically engineered for enhanced sensory perception, a fortunate trait for assimilating into Earth culture as quickly as he had. He'd wondered which of his Klaqin qualities, real or artificial, would naturally dominate in his son. It had soon been apparent that Alex functioned around Selina much like a trained service animal, alert to her health problems, physical and mental. But there was something more. He saw it now as Selina pressed her face against Alex's chest and Alex held her tightly. When she looked up into Alex's eyes, Nate recognized the truth as she made time slow down to its barest passing.

When at last she touched her nose then stopped her time-bending Nate intruded. "Selina, Alex, both of you move behind me." He held the arc-gun out toward Coreg and Marcum who came around the ship and whose faces both frightened and gladdened him.

"Third Commander?" Coreg spoke in Klaqin, hesitant, wary.

"I'm actually *Second* Commander Enrimmon. Show some respect." Nate's face didn't betray his lie and his demeanor mimicked the Second Commanders he'd trained under. He needed to convince these young warriors he was one of them, and that they should obey him as their superior.

Coreg and Marcum kept their arms tight to their sides. Nate went on, switching to English, "You're the spitting image of a man named Merlig." He stared at Coreg.

"Yes, Second Commander, Merlig was ... is ... my father." His face paled to a sickly green.

"The white hair, your face ... easy to see the resemblance. Your father was my instructor; he tried his best to get me to time-pace." Nate gave the closest thing he could manage to a chuckle. "We have some negotiating, er, discussing to do, men." He waved the arc-gun at them both. "Let's get in the *Galaxer* before the sun completely sets."

❄ ❄ ❄

ALEX HELD MY hand as we stood, backs to the screen, and listened to his dad explain the options. Mr. Rimmon couldn't keep my attention and I probably didn't help things. I started messing with time in order to concentrate on the feelings my fingers were relaying to my brain: warmth, tingling sensitivity, some rough spots, little squeezes from Alex when one of them mentioned my name, and mostly joy. If there'd been a way to hold his other hand, too, that would have been heaven, but his right hand cradled a Klaqin weapon.

I totally zoned out—not terribly uncommon for me, a daydreamer—and let myself bask in the truth: I had a boyfriend. It was like coming out of a deep, dark cave into brilliant summer sunshine.

"They will send ... abductors," Marc said.

Great. Way to put a dark cloud on my mood. I swallowed a hiccup.

His eyes softened as he looked at me, then they hardened when he said, "It has already been ... decided ... that she will mate—marry—Coreg to produce a new ... race." Marc's halting English brought the rain, totally flooding out my temporary high.

My eyes flashed to Coreg. No freakin' way would I ever marry an alien. Well, maybe I'd consider a half alien. I held tighter to Alex. So this was what they had up their sleeves. Coreg had kidnapped me and my brother planning to take me to Klaqin as his bride—*screaming exclamation points!* I crushed the tiniest sliver of a flattered thrill with a mental foot stomp then put my brain into Mach negative ten speed to try to compute a solution.

Wait. What was that name Mr. Rimmon used with Coreg? Merlig! I couldn't marry Coreg, for pity's sake, not if his father was the Merlig my grandfather told stories about, a cherished son with one arm. Was I remembering right? Was I grasping at straws?

"Guys, guys," I said, ready to stutter out my jumbled thoughts. Oh. My. Gosh. Coreg might be my cousin or something. *Cut to maniacal laughter*—I put it all together in an instant. Grandpa Turlek used to tell Buddy and me stories of a family he had to leave behind *in the old country*—he never named that country, I always thought it was Italy—and his sons named Merlig and Covill he never saw again. Those definitely were not Italian names. I never questioned anything. Like, what happened to them? Like, how did he get the last name Langston? Like, how soon after he came here did he meet grandma and have my dad? Oh, brother, this explained my father's secrets, my failure to fit in, my "special" ability, my brother's specialness, and on, and on, and on. Grandpa's hair had been as white as Coreg's for as long as I could remember. And Buddy mistook Coreg for Grandpa when he saw him through the peephole. Oh, crap.

Okay, everyone looked at me. I lined up my thoughts and opened my mouth, half hoping that Coreg would time-pace so I'd get this out fast. "My grandfather, Turlek Langston, had sons named Merlig and, oh my gosh ... Coreg, if you have an uncle named Covill then we're related."

The silence grew tense. I got chills contemplating all the implications. But what if no taboos existed on Klaqin against marrying your relatives? I'd end up like a dog in a puppy mill, popping out litters of sixty-two-and-a-half percent pure aliens if I had to *mate* with Coreg. Mr. Rimmon gave me the oddest look and went lax on his gun-pointing. Marc frowned, Coreg moved backwards ever so slightly, and Alex, well, Alex continued being Alex—there for me and not afraid of my spastic outburst and able to endure the mashing my hand was giving his hand.

"Yes," Coreg slowly stated the fact. The silence clanged around me. What was he saying *yes* to? Oh, right, we were related. No wonder I noticed something familiar about him when we went to the language lab. Good news, Mingzhu, you can have him. Oops, bad news, he was returning to Klaqin. If we didn't die here.

Everybody started speaking at once in at least two languages. I tottered on the verge of freaking out. Wait, who was I kidding? I *was* freaking out, but Alex never let go of my hand.

CHAPTER 25
#HereComesTrouble

MARCUM'S HEART RATE, slow by nature, defied his calm demeanor and began to race. Selina had spoken a mystery nearly as indecipherable as the Shakespeare play that had slid across the floor with the other textbooks he'd saved. He didn't understand her any better now than he had at their initial meeting, but his comrade-turned-rival, Coreg, repeated most of her strange conclusions under his breath. Between some of her words and Coreg's mumbled commentary he realized the impossible situation they were in.

Earlier, when he had given her the liquid to drink, he had made the choice to betray his planet, save this amazing girl, and return her to Earth. There he'd take his time, hope she would eventually reciprocate his affection, and then, and only then he could—if she was willing—fly her to Klaqin to fight alongside him in the Gleezhian Wars. Win the War; win her heart; win a wife.

He was fearless, born and bred to be intrepid. But with the sight of her holding the Earth boy's hand etched into his golden retinas, and with a racing heart, he was tempted to make another choice, totally contrary: to betray her, the others, and himself.

Marcum saw the blips growing on the screen, but Coreg's view had been blocked by Alex and Selina. Marcum waited, dooming them all. He wasn't afraid to die; he wasn't afraid to be taken captive. Anything would be better than this awful breaking of his heart.

But then his compassionate side surfaced. He made the others turn their heads with a few words, "Hellew ... attention. The screen."

"Quick," Coreg shoved Marcum and spoke in Klaqin, "turn on the *Galaxer*'s camouflage. I'll do the *Intimidator*." He dove for the passageway.

❄ ❄ ❄

OH, NOT AGAIN. The trembling started and I knew instantly that I was in trouble. But something else was happening, too, and Coreg shot out of the *Galaxer* like a cat while Marc fluttered around the control panel simulating computer geek Niket on a frozen keyboard. Perhaps Mr. Rimmon knew what the words leaking out of the side of Marc's mouth meant—Klaqin expletives maybe? I thought I should learn them as they seemed the most appropriate words to scream when you had a battalion of space monsters heading your way.

Alex croaked out, "Dad, how much time do we have? What if they can't get the camo to work?" He let go of my hand and pulled me into a sideways hug, gun over wrist at my shoulder. Strangely calming.

Mr. Rimmon answered him with a get-out-of-the-way wave of his hand. We stepped back together. Mr. Rimmon opened the *Galaxer*'s door and went outside. Through the dusky gray I watched the side of the *Intimidator* flick from its spaceship form into a semi-transparent approximation of the surrounding planetscape. Coreg must have exited his ship by the doorway and come around because he appeared next to Mr. Rimmon then moved off. The trembling that had me knocking my knees turned into a full blown panic attack. Hence the reason Alex was holding me like he used to when these seizures haunted me through middle school.

Way to be a superhero. Stronger arms, tighter hug. Muscles. Hmm, probably not a good idea to time-bend now while star cannibals raced toward us.

The doorway slowly reversed into a smaller opening and I wondered if Marc would make the *Galaxer* invisible and then lock Coreg and Alex's dad outside. My trust in him wavered. Coreg's head appeared and the door widened. He and Mr. Rimmon hopped in bringing cold air, dirty snow, and bad news with them.

"The port side of the *Galaxer* caught some electrified rubble in the battle. If the camo works at all it won't cover the port side."

"So we're sitting ducks." Alex's statement was met with questioning looks. Guess they didn't have ducks on Klaqin. "Easy target," Alex rephrased and Coreg nodded.

My body-quaking slowed and Alex relaxed along with me, but kept his arms around me. Nice. "So," I said, thinking aloud, "we leave the *Galaxer* here and sneak away in Coreg's invisible spaceship."

"Too many of us."

"Then we hide somewhere while you take your ship up, in camo mode of course, and shoot them as they train their attack on the *Galaxer*."

"Too many of them."

Sheesh. Was I the only human with ideas? "Okay, how about we contact them and surrender—you must speak a little Gleezhian, right?"

Marc grabbed the helmet and screwed with the controls. Well, I guess someone liked my truce idea. Over the speaker we all heard static and space din until he adjusted it to ooze slow syllables soaked—I imagined—in Gleezhian venom. Mr. Rimmon put his hand on his back and sank into the chair. Coreg and Marc focused on each other and repeated bits of this alarming new language, then my, uh, *cousin* translated.

"They're desperately hungry. Do you still want to surrender?"

❄ ❄ ❄

ALEX ANALYZED THE blips on the screen. He counted twenty-one flying in formation—seven sets of three. Different colors indicated how spread out they were and how far away. He started counting seconds. It was half a minute before the front three changed to a closer color. "I need to figure something out," he whispered into Selina's ear. "Can you do your time-bending thing for a minute?"

A blend of chess moves, basketball plays, and video game strategies along with the geometry of pool and bowling churned around in Alex's head. He dropped his hands from Selina's shoulders when he reached a conclusion. "Thanks."

Marcum repeated the same quick word of gratitude. He had used the extended time to treat the bio-metals.

"The *Galaxer* is ready," Marcum said. "I fed the bio-metals. The camouflage should work."

"I have a plan," Alex started, "it's risky, but chances are they've never experienced anything comparable."

"Wait." Marcum shook his head, adjusted the comm feed so the alien voices came through again, this time with no static. He began short halting translations as he worked through Gleezhian to Klaqin to English. "Heading ... star forty ... arrival ... preliminary harvest ..."

Coreg interrupted, "Star forty is Earth. You missed the arrival time, Marcum; it was twelve nine seven seven. That's eighty of our time units or two days to get to Earth. They don't have any captured pacers to force their speed. Also, there was no mention of us."

Nate Rimmon spoke up, twisting painfully in the chair to say, “Preliminary harvest—that can’t be good. Earth’s in trouble if we don’t stop them.”

“Two against twenty-one?” Coreg snorted and added a clicking noise.

“I have a plan,” Alex said again, this time louder. “Can you keep the camo working in flight? Will we show up on their—whatever they have—their scanners?”

“The *Intimidator* has that ability for limited use. I can fly it up their noses two or three times and not be seen.” He took on a cocky pose then shook his head at Alex. “But the *Galaxer* will barely hold a shape on the ground.” He lifted his chin toward Marcum.

“Okay, okay,” Alex went on, “this’ll still work. Coreg has to fly in tandem next to the lead ship ... with Selina.” He outlined his simple plan that left his father and Marcum grounded in a camouflaged *Galaxer*. He wanted to double the pacing with Coreg until they needed Selina’s time-bending to calculate trajectories.

“I don’t like being separated from you, son.” Nate stood slowly. “But I don’t see any better way. Fifth Commander, you bring them through this battle, understand? If you do, I’ll personally see that you proceed through ranks from Fifth to Third as soon as possible.”

❄ ❄ ❄

SO I GUESS I owed every video gamer an apology for labeling them geeky-loser time-wasting couch-potatoes. Right now I totally wanted to be nerdy and get in that seat in the *Intimidator*. I’d show the guys. I’d get a perfect wipe-out score. With Alex at my side I figured I might tolerate Coreg a little longer and it would be less awkward than having to endure the moon-pie looks Marc kept giving me.

A loud rumble rattled through the *Galaxer*, like the bio-metals were burping. A second later all five of us were thrown off our feet as a sonic blast rocked the ship. What in the world?

Poor Mr. Rimmon cracked his head against the corner of the chair, but I didn't see any blood. I grabbed the arm-rest and hung on as the ship tilted sideways toward where the door had opened before. I noticed some textbooks sliding past my knees. When they stopped moving I tried to rise.

"What's going on?"

"Atmospheric rectification," Marc said. Big words. I didn't understand. A small auxiliary light popped on and the ship shuddered like a dog shaking off bath water. Then the ship leveled itself, thank goodness.

"Is this bad?"

"No, but you better use the hatch." He nodded at me and Alex. Coreg had already started crawling across the floor toward it.

I whispered to Marc, "Can we trust Coreg?" He gave me a despondent smile with a nod, not the most reassuring endorsement. But it had to do since we were out of options. And I was proud of Alex's plan.

"Let me go first," Alex said. I wasn't going to argue that. He must have had a reason. It was always *ladies first* in every game we'd ever played, but obviously he didn't trust Coreg to pull me through and then not seal him out. I was okay being third.

His strong arms were there to help me out at the other end. Coreg didn't waste a second unlatching us from the *Galaxer*. Amazing how those bio-metals responded, like they were reading his mind.

Space was tight around the controls with three of us, but lucky me, I got the chair. Alex tucked the arc-gun into his pants and strapped himself into the extra seat when Coreg showed him how. Then Coreg planted himself into his standing pilot position and scared me and probably Alex too with a reverberating battle cry at lift off.

Rocketing into space once again went smooth as silk. I kept my eyes on the screen. Night on the cold planet—I should name it something pronounceable—turned as black as coal with faint glows coming from the larger patches of snow. One of those patches was, I assumed, the *Galaxer*. Then the *Intimidator* reversed course—I hadn't realized we'd been flying backwards—and put the planet—I started thinking of it as Mars 2—and the *Galaxer* behind us, out of view, and the stars and the starships front and center.

I tensed.

"Not yet, time-bender."

I didn't mind him not using my name. I *did* mind him pointing out my accidental bending. "Sorry." I stifled what must have sounded like a baby seal's cough.

The chair tightened automatically and we went into weightless mode. I was so over that thrill. I had contradictory expectations and felt as though I was fighting feathers. A totally different thrill was on my mind and I realized if we got wiped out—those were the odds, by the way—then I'd never get that all important first kiss that writers write about, singers sing about, dreamers dream about, and fantasizers like me fantasize about.

"I said not yet. You keep slowing us down." Coreg scowled at me.

"Sorry, but I need a moment. Can you pace us to the dark side of that planet and give Alex and me some privacy?"

Whoa, way for an alien to show surprise. Yeah, the albino geek, aka alien cousin, knew what I was talking about. I had to control my own look of astonishment when he changed our course and took us to what was now the sunny side of Mars 2.

"Go ahead, get it over with." Coreg turned on the artificial gravity and walked to the end of the cabin.

Unfortunately that wasn't more than a few feet away and he'd likely hear any lip-smacking that hopefully would occur in my immediate future.

I looked at Alex.

Didn't need words.

The chair wouldn't release me.

He unbuckled himself and knelt next to me.

Rubbed his nose.

All right, so I'm not going to explain in specific detail what took place next.

Cue the curtain.

Add the sound effects: romantic music, sighs, quick gasps—use your imagination.

Of course I engaged in a bit of time-bending. On purpose. Oh yeah. Though it didn't seem to work much and luckily I didn't hiccup in the middle of things.

Time to admit: I liked a lot of stuff I didn't like last week: video games, half aliens, and ... you know.

I still didn't like Coreg. Especially when he interrupted us by rudely pacing. He stepped into standing pilot position and told Alex to strap in. Jerk. That ticked me off, but at least it got me in a new mood, one to do battle. All the energy I used to put into avoiding people and situations I re-directed into the will to fight.

The ship lurched.

Before now traveling in space had been smooth, but Coreg left the gravity on and I swear I was riding the grill of a high speed train barreling through a dark tunnel.

Alex shouted. He didn't need to yell, but we were excited, *ahem,* though not quite as excited as I thought I'd be after a first kiss. Honestly, I wasn't sure it had actually happened. It seemed like I missed it. Anyway, he shouted commands for pacing and bending and coordinates and reminders about keeping us invisible. We lined up beside the middle lead Gleezhian ship. I have no idea how Coreg did it, if he was flying backwards or had switched the viewing screen to aim behind us or what, but I trusted that when Alex yelled "Fire" the triggers would release the anti-flames or freezers or defender thingies in the right direction. It took all of my concentration not to think of my bladder, my heart, my stomach, or the growing nausea and to bend, aim, fire. Release, wait, watch.

Somebody needed to cue the sound effects because, seriously, it was impossible to understand that I blew up a sixth row Gleezhian ship that then hurtled at the precise angle Alex projected and knocked out two ships in the last row. Poof, gone. Poof, gone.

Then he ordered targeting a fifth row ship that exploded on impact and took out both remaining sixth row ships. The last of the seventh row flew into the debris and ... poof, gone.

Way to economize the weapons, guys. Two shots, seven Gleezhian vessels obliterated. A third of their force disintegrated. I took a quick glance at Coreg whose smirk had morphed into an arrogant smile. He intended to take all the credit. Fine. He could tell his leaders anything he wanted.

The two furthest ships remaining in the fifth row rolled away from each other. They were on to us and had anticipated our next move. Coreg hit the comm and listened to the chatter while piloting and pacing us away. Okay, so he is pretty awesome at this. Promote him to First Commander or something.

"Don't bend, Selina."

Huh, he used my name. I closed my eyes, opened them to a new screen. We'd paced away, closer to Mars 2. The fourteen remaining ships had spread out into an arc, but not an even arc, they were staggered up and down. There was no way we could hit one and hope it would take out another.

"Are we still invisible?"

"Yes."

"What are they saying?"

"They believe they have been picked off by Earth sentries."

I looked at Alex and mouthed, *"Do we have Earth sentries?"* Maybe my dad, being half Klaqin—thanks to Grandpa Turlek—patrolled out here somewhere. No, impossible. Stupid imagination.

"So we can, like, wait them out and maybe they'll turn around?"

Coreg switched the gravity off. His way of answering I guess. Yup, we were waiting. My hair floated past my nose and I pushed it away. Then I rubbed my nose and giggled at Alex. A little space levity. Levity, get it?

But space battles allowed no time for humor. A new blip came on the screen. Oh, crap, if that wasn't the *Galaxer,* who was it?

CHAPTER 26
#SpacedOut

NATE AND MARCUM inspected the outside of the ship shortly after the *Intimidator* left.

"I'm surprised," Nate said, stretching his memory for the nearly forgotten Klaqin words, "that they still make *Galaxer*s after all these years."

"They don't. This is old. We trained on even older ones than this. Good design. But Fifth Commander Coreg's ship is top of the line." He shivered. The temperature had dropped with the setting sun. He bounced on his feet to keep warm and ignored the puffs of air that jetted out of his shoes' soles.

"Well, look at that." Nate stood next to the port side damage. Right before his eyes the bio-metals repaired themselves into standard siding and sheathing, but then they flickered and changed to match the surrounding bio-metals to complete the camouflage. "All right, we're good to go."

"But, sir, your son's plan will only work if we stay positioned here to shoot out the interceptor rockets. The *Intimidator* will be untraceable ... invisible ... for no more than three or four attacks. In training we used camouflage as a last resort. He is using it first because the odds are against him."

"I understand that," Nate took the lead following his previous footprints around the ship, "but I'm not about to sit safely down here and not go up and cover his backside when he shows up on their scanners."

"But we don't have a pacer on board." Marcum touched the side of the ship and increased the size of the opening. He gave the man he now believed was indeed his senior officer some assistance climbing up.

"I've got a little secret, Fifth Commander, when I said that Coreg's father tried to get me to time-pace, I implied it didn't happen. Well, I meant it didn't happen then. Not until I reached Earth did I discover my time-pacing aptitude. For a while I honed the skill, then I got married and Alex was born. I haven't paced since, and the skill didn't come back to me when we were in the *Galaxer*...needed a little outside help to teach my son...but now I think I can pace at the right moment."

Marcum nodded and took his place in the standing pilot position while Nate lowered himself gently into the cockpit chair.

They watched the screen in silence as some of the twenty-one Gleezhian vessels began to disappear. When the count went down to fourteen the Gleezhian chatter on the comm burst into overdrive. Marcum tried his best to listen for clues.

"Third Commander, they keep reporting they've been picked off by Earth sentries."

"Good. The *Intimidator* is still invisible, even to our sensors. Wait. Look, the Gleezhians have rearranged into a defensive arc."

"Your son's plan will fail now unless ..." Marcum put the *Galaxer* into the air and finished his sentence, "unless I can force the *Galaxer*'s camo to override the—" He stopped talking and reached for various levers. "No, it's not going to work. Sir, you must be ready to pace us away after every attack."

"Right." Nate took a breath and watched as they instantly left the planet's seventh atmosphere and joined the battle.

But before they positioned themselves for an attack, a new blip forty degrees above the center ship appeared on the screen. "Is that them?" Nate instinctively reached for the control to change the colors to shapes.

"That's not the *Intimidator*," Marcum said. "And it's not a Gleezhian ship either."

"I don't believe what I'm seeing." Nate hit the switch on the comm and spoke in standard Klaqin: "*Fighter Five*, identify yourself."

❄ ❄ ❄

"WE'RE STILL INVISIBLE, right?" My nerves rankled in response to this anxious waiting game. *Bring on the slowly increasing drum beats*—no, scratch that, it was time I gave up my mood-lightening habit of stage directions and voice-overs. *Grow up, Selina Marie, get serious. Concentrate, don't time-bend.* "Why is the *Galaxer* showing up on our screen? That is the *Galaxer*, right?"

Mr. Rimmon's voice came over our speaker then, but I couldn't understand him. "So?" I shot Coreg my bewildered expression. "Come on, translate."

First he nodded toward the screen and then he spoke. "It is not them." A second, fast moving blip traveled across the coordinates, heading straight for us. "That's them. The Third Commander is ordering the new ship to identify itself. He believes it is an antiquated *Fighter Five*."

"What? What does that mean? Is it friendly?" My armpits were damp with perspiration and my heart was beating loudly enough to drown out all other sounds.

"It is one of ours."

A voice came over the comm in answer to Mr. Rimmon. The words were utterly unintelligible, well, to me and Alex, but the voice brought tears to my eyes. I was so not expecting that sound to follow me into outer space. "What's he saying?" I would have grabbed Coreg's sleeve and broken his arm to get him to answer if he'd been within reach.

"He says he is Second Commander Langston. Is that not your name, time-bender?"

I sucked in air so fast I got a lock of hair in my mouth. It was hard to spit it out and speak at the same time. My dad was an Earth sentry!

Maybe he did know an actuator from a transducer.

"Dad! Don't shoot. I'm in this ship, so's Alex. And Mr. Rimmon's in the other one. Shoot the cannibals!"

I never thought I'd ever say anything that sounded more ridiculous. Luckily Alex had more sensible things to say. He told me to bend time for a minute, specifically to make five seconds last sixty, during which he found out that his dad might be able to pace, too. *Caramba*. Mr. Rimmon had a new plan. What a genius. I stopped bending and Marcum flew the *Galaxer* to the *Fighter Five*'s side and latched on. Coreg obeyed too and, taking the *Intimidator* out of its stealth invisibility, he flew us to the other side of the *Fighter Five* and latched on. With some unbelievably quick calculations, probably one of the guys was pacing, we lined up our three noses at precise angles to take out three Gleezhian ships at a time. Best. Team. Sport. Ever.

Missiles and rockets and flaming whatevers flew over and around us, but we managed to triple-pace away on my dad's command. His old ship was larger and fatter and longer than ours. Picture a super-galactic butterfly and we were the wings. Coreg, Alex, and his dad did the pacing and my dad did the flying. As soon as we flew to a new position it was up to me to give us some added time to target three consecutive ships. On my dad's command we fired and I instantly released my bending so we could pace away to a new position.

It worked perfectly the first and second times. I missed my target on the third line up even though I was bending and releasing on cue. Nobody's perfect. But eight of the fourteen Gleezhian ships were annihilated. That left six. They fired at us nonstop and I wondered if, since we were latched together, the bio-metals might be able to communicate with each other.

"Coreg," I said, "turn on your camouflage." And he did.

The stars were lined up, must have been, because the Gleezhians stopped shooting at where we were and began randomly firing in other directions.

We targeted three ships without me needing to time-bend. Poof, poof, poof, gone. Only red lines showed fleetingly on the screen, outlining blackened shells.

Three ships remained.

Once in a blue moon I get a good idea. "Should we let them go?" I asked. "You know, to go and tell their leaders to never send another Gleezhian toward Earth?" The cannibals behind the blips on the screen were obviously thinking the same thing. The colors were changing; they were turning tail and running. Alex shouted one of those military boo-yah cheers.

❄ ❄ ❄

NATE WAITED UNTIL the battle concluded to speak. "Rudy? Is that you?"

"'Fraid so, neighbor. Let's stay latched and I'll land us down on the morning side of the nearest planet. I suspect each ship is in need of some galactic lard and I happen to have a stash of it below."

Wide eyes and raised eyebrows were the pattern among the five on the other two ships. No one said another word the entire time it took to land; no one time-paced.

The landing spot this time was clear of snow. Bright green grass and blossoming trees dotted the landscape. Mr.

Langston brought them to within a few yards of an iridescent creek that twisted off into a wooded area. He retracted the latchings and exited his craft.

The *Intimidator*'s door widened next and Selina pushed past Coreg to run into her father's arms. Alex went to his dad's side and the two embraced as well. Coreg and Marcum stood together, one scowling and the other pressing his lips closed with the greatest effort.

When Selina let go of her father he whistled out a huge sigh and pulled her in for another kiss on her forehead. He whispered something to her then held her at his side and addressed the others. "Men, that was an unbelievable show of force. I've never had help before. Thank you. I've held off as many as four Gleezhian ships, but that was the first time they sent such a large fleet. It was a miracle that you were here first." He nodded toward Nate and Alex and then the two others. "Let me introduce myself. I am Second Commander Rudy Langston, son of Turlek Langston, who was known on Klaqin by a single name: Turlek. Probably no chance you ever heard of him. He left a long time ago."

Coreg spoke low, "My father is Merlig."

Mr. Langston, took an involuntary step in his direction. "Then you're ... we're—" He squeezed Selina's shoulders and looked down at her.

"I know, Dad, we're cousins." She tried for a smile, but it turned into a smirk. She fidgeted with her jacket's zipper.

"My father and several others came here—to this planet we're standing on, Azoss—on a secret mission to get help in the fight against the Gleezhians. But no humans inhabited this planet so they moved on to Earth. Their time-pacer died suddenly, shortly after they arrived. There was no chance to return without a time-pacer so they settled in, had new families, and did their best to defend their adopted planet. They passed the job and the spaceships on to my generation." He paused and looked from Nate to Coreg. "But I guess the government of Klaqin kept sending ships this way. Right?"

"Not exactly," Nate said. "I escaped a Gleezhian battleship in an emergency pod and must have unconsciously paced myself here. Can't believe I ended up being *your* neighbor. Of course, it may have had to do with my old comm ring I used to wear. It started to glow when the real estate agent showed us your neighborhood. I took it as a lucky sign..." Nate gave a snorty laugh, "...but it must have picked up on your Klaqin blood."

Mr. Langston nodded along with him then turned to the boys. Coreg grunted and spoke in Klaqin to hide the truth from Selina and Alex, "Marcum and I are Fifth Commanders. We are absent from command without permission. We suspected we'd find a time-bender on Earth. We had studied radio waves, phone communications, and television broadcasts." He clucked his tongue and nudged Marcum.

Marcum spoke, also in Klaqin, lowering his eyes. "We intended to kidnap Selina. The government can breed her with Coreg and create a new race able to bend and pace at will." He lifted his eyes and his voice. "We will wipe out all the star cannibals as easily as we took out eighteen ships tonight with very little weaponry."

Mr. Langston held his daughter more closely. She looked up at him. "What'd he say, Dad? That they tried to kidnap me and Buddy?" She pulled his head down and whispered in his ear, "I don't trust Coreg."

❄ ❄ ❄

I HAD MORE to whisper to my dad. Like were there any more secrets I should know? Like, did Mom know where he was? Like, could he call her now and tell her I was fine? I was going to topple over with questions. Wait, what I desperately wanted to know was: where was the bathroom?

I stood on tippy toes and whispered again. He pointed toward some bushes a few yards away. Crap. What if there were Mars 2, or rather Azoss, flora and fauna as menacing as the star cannibals behind that bush? Too bad, they would just have to watch. I cast a shy glance at the other guys and tried to slink away. Back step. Back step. This was no time to time-bend. I hurried behind the bush and took care of business. I had a sneaky suspicion that Alex was practicing his time-pacing because I finished in next to no time.

When I came back around they all scattered off to do their own thing. All except my dad.

"Honey," he said, "I'm not mad, but I want a full report from you. Should have expected something like this—it's in your blood." He nodded toward the ships. "After they're done feeding the bio-metals Alex and Nate will come with us and we'll let the Fifth Commanders go to Klaqin and face the music. They'll probably get prison time."

Huh. I wasn't sure how that made me feel. They didn't deserve prison.

"Why don't you sit down over there by the creek—looks safe enough—and I'll get you when we're ready to take off."

"Sure, Dad."

There were no paths indicating the presence of animals like deer or bunnies, but there were some rocks unnaturally positioned to make an adequate bench, as if somebody had stacked them to sit and watch the water flow by. I swear I spotted some fish. And I heard birds singing. Definitely whistles and tweets. They got louder and a flock of birds, like starlings, came and perched in the nearest trees. Alex would say they were squawking, but I decided they were singing. More rocks and dirt than grass made up the majority of the landscape; most of the boulders were painted with bird droppings on the top and tinted red and purple underneath. Maybe this place wasn't so barren; it certainly was, if not peaceful, interesting. I plopped myself down on the stone bench and faced the ships. Coreg jumped out of the *Intimidator* and carried something to my dad's mammothly larger space-tank. Marc appeared then and started walking slowly toward me. Yikes. Oh, crap. I'd lapsed into automatic time-bend. *Way to stretch out the awkward moments, Selina. Get a grip.*

"Hellew."

"Might as well sit down," I said. "We've got some good-byes to say." I wondered if he'd have a funny way of saying that. "Wish I could send some pie with you." He smiled at that.

And then he sat, leaned in, and put his feverishly tropical lips on mine.

Okay, time out. What was going on? My pulse didn't rocket like this when Alex kissed me. Where, oh where, did my breath go? And those birds? I couldn't hear a single squawk.

I pressed my lips onto his. In fact, my arms found their way around his neck and the heat off his body wrapped itself like a blanket around my entire being.

Alex didn't put his arms around me like this. Alex didn't melt me like this. It was a good thing that I was sitting down because my knees were rubber.

Oh.

I got the tiniest breath in and let go of my feelings for Alex. I focused on Marc Marcum, unbelievably insane lip-caressing hottie. Holy cow. It was like we stepped completely outside of time's restraints.

Talk about being torn in half. It took the rest of a time-bending age, but I managed to pry my eyes open and look at him. Now what was I supposed to do? My heart had started ripping apart as soon as our lips unlocked. He was going to fly off millions if not billions of miles away.

Something else was stinging my heart.

Something about choices.

Was there even a choice to make? That is, one that I'd be allowed to make?

I looked over his shoulder and saw Alex standing halfway between us and the ships. Standing. No hands on hips. No arms crossed. No frown. No anger. Like his body language was telling me he was okay with me kissing someone else.

No way.

He smiled, but that didn't hide his shattered soul. He rubbed his nose and turned away.

What had I done?

If it was even possible, I just broke my own heart.

❄ ❄ ❄

ALEX TURNED HIS back on the upsetting scene and stood still, vision blurring, heart breaking. He could never be angry with Selina, but he felt infinitely disappointed. Somehow his feet took him to the *Fighter Five* and he found his father and Mr. Langston deep in a conversation full of revealed secrets. He leaned against a set of toggled panels and joysticks and pretended to listen, but his mind settled elsewhere, a mental playlist of sad songs crowded out the singular sound of Selina gasping for a breath.

He wondered if she'd kissed him earlier because she thought they were about to die. That kiss had meant more to him than to her, obviously. To him the kiss was poetry and song lyrics; it was flying a spaceship and pacing time; it was holding a hollow breath and coming up for air all at once. She'd started to use her time-bending, he was sure, as soon as Coreg had turned his back and he had knelt next to her, but he had inadvertently paced, sending their special moment into hyper-speed. It was over too soon. Not like what he witnessed at the stream.

He tried to get the scene out of his head. He concentrated on listening to his father and Mr. Langston. When that didn't work he began evaluating the old cruiser. There were three staggered workstations, a standing pilot position, two chairs, and three screens. The walls reeked of the oily smell.

All of a sudden he caught a movement on one of the screens. A sonic boom punctuated his alarm.

"They're coming back." No time to say more. A sudden burst of fire, a horrendous cracking explosion, and ten or twenty quick spurts of energy assaulted the ancient ship.

"We have to take off," Mr. Langston yelled.

❄ ❄ ❄

I JUST GOT kissed by an alien. Well, there's another cool thing I never imagined I'd say.

But I couldn't stop staring at the spot where Alex had disappeared into my dad's spaceship.

I looked at Marc. "So ...?" Hmm, what did a shy girl say after that kind of thrill? After that kind of guilty rush? I needed to talk to Alex.

Marc fell into his pattern of short responses. "So," he mimicked. He smiled, too, then looked down at his feet. My eyes followed. The ground was covered with thorns.

My stomach rocked and rolled then and not in a good way. Chocolate would've helped. Something, any-thing, to stop that creeping sensation that not only had I done something unforgivably bad, but that I was going to have to pay a high price to right an intergalactic wrong.

That was the moment they struck.

I heard the boom and fell flat on my face. Marc, too. Then he jumped up and raced for the ships. A strafing of blasts came through the woods, setting trees on fire, shooting creek water and rocks into the air, and showering debris across the area.

Debris. Like bio-metals. And Marc left me here!

I saw my dad's spaceship shudder. Alex jumped out right before the ship lifted off the ground and shot straight upwards with an ear-splitting blast. I couldn't believe that my dad would leave me here like that.

Alex didn't hesitate as Marc ran by him. His arm shot out, his fist connected with a very square jaw, and Marc collapsed and rolled under the *Galaxer*.

So ... probably a good time to do my thing. I was *the* Time-Bender, the only time-bender around to my knowledge.

Okay. Bending. Analyzing what I just saw. How did I feel about that? Alex decked Marc with one face-smashing, butt-kicking punch. It was incredible. Too incredible to dwell on. Changing focus. Ignoring pounding heart. Looking at the debris. Do bio-metals bleed? Red stuff. Ick.

Keep bending. *Keep repeating: dad's coming back. Dad's coming back.* Sheesh, what were the chances I'd get to borrow the family spaceship? Oh, yeah, like Z. E. R. O. I was still grounded.

Walk to *Intimidator*. Surely Coreg could shoot into outer space from here.

The *Intimidator* was hit. Bio-metals wormed around in circles. The doorway pulsed open and closed and I couldn't see Coreg or anyone else inside.

Steal glance at Alex. Block out thoughts of him hitting Marc. Clear throat.

"Alex! Where's your dad?"

He rubbed his fist then pointed skyward. The heavens blurred with lights and fireworks, but the sounds didn't reach our ears though Alex cringed a couple times as if he heard the blasts. I had no idea which of the two ships held my dad and Mr. Rimmon, but the space fight above us displayed a mass of contrails and streaks, fireballs, and—

I stared at Alex, stuffed my fears—and my guilt—into the basement of my mind, and said, "Don't worry, they'll stay out of the Gleezhians' way. There's only one ship that came back to attack, I think."

"Looks that way." He nodded toward the *Intim-idator*. "That's not going to fly again."

Marc pulled himself out from under the *Galaxer* and peered into the *Intimidator*. "Only ashes," he said.

I was still bending, but it didn't affect the fight above. They couldn't seem to get their aim straight. Two old men, our dads, were battling star cannibals in my grand-father's spaceship. This couldn't end well.

"Alex, we need to get up there, latch on, and help by pacing and bending."

"I know, but Coreg's ship is toast and Coreg is MIA."

Marc mumbled again. "Only ashes." His face sported a reddish bruise on the left side. I hoped the fight was one of those guy things that had to happen and was quickly forgotten.

"What do you mean ashes?" Alex said.

"An energy force hit the *Intimidator*. The bio-metals conducted the force through their systems to protect the ship. She's crippled, but she'll fly. Coreg took the full effect of the energy. He's ... gone."

CHAPTER 27
#Endings

I TRIED TO wrap my head around Coreg's death, but that was pretty much impossible. I didn't know what I felt—some combination of disbelief, panic, and sadness. Marc seemed to be taking it rather coldly, holding his thumb up to his lips and droning meaningless syllables into his hand. Alex and I stood there in temporary suspension of our vital functions. At least I did; I couldn't hear or see anything but a memory—a shadow of something lost.

It was a totally shocking surprise when two more Gleezhian craft came shrieking in along the horizon, fifty feet off the ground of Mars 2, I mean Azoss. They glittered and sparkled to a stop, hovering above our heads like fancy decorations. Deadly ones.

I started imagining tractor beams and invisible ray guns. I expected the monsters to walk out onto a platform above and levitate us up to be their lunch or supper. I imagined them tearing the meat off our bones with their six-fingered hands.

Alex whispered at my side, "Good job, Selina, keep things slow. On the count of three release and I'll pace. We'll jump into the ships and start shooting.

"One."

Oh crap. Should I go with Alex or Marc? I knew Alex could fly the *Galaxer*, but Marc might have trouble getting the *Intimidator* working. He might need me to help.

"Two."

No, I had to be loyal to Alex. Alex was my best friend. Marc could fly and shoot by himself; that was what he trained for.

"Three."

Alex pushed me toward the *Galaxer*. I moved as slow as mud at first, then I released the bending and flew into the cockpit, stumbled over some textbooks, and slid into the chair. Surprise, surprise, Marc came with us. Yay, we made it. Maybe we were destined to fly out of their reach.

The bio-metals crackled. Really. They crackled. Think dry twigs on a campfire.

Marc choked out the bad news in monosyllabic fashion, starting with that strange word he produces in the back of his mouth. "*Ehk*. Too close. They paced with us. Shot first."

I had mental images of our ashes swirling around the cabin.

"The bio-metals failed."

Failed? Failed? That was actually good, wasn't it? They took the force of the hit and we didn't get incinerated.

Marc looked to the doorway which hadn't closed. There were beings there. Alien, six-fingered beings. The enemies had landed. And they weren't too terribly scary-looking after all.

Thoroughly human. But overly bearded.

And angry. Angry bearded humans.

I couldn't have moved a muscle if I wanted to.

❄ ❄ ❄

MARCUM HAD TRAINED a few times for a hostile Gleezhian encounter. Facing authentic Gleezhian commanders neither raised the hair on his neck nor rattled his thoughts. He was, as always, fearless. The many practices he'd participated in served him well. He spoke in a rehearsed prattle of standard Gleezhian dialect, something to the effect of *we surrender and will supply, most willingly, any and all Klaqin state secrets by which these far-traveling spaceships operated.* The standard untruth. He knew a hundred other Gleezhian words, but none came to mind.

One of the five hairy, colorfully dressed Gleezhian commanders, the obvious leader, responded with a gargled laugh and a handful of syllables. Marcum spoke again, gestured to Alex and Selina, and answered—in Gleezhian—a series of questions.

"What's he saying?" Alex asked.

Marcum motioned for him to be silent. The leader stepped forward.

"He was bargaining for you," the leader said in quite astonishingly good English. "Do you understand me?"

"Yes."

"He claimed all three of you are from Klaqin, and I see by your eyes that is true for you, and yet you speak a language of a different planet. Why?"

Alex bobbled his head from Marcum to Selina and back again to Marcum.

❄ ❄ ❄

OH, BROTHER. THE lead alien was straight out of central casting, but he sounded like someone trying for a fake British accent. In spite of that his face was scary, like he just ate barbed wire for breakfast and liked it. "Hey," I said, totally ignoring my panic and not giving Alex a chance to answer, "Marcum's from Klaqin, but not Alex or me. We're from Earth." Where was I going with this? Well, maybe if I slowed things down, lulled them into a false sense of superiority then my best friend might finish finagling that arc-gun out of his pants. I hoped to heck he knew how to aim and shoot the thing. I wasn't sure how to tip off Alex as to when he should make his move but then one of them turned sideways, looked out at the sky, and I got a silhouette view of his humped back. It made me think of a certain chess piece. Perfect. I knew the clue to use.

The leader nodded, ever so slowly. "We were headed to Earth, but they are more hostile than the inhabitants of Klaqin."

His eyes drilled holes in my head, well, not literally, but I could swear he was challenging me to confirm it. Ha! They blamed our devastating destruction of their fleet on Earth. Good. I decided right then and there all that adrenaline surging around my body wouldn't go to waste. I pointed a trembling finger at the book near his feet. "Do you know what a book is?" He signaled an affirmation. I continued, "That one will blow your mind ... like a berserker." Oh, I so hoped that Alex got that reference to chess. He needed a wild opening move and between my enigmatic clue and the phrase *blow your mind*, he shouldn't need but one more long moment ... and ... "Alex, pace," I screamed.

I released my hold on time and he took over, instantly pacing. He swung the arc-gun out and fired off a series of shots in a fraction of the time it took me to grab a second gun off the wall and thrust it at Marc. An arc-gun fight in close quarters was not something I ever wanted to experience again. Not to mention dead and dying cannibals in color coordinated duds. The cries rang out in gut-wrenching shrieks ... totally unearthly ... well ... yeah ... and the blood spouted red and black. Not cool. But hey, I might be rewriting that paper on conscientious objectors. War was war. Them or us. I voted for us.

Over almost before it began, one alien body rested across the threshold, four more lay smoking across one another. Literally—smoking. Whatever those arc-guns used it made a stinky mess of the Gleezhians. They'd become mangled bloody chunks of meat. I couldn't stare for more than a few seconds. Alex stopped pacing and I resumed bending so we could seriously assess the circumstances—but not look at what we'd done.

Some dim recess of my brain, not occupied with immediate survival, time-bending or the shock of our current circumstances, speculated that the math of this situation did not add up. "There were two ships," I said. "Do you think all five of these ... people ... were from both ships? It's an odd number."

A groan from the deformed one alerted us to his subtle movements. His exposed skin paled in the Azoss light, his hair saturated and pasted against his scalp. His plump chest rose and fell with slow labored breaths. Marc reached for the moaning alien's bloody hand which held a box. But before he could take it away the dying Gleezhian pressed it and one of their ships nearby exploded.

❄ ❄ ❄

IT ALMOST TOOK too long for neighbors Nate Rimmon and Rudy Langston to learn each other's rhythm in a star battle. But with unpracticed time-pacing paired with frugal, well-aimed anti-flames and high voltage rockets, not to mention the added microwaves that Langston had retro-fitted onto the *Fighter Five*, the men finally caught the upper hand in the battle. They watched the targeted ship disintegrate then flew a well-paced light year ahead looking for the last two Gleezhian ships.

When they reached the edge of the range Langston deemed adequate, he turned the *Fighter Five* around. They were within the gravity of Azoss when the craft's detectors warned of the proximity of two enemy spacecraft. As they closed in on the landing site a ball of fire erupted and black smoke clouded the area where they'd left their children. Nate feared the worst.

"The Klaqin craft are where we left them," Langston said. "I'd say that ship self-destructed; that's my assessment. But a second ship has landed beyond the woods."

"I'll pace, you aim."

"No, can't chance it. Our kids might be on board."

"Land! Just land this thing!"

❄ ❄ ❄

LOUDEST. EXPLOSION. EVER.

"Stay here," Marc commanded.

He and Alex jumped out over the fifth, not quite dead, body. Oh, that was so not good. I glanced around to find something to defend myself with against the surviving Gleezhian. There were weapons on the wall, but who knew if I'd be aiming at myself if I grabbed one. Two of the lifeless aliens still clutched small boxes in their overly fingered dead hands, and two more boxes—remote explosives, I presumed—lay close to the ghastly corpses. Not going to touch them. So not liking this. Okay, looked like a heavy history textbook was my only choice. I could bash his skull in. Maybe.

I bent to pick it up and the horrible almost-dead Gleezhian groaned. I jumped. He mumbled incomprehensible nonsense. His mouth gaped open, exposing evidence of a distressing lack of concern for dental hygiene and for a fleeting instant I felt sorry for him. But I was not going to get close enough to hit his head, let alone allow him to grab my ankle—classic heroine misstep.

"Hic!"

Holy crap, I was probably slowing things down for the guys. I closed my eyes and let go of my thoughts. I stayed very still and held my breath. Time rushed at me then. I opened my eyes to find all five bodies gone. What the—

I looked around quite calmly, with that eerie sense of detachment that comes with awareness of impending disaster.

And then Coreg appeared. I could see a huge vein down the side of his neck, throbbing with a steady pulse as even as a ticking clock.

I closed my mouth after a second and found myself feeling the teensiest bit relieved that he wasn't dead. His face was dark and puckered and the foreign words passing his lips were obviously obscene though the words were spoken just below the level of both my hearing and my galactic language comprehension.

"I should leave Marcum and take you back right now, but," he used his eyes to nod at all the arc-gun blast holes that had shattered the non-bio-metallic equipment, "this clunker will probably never fly again." He dropped his rough demeanor and seemed softly human.

"We thought you were dead."

"My plan exactly. Nobody is more cunning than Coreg." He resumed his rigid posture. "I burned a book on the chair. I knew the Gleezhians were returning. I hid myself and—" The look in his eyes unmasked him. He wasn't so bad after all. Maybe I'd misjudged him.

He turned and looked outside. A couple seconds later Alex and Marc hopped in, equally surprised to see Coreg.

Coreg smirked at them. "You found the other ship and are here to report that all on board are mysteriously gone. Thanks to me they are already fermenting into galactic lard. Also the five you left here are in the *Intimidator*'s processor as well."

What? He'd paced around me doing all that while I'd zoned out. I barely had time to process that bit of information before I heard a couple of fatherly voices yelling for Alex and me.

"We're all right," Alex yelled back. Ten seconds later our dads appeared and five of the six of us started chattering like monkeys, describing the fights, the explosion, Coreg's fake death and his stealthy and ruthless attack, the "disposal" of the bodies, the sad state of the *Galaxer* ... but one of the six of us was very, very quiet. It was either Alex or me. Not sure, because I may have said something about lard, or maybe Alex talked about pacing. But mostly I looked across the mess and stared at those honest eyes and rubbed my nose and hoped and hoped ... and then my eyes closed and things went black. Again. Like a stellar black hole. And someone's arms caught me.

❄ ❄ ❄

"I'LL TAKE HER down by the stream," her father said, "and get her out of this smoky air." He turned to Alex. "Want to give me a hand? Your dad has a bad back."

Alex stepped up, lifted Selina from where she had slumped against Coreg, and carried her off the ship. Nate stayed behind to discuss their options with the two Fifth Commanders.

Selina's father strode alongside ready to help, but conceded to Alex's easy undertaking of the task.

Before they reached the stones Alex hesitated, moved upstream a bit and picked out a grassy spot to set her down. He took off his own jacket and tucked it under her head. "I've done this before, Mr. Langston. She'll be out for a few minutes. Faster if you want to see me time-pace. I'm half Klaqin, you know."

"Like me. I was your age when I found out. It's pretty overwhelming."

"Blows my mind. So ... did you know about us?"

"Not a clue. Selina's grandfather mentioned something once several years ago, when he baby sat for Buddy and Selina ... you came over to play and he told me later that he saw something in your eyes ... something that convinced him you could forever be trusted. You were maybe eleven."

"You *can* trust me. I'd never let anything hurt Selina."

Mr. Langston held out his hand and shook Alex's. "I know. I trust you. The thing is we can't blindly trust those Fifth Commanders. We've done a great job eliminating the threat of the Gleezhians, at least for a while, but you should know ... the star cannibals aren't the only problem."

Alex cocked his head, glanced at Selina's fluttering eyelids, and whispered, "It's us, right? Coreg, Marcum, me, my dad, you ... we're as dangerous as the star cannibals, aren't we?"

"You're a smart kid, Alex. Too smart. You learned to pace in a fraction of the time. You figured out a way to eliminate eighteen of the twenty-one star craft with a minimum of weaponry. I don't think you need me to tell you that our people out there," he looked up, "need someone like you ... like you and Selina ... to put an end to the wars. And an end to the cannibalism ... whether they eat us or our galactic lard machines eat them." He sighed, stroked his unconscious daughter's hand, and finished, "I'll make your father understand. He needs to let you go with them ... to fight. To keep them all away from Earth."

❄ ❄ ❄

THERE WAS NO way I'd give up everything I cared about to go up in one of those rickety old spaceships and fight. Wait ... my dad wasn't talking to me, he was talking to someone else ... I opened my eyes and lifted my head and said what they probably expected me to say, "Where am I?"

Reality slammed back hard after a second and I sat up.

"You had one of your, uh, episodes," Alex said.

My dad was petting my hand, but he stopped, let go and said, "Selina, you're special. You and Alex both. You must have inherited the right DNA from your mom and me to develop this time-bending ability. And Alex inherited time-pacing. It's phenomenal and shouldn't be wasted." His words were as soft as the rushing of the brook nearby and pretty much as indecipherable. I tucked a wad of unruly hair behind my ear.

"What are you saying, Dad?" He reached for my hand again and this time he held it like he had to give me some awfully bad news, like *your dog died* or *your mom's got cancer* or ... or ... *you're never going to see Earth again.* I reached my other hand out to Alex and he held it.

"Alex has to go. If Coreg and Marcum don't take Alex with them there will be others, higher up Commanders, who will be commissioned to visit Earth to seek you both out. They'll bring the war to us, on Earth."

"No!"

"It's okay, Selina," Alex said. "I'd do anything for you."

"No, you're not going without me."

"Honey—"

"Dad, no."

"Wait, Mr. Langston, think about it. Selina and I were awesome in battle. It was like we were meant to work together. We should both go."

"Yes!" That was my voice, right on top of my dad's firm "no." I sat up a little more and my dad drew back the same distance, but didn't let my hand slip out of his.

"I can't let my precious daughter go and fight for them."

Alex squeezed my other hand. "Please, Mr. Langston. We're probably the only chance that...uh, their planet and our planet have. They want a time-bender. I won't be enough. We have to *both* go. You know I'm right."

My dad closed his eyes for a long time. I didn't make it longer. When he spoke it was barely audible, but he looked right at me super intensely. "I don't see any other way than to send you to fight for them." He sighed. "You and Alex."

Whoa, he agreed. I could hardly believe it. "And you'll tell Mom and Buddy and Alex's mom that we'll come back as soon as we can?"

He shook his head. Super sorry facial expression. "I won't be far behind. I promise."

Holy crap. "But ..." What could I say?

Alex squeezed my hand again, held my gaze, and tried to look strong. He didn't fool me. Then he whispered, "We can write a note and say we eloped." Despite the fact I knew he was kidding—wiggling his eyebrows gave that away—it made my hair stand on end. Elope? Blushing emoji.

Elope? *Full on body shiver*. Hmm, let's see. Leave a note, fly a billion miles, and fight aliens. And my dad approved? Funny, but I had a totally opposite reaction from when Coreg and Marcum tried to kidnap or seduce me into going. A big old thrill built steps up to my heart, shook my insides, and then settled into an awesome and perplexing contentment, like finding a chocolate stash I'd forgotten about.

I had never fit in at school, but I fit in out here. Serenity. Satisfaction. I was going to do it.

And then reality slapped my face. I pulled my hands out of both of theirs. "But dad, I don't have much time left ... uh, you know ... my days are numbered ... the doctors don't think I'll live past eighteen."

His laughter started and stopped in an instant. "Oh, honey. That's not true. Yes, they found a bewildering anomaly in your blood and yes, you have blackouts that *they* can't explain, but they never said you were going to die."

"They did, I heard them. At least I think it was them. I was about five, sitting on the porch..."

Dad's face broke into a slow smile. "Oh, I remember that. Baby, the only one who ever said anything about your days being numbered was me. You must have overheard me say that to your grandfather a long time ago."

Ordinarily I would have found it embarrassing to be called "baby," but under the circumstances, it was oddly comforting. He looked skyward and I stared at him. I knew exactly which conversation we both were trying to remember. He'd told my grandfather my days on Earth were numbered and by the time I was eighteen I'd be in the heavens. As a violet. Hmm, I guess I heard wrong. He must have said pilot.

❄ ❄ ❄

MARCUM LISTENED AS Nate briefly grilled him and Coreg on procedures. He didn't believe that this man was still an acting Commander; it was obvious he was pretending and Marcum saw through it. It was also obvious that the man was in a lot of pain.

"Perhaps you should sit in the *Fighter Five*, sir. You may have sustained significant aftereffects from your battle."

Nate nodded. "Yes, thank you. Help me, Fifth Commander Coreg."

Marcum watched them begin to head for the ship, then he turned toward the sounds at the water's edge. He moved closer and listened. The three on the ground were huddled in deep conversation. The emotional vibrations almost knocked him back. Should he believe his ears? Was the time-bender agreeing to go willingly to Klaqin? To fight?

His heart sank when he assumed she had also agreed to marry the new time-pacer.

He watched the three of them rise, saw Selina hand Alex his coat, and noted the affectionate embrace the father gave his daughter. For a brief instant Marcum let himself melt into a despair that took him outside of the confines of time. He examined the situation from a thousand vantage points all in an instant. If only he could disappear. Then, as soon as he regained control, he strode toward them. "Second Commander," he shouted, "I request permission to join your force on Earth and work with you to repel any and all intruders. I have skills that will be of use. I can repair the old moon-chaser, the *Galaxer*." He kept his eyes on Selina's father and didn't dare glance her way.

Langston nodded, walked forward and clucked his tongue at Marcum. They walked to the ships together, leaving Alex and Selina alone.

❄ ❄ ❄

I NOTICED HOW Marcum wouldn't look at me. He essentially told my dad he'd give up his Klaqin citizenship and help Earth. Wow. I flashed on that kiss we'd shared a few feet away and wondered if he was giving up every-thing—oh, the irony—for me.

Alex slipped his coat on and put his arm around my shoulder, effectively turning me away from watching them head off.

"Let's walk into the woods for a second," he said.

"Do you have your arc-gun?" That black wall of imminent death had been lifted from my soul, but caution reigned.

"I know what you're thinking," he ushered me forward, along a narrow path, "but there aren't any animals or monsters or aliens that we can't use our super-powers against to keep ourselves out of their reach."

"Right." Hmm, that was true. And funny. Incredible, but funny.

I supposed suddenly being in the middle of the woods meant that Alex had used his super-power and walked me in time-pacing fashion to a totally and completely private spot. Not to mention somewhat romantic.

Okay, I was ready. Not going to take it slow or fast. No bending or pacing, please. I looked up and he held both of my hands. This was the guy I was going to go off with into ... parts unknown ... places unseen ... battles unimagined ... and I was not afraid.

No regrets. No fears. No doubts. I knew with certainty that the mental wobble I'd experienced kissing Marc had been imaginary, fake, and only some cheap imitation of ... of love.

I completely blanked out for a second, erased my memory of Marc's kiss and erased my first kiss with Alex too—I didn't have much of a memory of it anyway. I stood up on my tip-toes for what can best be described as butterflies and stars, fire and sparks, Hershey's chocolate and Alex. Yeah, so good. Sweaty palms and racing heart good. Time stopped and his lips pressed softly on mine and I knew his heart and his mind and everything good about him. My best friend, my favorite person, my rock, my protector, my healer, my angel.

My eyes stayed closed, but my heart opened wide. I could have done some time-bending, but I didn't need to. The kiss lingered on its own. And about those butterflies: we were probably in the Butterfly Nebula. When our lips parted we both opened our eyes and broke into smiles. His was heart stopping. He looked down at me, tears arching to dive off the lashes of both his eyes.

I did do some bending on the walk back to the ships. We needed to say some stuff. Important stuff.

And then we reached the others. Goodbyes were strange, but they weren't forever. I was sure of that. Calm about it. Our dads assured us that our moms and Buddy would be told the truth in a way that wouldn't break their hearts and also give them some hope of seeing us again.

It began to snow and that, of course, reminded me of home. I repeated to myself that I'd see home again: Mom, Buddy, Dad, Mingzhu, Niket, the language lab, well, maybe not the lab.

We climbed into the *Intimidator* with Coreg and I tried not to think of the galactic lard. Our dads took Marc with them in the *Fighter Five*.

I settled into the chair, Coreg stood in place, and Alex took the small seat and clicked the arc-gun into a spot on the wall.

Cue the music. I took some deep breaths. Did a bit of time-bending long enough to exchange smiles and secret gestures with my special someone.

The seat tightened up.

All right. I nodded to Coreg. I'd have to trust him. He gave me a tiny smile and tugged at his ear. I turned to Alex. Big smile and ... three, two and a half, two, one and a half, one ... the *Intimidator* took off.

THE END. Not

The adventure continues in the sequel:

THE TIME PACER

Alex's feelings for Selina are too great to let her go across the universe without him. He accompanies her into a far distant society on a planet of eternal sunshine, where schooling is more than indoctrination and their interstellar enemies are closer than they realize.

Marcum follows, powerfully revealing his own one-of-a-kind ability and eager to win back Selina. When the three of them discover a secret peace treaty that would deliver Selina to an alien enemy, Marcum comes up with a plan that will either doom his own planet or Earth, while Alex risks everything to stay at Selina's side.

CPSIA information can be obtained
at www.ICGtesting.com
Printed in the USA
BVHW042147111219
566432BV00016B/398/P

9 781546 559986